MW01113388

Love me, Loudly

Love me, Loudly

JESS KOLBE

Copyright © 2020 Jess Kolbe
All rights reserved.

ISBN
9780648933601 (Paperback)
9780648933618 (eBook)

This is a work of fiction. Names and characters are the product of the Author's imagination and any resemblance to actual persons, living or dead, is entirely coincidentail.

All rights reserved. No part of this publication may be reproduced, stored in a retrieval system, or transmitted, in any form or by any means, electronic, mechanical, photocopying, recording or otherwise, without the prior written permission of the publisher.

A Cataloguing-in-publication entry is available from the National Library of Australia.
www.trove.nla.gov.au

I am forever indebted to my beautiful parents who love and support me, with uncompromising belief.

They are two genuine gifts in my life that I am so lucky to have and cherish every day.

Bree Downes-Smith, who understood what I am trying to achieve and her willingness to always show up for Love me, Loudly.

Enromous thanks for the woman she is and the woman she will be.

I hope you feel a little less disconnected and a little more heard. To be emotionally bare, is love accepted, of self.

♥

PROLOGUE

He stands before me, bare, peeled back. Naked in heart and soul, something we have both grown accustomed to. Being emotionally naked. I take in his body, drinking in every line, every muscle, lingering in all his special parts, the ones I love. The room is full of our scented energy, salty sweet, with earthy undertones encouraging our raw selves to reveal themselves. His manhood hangs heavy and full, glistening with the glow of me. He allows me the time to take him in completely. His body is moulded by spectacular genes and a life lived of hard physical work. It shows in his body and face, a man put together well. He is all mine and I entirely his!

I never knew love could be like this. I never thought that I could be loved. Love didn't feel like an option for me. I could never have dreamed us, nor even considered the love that exists within me. I didn't truly understand the friendship that comes with love, that I could be accepted in both my known self and my wounds. I thought I had to get a man, desperately cling to him and hope he never finds out how broken I am. I mean, who could love someone like me?

I was so very wrong. I discovered a capacity within me to love, and to learn to receive love, to be comfortable in all my insecurities, my demons, trust and need for control… These are what I have found made me the perfect woman for my love and his history, the perfect man for me, a gift in this life for both of us.

I told myself that if I started journaling my experiences it could protect him from my broken parts, my manic mind. I needed to put my fears somewhere, and writing became my freedom and our story together of learning to love.

Our lovemaking has evolved immensely in trust and emotional vulnerability. This is how I find myself on the hard timber floor, him manoeuvring my hips to his liking, hands purposefully gliding over my skin, waking my every sense, calling my body to him. I lean, allowing him in, trusting him unconditionally. I am open, exposed and submitting to his will, to his passionate heart. We experience unspoken moments where we exist in body and in heart, safely exploring our felt emotions and each other, at times in tender touch and others in mind-blowing love making.

A year ago, if you said this would be me, I'd call bullshit and yet here I am. You see I was damaged with pieces of me broken off and drowned in the depths of a shivering abyss. Then I found a strength that I never knew had survived within me. I fled from everything external, from everyone trying to fix me, to find my own internal courage and to learn that I had all that I needed to be freed from my caged heart. I rose up from the depths of pain into a strong woman who could be grounded in her real self and true to her wounds with grace.

The universe presented me a gift in this man, Sam, and my monsters came back with a vengeance, attacking me in the dark scratching at my soul, tearing my heart, dragging me back to that dark abyss…

My thoughts are stopped in their tracks with one look from the man I love ever so deeply. He catches my eye, eagerly awaiting my encouragement before holding my gaze and pleasing me. Heat swirls around my throbbing thighs, aching for his sex, collapsing into him, savouring every touch, relishing his strength. His eyes are alive with purpose, the heat spinning around us as he watches me admiring his every move. Our intensity increases with our love.

Our connection is interrupted by my battling thoughts again - how the hell did I get so lucky? I feel the joy rising in me as the sensation of my love brings appreciation to my heart. Joy comes bounding out of me in this moment capturing me as we build our love making together. Sam feels it too. I move to tame my joy, falling to my knees in front of this man, in complete faith. I am love expressed in this instant, in him, in us, for this man loves me ever so loudly.

H E R | One

For my sanity and to slowly drip feed my love to my crazy I began to write. Creating a place where my fears can flourish rather than controlling me from the corners of my mind. I instead release it all in words, allowing the idea of writing to someone help me to let someone into my pain, and to practice being with my pain.

Monsters are real and terrible things happened to me. I lived my fears and fought hard to not be controlled by what happened to me. I truly have never known the love of another, and I want to.

I need to let my anxieties and trauma out, let them run through what they need to, in order for me to function as best I can and not have the anxiety monsters ruin my life.

Before we begin my love story, let me tell you how I got here. I must share with you, how this curvy and oh so sassy warrior, found a love she didn't know existed within her. I don't always feel enough in my life and I am learning to accept that my best is enough.

My life has been a warzone and because of that I am always on, like a simmer. Truth be told it's more like a long bubbling boil. Ready for anything, my brain only seems to experience "on" mode, awaiting the next blow. My survival mode can be a foreign thing for me, only realising I am, at times operating without quality control, spending too much time in my thoughts and thinking everyone is out to hurt me. Stuck in survival mode, no one's ever getting too close. My only motivation in life was survival. I only focused on potential dangers. Everyone was a threat. Thought patterns letting me think I am my thoughts and that every thought is a truth. I'd then process my life according to the data those thoughts collected, whether it is rational or not. Logic doesn't matter to the survival part of me. My adrenaline fuelled thinking compelled me to predict the world and manage the next punch, either from myself or an external threat. Essentially, my brain operates to survive life; to endure, not to thrive; not to live loudly. Living a life where fear is in control and I'm operating to avoid being hurt again. I learnt and ran from the so-called "experts": professionals who tried discovering my broken parts to "fix me" as I was broken, or I didn't feel properly in order to heal.

'Perhaps, I was not broken. Maybe bent a little - more a sign of the fighter in me,' I thought. I was doing my best considering what happened to me. I have discovered that there is actually no fucking "right" way. There's no unlocking some part of me in the deepest of holes that could free me.

I found I could trust myself and show up for me, whatever that looked like. I didn't trust that my feeling could be right. I had to express, I had to tell my story, daily, to be free of it in my way. I had to stop arguing with myself. I had to start choosing the life I wanted, otherwise I wouldn't make it.

So, I did.

I stopped engaging in mindless bullshit of what I was meant to do, because I was failing at that too. I had to listen to my screaming heart. I just couldn't keep failing at healing. I was teetering on the edge, not sure if I could come back. I wanted to *live*, not just survive this ever-present pain, which was numbing me to my core. I could no longer stand the pain. I committed to be present in my feelings and in life, basically to show up in what was authentic and real for me.

This meant I had to learn what was authentic for me. My monsters had even switched me off from myself and who I was under the weight of my scars. If I was sad, I let my body shudder, I was just fucking sad. If I felt down, I allowed it in, I'd weep. I'd argue with my body, tear at her agony. I'd find that feeling within my body and just sit with it, hold it, like a mother would with a toddler. I taught myself to discover what sad could look like beyond being frozen in petrified bodily fear. I learnt what happens when I accept my fear, when I accept my body to freeze, what happens if I comfort and allow acceptance of what I am feeling, rather than fighting it away, pretending as if it's not happening. This is where I found freedom, by designing and creating ways to spend my feelings. I freed myself from the cage that I was locked in.

I don't design my feelings. They're a truth to my experiences, my pain, an old scar, an old belief, reacting to my environment. If we weren't meant to feel, why are our first few years of life lived in feeling only? This became a mantra in the dark times to allow the feelings to exist. I just let them be, without judgement, and they stopped owning me. I learnt to emotional process by chance. I stopped battling myself as to what I should or shouldn't be thinking, feeling, being, healing. Fuck that shit. I realised I never failed me. I never let myself down. I was fighting for myself every day. I write my own fucking story. Somewhere in all of my mess I showed up and discovered how to spend my emotions, not just acknowledge what I am feeling. To find ways to put physical action to my feelings and this, was my freedom. I came up with an encouraging mantra, allow, accept, and spend.

I have had extreme versions of all emotions. Expressing these is not the easiest of options and I have previously preferred to run from, ignore, push down or attempt to lose myself in other things to feel something other than what I needed to feel.

NOT ANY FUCKING MORE.

I am that crazy chick that hums to her own tune, smiles at the world and feels whatever, wherever. I have an ongoing relationship with myself and my past. I have good days and bad. The more I allow, accept and spend, the more skilled I become at understanding me and how I react to things, in that I have a history that follows me around and the world can still be a harsh place. I am beginning to trust myself to have my own back, and work through whatever I am faced with. I have already survived so much.

Everyone has a story. Their traumas, anxieties, mental health, depression, PTSD… the pain is yours and only yours. Every person at one time or another has wanted it all to be over, or to end. My realisation is not new, nor is my battle. I'm not fucking special in what life has dished out to me, not to make any of it okay or justify actions that hurt me. When I allowed myself to stop trying to get over my life and began a relationship with myself, from a perspective of kindness and learning, it all changed. Rather than 'I should be this' or 'should be that', I became curious about how my body and brain processed things. I learnt a lot, as rather than telling myself what it should be, I actually listened to what I needed. No-one was going to ride in on a white stallion and save me. There's no fucking knight in shining armour in this story. So, I needed to goddess the fuck up and find my own armour. There are no miracle answers. I had to create, not wait for something external to fix me. I would have been swallowed by my monsters lost in their torment, tearing at my heart. If I had waited one more day.

I refused to be on the same gut-wrenching merry-go-round spinning out of control. I stripped my emotions bare, finding a way to me and accepted her as whatever she needed to be. So, in letting go of a design of what should be, I found the evolution of a woman who could be happy, strong, and that she evolved in her style, not perfection, nor broken, just being and contentment poured in, with moments of pure joy. I stopped letting my past attempt to control my future. I had to free myself otherwise I would end it, end the suffering and I wanted to *live*. There's more, there has to be more to life, and I wanted it! I clung to hope, as the opposite was death. I stopped engaging in this mindless bullshit of 'should'! Should be healed, should not be depressed, should be over it by now, should change medication, should listen to this podcast, should find a man, should be happy, having it all together, picture-perfect white picket fucking fence and let go of all those shitty expectations and knowing that white picket fences were never going to be my thing. I ran with kindness and a gentle approach to myself. I learnt to be ok with my emotions, as they are not my enemy and they had a right to exist in my world, because fuck me, my horrors petrify me into disbelief. I found that I didn't break, I felt release. I didn't get lost in my darkness anymore, I spent less and less time there, while discovering that my darkness is how I coped, actually my own protection system and the safest place in the world for me. I stopped trying to hide my feelings, stopped trying to prevent them from being expressed, and stopped holding back the tidal wave of pressure. I accepted and acknowledged that they have a right to be in my world because they reflect the depth of what I have lived and are the way forward in retaking my life.

That was a few years ago. It took a few months to get everything out of my system. Warnings should be compulsory for what antidepressant withdrawal is truly like, how you attack yourself internally and after that horrible time, I have not looked back. I am me in compassion, not judging myself harshly. I practiced not fighting with what should be and allowed my body, mind, and brain time to heal. I got out of my own way and trusted myself. Something, a long time ago was taken from me and I fought so very hard to live through. My shame consumed me. I was wrong on the inside. I couldn't trust myself, so I had to trust others and I listened to everyone, desperate to get away from me. I did what I was told, even when everything in me was saying no. If you scream 'No' long enough it loses its meaning. Not even heard by me, when I was still attempting to speak, and no-one was listening! No-one truly heard my empty screams muffled by my own compliance with fear.

I've had it all, therapists, shrinks, pills, spiritual healers, mindfulness shit to a near fucking exorcism and the stupid thing was everything was external to me. No one said I had the power! It felt like not one person, including me, believed in my ability to heal. I couldn't comprehend what happened to me, let alone figure out what to fucking do. So, I made a promise to strive to feel in control of myself and that's how it started. In search of control and choice, I discovered my freedom. I learnt to allow and accept my body's expression of my emotional experience when I am triggered. This was my biggest hurdle, to learn to trust myself to be out of control and trust I can put myself back together. I discovered that I always did, I could always come back to me, even if that looks like a fumbling mess sobbing uncontrollably on the floor, or, to frozen in a zombie like state, or to walking around as if nothing in the world affects me. All of it is me working ridiculously hard and successfully because I am still here. I used to fight myself and hide my hands shaking, ignore my heart thumping so hard it feels like it is going to break free from my ribs that contain her. I would force a shutdown to contain everything internally, while inside silent screams rained down on me. And yet, I would deny it, tearing away at my insides! I was scared to feel, frozen by fear. Frozen in a false sense of control, that made me feel safe. I thought I could break out of that. I had the illusion of control. Now, I feel with my body and heart. I learnt to allow space, to allow time to nurture my screams, to scream until my screams ran out or my hoarse throat pained me so. Through practice and self-trust, I discovered that breaking a little was the best thing I ever did. No resistance.

First, my trust was ripped from me, and then I handed it away in order to 'heal'. This ultimately became the source of taking back my power, in realising I had the power within me. It is far from ideal and I don't want it to be, I'm proud of me both in my mess and my grace. It is my choice and I have one, a choice for the first time, in a long time. This type of surrendering to self, means I'm in the driver's seat and growing stronger and happier every day. It's far from fucking perfect and I have called it an epic fail in the middle of the night while being tormented by my past and yet survived to stand on my own two feet in the morning. I still have days where my brain is running the fear show and my thinking is off on mad thoughts based in fear or whatever I'm struggling with at the time. I've come to realise I am not alone in this. We all as humans experience this. I thought there was something very wrong with me. Some of us have fears that are real, the monsters in the dark are really, there, attempting to tear our souls from our bodies. I want to make sure my fear response protects me in the future when I need it too. Bad things happen all the time.

So, I needed to change my relationship with fear. To move from fearing everything and everyone, to determining for myself what fears are real and warranted and those that are not. Which fears are those that my monsters convince me of, like, "People only hurt me." We are like a representation of how we feel and deal with emotions in our worlds and, like everyone, I'm trying to find my own way in this.

I like to think of it as our inward emotional temperature matches the outward experiences. I handed my temperature control to others but now I'm setting the temp. I've learnt ways to trust myself, and to do things that help bring me down into my body, so that I'm not caught in the fears of my thoughts and allow the emotion to be expressed in my heart. I developed a way of making sense of what happened to me and how I could learn to live with my past. There is a part of me that I picture as a scared little girl. She's the one that requires to be nurtured and protected as I get stronger. She is the part of me that suffered, her spark snuffed, but she endured. This beautiful, delicate part of me, holds all my hurts and damage. When I'm frightened or in the depths of my darkness, she comes out and freezes us both, which helps me to disconnect from the world that is hurting me. Together we found safety in the dark, and I truly began to have a relationship with myself, in a way that acknowledged what happened. She and I have been together for a long time and she has protected us in the dark. She has also taught me to love my darkness as much as I love the light.

There is pain and safety in my darkness and sometimes a comforting solace and I am thankful for all of my aspects, as they are all me.

Occasionally, my warrior self has shown up in the deepest of places to protect us both with her armour. Sometimes, my little girl has complete control of me. She's very irrational and scared of the world and this literally means fear owns my mind, body and soul. Now, I fucking know this is my imagination! It is my way to make sense of what is happening to me and my thought processes, giving my fears a face to work with and become strong, for fuck sake I'm crazy, not psychotic! Perhaps debatable with a professional. I do have to have a relationship with my hurts, fears and torture. I learnt to listen and trust my voice by responding to myself with love and a gentle heart. Often I'm scared, and I need her to comfort me in the dark and then there are times that I help her from being terrified of the lightness in the world and you know what, altogether we are a stunning mess.

The mess that is life for me is truly about practising living with my demons, learning how they show up and how to overcome them. Opening and closing ourselves to the world, based solely on what feels right, on our past pain and hopes for the future. We all exist within the past, present and future of ourselves, but the key to being human is managing the balancing act. I feel like within us all is a spinning hot mess of chaos and we spend most of our lives hoping no one will see the depths of our mess when really, it's this mess that makes us fit into this world. I accept myself, in mess and wonder, in knowing that it is all of my experiences that make me unique and the woman I am. I don't want to live defined by pain. I'm trying to show up in every way of my choosing.

I practice choosing to see the good and kindness in myself and the world around me. I try to be present with accepting and liking myself, so I am most happy to hum to my own drum. I'm the one that smiles and says hello to everyone, even though this level of exposure was complete torture for me at first. I wanted to learn to be comfortable with all things uncomfortable to me. You smile at the world and the world smiles back, it mirrors you. It's how I began setting my own temperature, practicing the type of person I wanted to be before I was taken from me. I knew I wanted to be kind, and someone who was strong. So, I practiced being that person and noticing it when I saw it in others, even when I didn't believe I was strong. It has been an ongoing relationship with me, and writing has helped so much.

My relationship with Sam is different. I'm struggling with some powerful parts of me, including my trauma. For the first time, I'm wanting someone in my life as an equal, and I need help. I'm doing just fine, but love, a giant wave of love is chasing me. I'm caught drowning in the breakers, gulping salty air and need someone to reach down and help me tread water. To teach me to not fear the next wave, to read the waves and make it through the current, not return to shore. I don't want to live a "fine" life. I want this, I want extraordinary! I'm petrified, not of drowning, not of being swallowed by the abyss, but of not loving. I want to learn to love and be loved safely.

A moment on the street, a glance, a smile, a man organically saying hello and for a millisecond, we are frozen in time. A single moment of possibility beating through your body and before you know it, you feel it, without even seeing him. The heat rising within your body bringing forth, the first wave of chemistry, the soft scent of him dangling within reach and that stunned recognition of meeting another passion. I don't want to run from him. I don't want to sabotage. I force my feet to stick to the ground. It's not the first time I've felt this, felt eyes, experienced that want. It is the first time, I don't want to run from that level of intimate chemistry, where words have not been shared and yet the intensity is overwhelming. That fire ignited within you, equally matching the fire that is searching for you, desired in his want.

Attraction reciprocated in this way is the love at first sight real deal. It's the stuff of magic, not fireworks around you, but if you're in tune with your body, your heart creates fireworks within you, every cell in your body switching on and alive. In one moment, his want and need for you pours out all over you. The intensity of that one second, freezes me in time and into a state that I have not known. For me, a man who is equally confident in his strength, his manliness and ability to express a softness at the same time, is a very sexy man. When a man can be manly, and authentic in his skin while also completely comfortable with being uncomfortable at the same time, he feels different, more genuine. I think our internal temperatures matched the external and we both took a chance to show up even if our voice shakes, with the same emotional vulnerability, the same level of self-acceptance. Not running from the emotional expression of that moment, instead meeting it head-on, feeling the excitement and the nervousness in the emotion, and facing those sensations, not running away.

Sam embodies this and has one of the best swaggers I've ever seen. His slight natural hip swing rhythmically calls to my womanly desires. A man who takes my breath away as he moves in balance with himself. He puts on a sexy show of 'this is what I've got' and loves my eyes on him, as I encourage him to express his rhythm. Before I've even had a thought, I'm walking towards him. Our bodies tune to each other, making their own decisions, as they feel the chemistry and react to the energy whirling between us. Immediately, there is an instant recognition between us. A glance turning into childlike giggles at the acknowledgement of the connection, as he feels important in some way. It is like our bodies have a hidden language I've never heard before, and I'm allowing it to lead me. A true reflection of two individuals living life on their own terms, allowing to be caught up in the wonder of someone else. Succumbing to our emotional experience being expressed, with our fears somewhat conquered and our chemistry driving us toward each other.

For as long as I can remember the way a man carries himself has been important to me, either a complete turn on or off for me. You can tell so much by the way someone carries themselves in truth, not being anything but themselves. I had to become an astute study of people for self-preservation. We all have varying degrees of confidence, self-trust, self-worth, resilience… things I've battled with my entire life. If you're a good observer, you can tell when someone has mastered the art of self-confidence by the way they authentically feel comfortable in their skin. To, simplify they trust in their own ability to show up for themselves. True confidence is someone who sincerely has trust in the love of themselves and is ok with not having it all together. A value I attempt to live by every day is that my best is enough. I feel that someone who is genuinely happy in themselves, is humble in their confidence, feels right for me.

The character of someone is important to me. I want a life lover, not someone to live my life for me. I've battled a hell of a lot to get to where I am, while I will continue to show up for me, I would love to have someone stand next to me. I don't want them to do life for me. Let's be clear, every human being is an incredible work in progress. You never really have it all together. We all have had hurts and worse.

I do think it is character that defines us as being willing to be genuine in our mess while understanding that the mess is what makes you authentically beautiful. Being happy in your present-day story working with all aspects of yourself. Perfection by design is decided by you after all, created by you, you make meaning out of things, you write your own story to things.

I've grappled with understanding what happened to me, and believing I am bad. I have worked on and battled, surrendered and celebrated, freed and accepted the mind, body and heart of me. It has been an epic battle between all those parts of me, trying to never be hurt again and to feel my pain. Petrified to completely lose control, to feel torn from skin and buried in fright between demons and freedom. Battling letting go and being lost, to realising how much my thoughts are lying to me but how my body never does. How stepping into my abyss to allow expression was my salvation, I learnt to trust myself and that this came from my body and heart, from within. It was not through thinking; it was feeling expressed. My trust built out of my bodily emotional expression, in that, I felt more in control the more I let go of control on what I should be feeling. Learning to love and embrace my darkness led me directly to my light, because my darkness was a protected place for me. I battled with it so much that I failed to realise that for me, my darkness was also a place of safety too. I do not have it all together, or have all the answers. I just stopped fighting to 'get over it' and felt with my body. I opened to the perspective of living with and stopped fighting with myself to get over what happened to me.

I think we all have this ability to go into surveillance mode to predict our environments. To what degree each of us can do this probably depends on what has happened in our world, and I really feel that every human needs this ability to protect themselves. Some of us have developed special forces tactics to survive. I know when it began - it was the first time someone hurt me. My unconscious and conscious brain both went into protection mode and hammered that survival button into overdrive. I knew then that I needed to protect myself in order to stay alive. My hurts spilled into all aspects of my life. I was at the complete mercy of what my fear response decided was a threat, often everything and everyone. I naturally became focused on never ever being hurt like that again. My threat detection stood in between me and everything. So, becoming strong, predicting people and situations became my survival tactics, even if I didn't know that then. People who have had to survive also had to find a way to actually 'do' the surviving and the 'how' is probably unique to each person. Yet we are similar in our evolution of survival strategies, and how we hurt. I learnt, I listened and practiced ways of knowing myself, building trust in me and developing a sense of self, which, of course, enabled healing and self-trust, as well as understanding that I am and continue to be a work in progress.

I have noticed that when I am in the grips of darkness, my negative thoughts and painful experiences become so loud it's hard to see a way clear of it. I've learnt the tricks my mind plays, always in the same voice in my head, reminding me that I am unlovable or weak. On a bad day, I suffer an assault of thoughts screaming 'you are not even worth living!' If you hear this enough, you begin to live your life according to that lie from the shit show that your anxieties bring out. When bad things happen to you all the time, all you see and experience is bad things, so you must be worthless. This is one of my shit shows favourite attempts to keep me locked in the darkness. Don't get me wrong, this is not a conscious thing I did to myself. It is an unconscious habit we do to ourselves and for me is at times, even now, so exhausting and so loud. I try to be a witness to these thoughts, often sobbing in the background, attempting to not get on my shit show train ride of worthlessness. I have grappled with my shit show and it has owned me before. By accepting the ride and not moving through my own emotions, I was previously stuck in the stories of my pain. Until I learnt to navigate my shit show, changing this story was so hard and I am still working on it. Although, I now know how it behaves, I try to be several steps ahead.

I've always been trusting, and, I hope, kind. I can be gullible at times, but I have always had a stubborn streak that I did not understand. Finding my breaking point showed me how much fight I actually have. I didn't understand why some adults were mean and hurtful for no reason. As an already impressionable teenager who had bad things continually happening without reason, I began to believe that this was normal. If enough people hurt you, your new normal becomes hurting yourself to ensure the 'normal' continues, as this makes you feel safe. For example, you get called a piece of shit long enough, you will begin to believe it and act like it. Then you'll walk through life with this belief, and never really show up for yourself, because why the fuck would you? You are a piece of shit after all. It doesn't matter what that core belief is, or what was said to you, or done to you, in that one moment where you needed kindness and got a piece of shit, scars run so deep. Often, it's about making themselves feel better, or abuse, or just fucked up people. As a child you only end up thinking bad things about yourself, adults can't be wrong, you are. I had to learn to take my power back, to gain my control and get their voices out of my head.

And I did! Oh, and how life has opened for me.

I also committed to never living my life by what 'should' be. I'm excluding bullshit, mediocracy and drama. I'm fighting for real authentic connection.

I'm getting lost in the telling of my story and forgetting to tell ours. My point is depth meets depth. The strength of his character, the feel of his manliness oozed out all over my body, in that one moment, our first moment, never have I ever, experienced that before. A gift of being more in tune with myself was discovered. I had desires, I had things that I found sexy in a man. That I could have likes, preferences, I could have needs as opposed to being unwanted, damaged goods.

Now, let's refresh a little and return to the sexy glide of a man in complete self-acceptance. I was telling you how his swagger rolled into my life. There is a lot you can feel from a walk, if they are genuinely comfortable with themselves and unconsciously attempting to find a rhythm, instinctively trying to connect and find flow with you.

Have you ever seen a happy person walking, enjoying the flow of their walk? That moment of balanced happy, written all over their face in one of those lusty smiles? Your walk represents who you are, in movement through your senses and depths of realness. Like the story of the buffalo, running at the storm, not waiting for it to build, facing the storm and chasing it. A stampede at the storm, using the strength within you and the strength of the storm to rise. A buffalo has an amazing strut!

I saw a swagger in him, that said, 'I'm here, watch me, feel me', while his energy wrapped around me.

So, I rise up and chase my storm.

H I M | Two

I live between the farm and my business, frozen in time. Six weeks have gone by in a blur. I am surviving on adrenaline and feeling numb, shut-down. I don't know how I'm meant to be or what to say. What am I feeling? I just get on with it, one foot in front of the other and don't fucking think. I haven't cried since that day, when I cried with my dad in his final moments. One day folds into the next. I move through the motions of what must be done - there is no one else. I think they call it backstroke in denial, or what-ever. It is easier to focus on Mum and Ruby than me. That's what men do, isn't it? Get on with it, over it. Fuck. It's like I'm emotionally vacant, zombi-fied. The world is operating without me, a sea of sympathy smiles and the same sad, blank faces, I'm blank. Everything feels useless.

I saw her. In that one moment she beamed colour back into my life, jolted me out of the greyness of the world, for an instant. She was sexy as fuck, with a full body, curves that would make a man stand up, dressed in busi-ness type with a side of flavour, bright red heels clearly more her style.

The intensity electrifying, she's pulling me closer to her, drawing me in to her. I have no control. I want to know what that body feels like. I grow harder under the thought of her body squirming underneath me.

The world has stopped spinning. As if on cue she touches her lips with the tips of her fingers as if considering my thoughts, well at least that is what I am telling myself.

Could it be?

Her eyes are darting around the closer I get. I can see my impact upon her, as those powder blue eyes keep searching. I'm willing her to find me, to look at me, pleading with her. She finds my legs, shit she is fully taking her time. She slowly traces my body with those eyes. I'm internally encouraging her - come on, yes, a little more, fuck she's a confident woman! She lingers at my groin. It feels fantastic and frightening. She's openly enjoying herself and I love it. My walk naturally slows, giving her time. She averts her eyes, and I ponder how I could play with her.

I keep moving past the table she is at. The world starts up again, returning to a normal pace, did that really just happen? I stop at the shop entrance, trying to work out what I am meant to be doing. I'm staring at the back of her, hoping she will turn, willing her to give me a sign and some encouragement.

She is utterly captivating. I can make her body out, hips that I can hold on to, caramel skin that has been kissed by the sun, healthy breasts that compliment those curves, lips that hold a beaming smile. I want to see all of her, I want to peel her back, hold her down and taste her. I want to know her.

The intensity of my thoughts shock me and I demand that I hold my shit together. I'm not in a position to be looking for anything. The reality of my life slaps me square in the face and it all feels wrong, fucking selfish. I berate myself for looking for a distraction. I move away and start back on the tools for the shop fit out, measuring twice, and cutting once...

From the corner of my eye, I see her moving from the table to directly opposite me. I can't avoid her. She feels great. I take her all in now, head to toe, her body, presented to me, curves for days. She is giggling innocently with buckets of nerves.

That smile hits me in the chest like a ball of warmth and comfort, fuck, feels like home, fuck she feels like home.

Then in one instant, she shifts from nervous giggle to standing bold presenting herself to me. Fuck, the sexiest thing happens, as a woman comes alive in front of me. The moment is hot as hell. I am rock hard and take a gulp of air, completely out of my fucking depth. I instinctively move towards her and we stare at each other, frozen, in this electrified space.

She breaks the moment and I need to move away. What the fuck was that...? Emotions rise in me, fuck, what is going on?

I seek out the privacy of the back room in the store. I feel stunned, it's all too much, fuck. I force my thoughts and emotions away. She felt strong, vulnerable. That nervous laugh, both scared me and excited me. It dawns on me that, I'm captivated by her, and I want to get know her. I robotically get up and search for her. She feels amazing. Why am I hiding? Is this real or am I just avoiding feeling the loss of Dad?

I'm searching for those hips, while considering how she would find her rhythm on my cock. I walk out of the shop, looking back and forth, a little more frantically than I would like. I feel like a lost puppy and also a bit stupid.

I know she's gone.

Fuck, well done dickhead, loudly reverberates around my mind. I turn back to the tools and promise that if I ever see those hips again, I will get their number.

My day moves on well. I feel a little different in that a really normal thing happened and it's strange that normal is uncomfortable. I know that its

Dad who is a constant in my thoughts. I realised I had a moment where he wasn't, instantly anxious at the thought of losing a little bit more of him, with a punch in the guts hitting me square on.

Dad would want me to be happy, I know that. He was always going on about me finding a good girl. Such an old school gentleman, he was.

She looked like she could be that.

A wave of loss hits me again, the sense of loss embedding in my throat. I desperately try to swallow it away, force the thought and emotion away, fucking aggressively demanding I pull my shit together and not lose control. Be a fucking man! I tighten my fists and push away the gaping hole in my life. I feel like I'm betraying him and the family, thinking of a random woman when everything is fucked.

It is so hard to look at Mum and Ruby. The pain on their faces and horror behind Mum's eyes from that day. It's still there every time she looks at me.

Desperate for my thought pattern to stop, I say aloud, 'just get on with it'.

Something I say multiple times a day to block out and get on with what I have to do, keep moving.

It's like he never existed. Like this enigma that we all know a story about yet isn't around. People don't say his name, or they try to catch themselves before they say it. Truly the worst is when people actually correct themselves and redirect the conversation as if both the comment and Dad never existed. I don't get angry when it happens. I don't know what to say either. They're the lucky ones as it's not happening to them and I'm grateful they don't have to go through this.

Really, I don't know what to fucking say to anyone about anything at all. I don't trust myself, even though I'm walking around pretending I do.

I am the man of the family now. What other options do I have? Empty, just empty. I should be sad or angry or have more feeling. There's nothing. I'm numb to the world and his loss, the thoughts painfully digging into the hole in my heart. My mind swims in looping negativity. I'm scared I am stuck here with no way out. The colour in the world has gone, just like Mum's face - hasn't found her rosy cheeks. Ruby sobs and sobs, she's taken leave from work and the two of them walk around the house like zombies. I think they're helping each other but it's hard to tell. Mum's really the only one who talks about him. Well she still walks around the house talking to him, still sets the dinner table and just sits staring at his chair. Ruby said yesterday she stopped making his dinner. Looking at their faces is fucking horrible, the shame I feel from what I did. I can't even look at myself, let alone them. Why would this woman even want a fucking bar of me?

H E R | Three

Today, I'm feeling confident. I've got my nice heels on, dressed business smart, with a slight flare as my personality must shine through so I feel comfortable and not like a fish out of water. It will help to give me the courage I need for this meeting today. A potential big design contract for me if all goes well. My time to pitch. I've gone over it in my head and feel at ease with what I'm going to present and then it will be up to the gods.

At first, I am shaking and allowing my nervous energy to be there. This is big for me, so I accept my nerves, embracing my hands shaking in sweat, taking a moment to remind myself I am enough, my best today is all I need. I settle into my feelings and things begin going swimmingly. The table is engaging with me and a nice flow is occurring. My initial concerns dissipate about requesting to meet at a coffee shop. They are as relaxed and responsive as I am, so we have a lovely exchange of information bouncing back and forth different design ideas and excitement builds for our project, hopefully.

My temperature suddenly changes, I'm excited in a very different way. I feel him in my body first, the sensation of something quite different. I feel exposed and aroused. I don't see anyone except a wave of energy lustfully pulling at me and my own desire scratching to get out, to be freed and play with the person coming towards me. The energy is full of heat. The table has its own flow about the project applications thankfully. I'm being pulled in another direction, overwhelmed, I need to look, I'm distracted.

Reality hits me like a slap. Please, Evie, pull your shit together, I'm screaming internally at myself. This contract is too important and could set me up for the rest of the year! My skin is covered completely in goosebumps, a hot flush is climbing out of my womanly self, turning the heat up. I could lose it any second. I'm trying to focus, find composure, be attentive, avert my eyes. I can't resist glancing over and seeing his strong tanned legs, navy work shorts, a smooth swagger and reacting to my eyes on him, he slows, to feel my desire. I must stop my eyes from moving any further up his body, inadvertently lingering at his crotch, being too bold. Who am I? This is not me, openly checking him out. The intensity of the moment overpowers me, and I demand composure from myself and pull away.

I force myself back to the discussion, listening intently, right, branding, scope of campaign. I can feel him behind me now. I know he's watching his eyes feel like his tongue tasting me. I'm hot, flushed and throwing my hair around like a fucking peacock. Two vastly different people are battling inside me, one trying to be serious and not fuck this up and the other skipping off in lustful naughtiness. The hairs on the back of my neck are standing up to attention. I tune into myself and I think I'm panting, fuck, am I panting? This feels different, maybe? The pressure to turn is unbelievable, to look, to feel him, the sensation of him is agony. Tuning in to reality brings me acutely aware of my senses, the smells, my situational awareness, the dryness of my mouth, tingling of my thighs, pheromones going crazy and one of the gentlemen at the table smiling at me in a way I don't want him too. Sensory overload. What is happening to me?

My pitch somehow appears to be going well without me, luckily designers are always accepted as eccentric. I'm staring at them all, attempting to demand focus from myself. Perhaps a little too intently, so, I take a deep breath, quietly acknowledging the overwhelming feelings in my body, seeking some internal composure. My phone rings, startling me almost out of my seat. I ignore it, I am on edge. There is so much going on, I want to turn and see him, my head is spinning, the hot flush now spreading throughout my body…

Thoughts are racing. What am I saying next? I've not even seen him! Control yourself, Evie! He feels like the warmth of the sun on my bare skin, to tattoo left calf muscle, strong legs. My brain is taking mental notes of him, of what I'm seeing, trying to imprint the most significant. Then mid-crazy thoughts, I'm thrown completely. His energy is gone, snap, the feeling is gone. I can't feel him, I turn and look in the direction of his energy and nothing?

Internally my fears are screaming, piercing my vulnerable heart. You're a fucking nut job. I take a sharp breath to steady my stinking heart, to refocus on my work, concentrate, don't blow it please, stay with it, Evie. Trying to make the encouragement louder than the looming sadness and smiling assassin internally smirking at me, saying 'SEE.' There is just enough left within me to swallow hard, force my monsters down, ignore the battle raging in the background and return to the meeting, trying to resemble a businesswoman. Thankfully, we are finishing up. My phone rings again and I answer, relieved to move away from everyone.

The caller is angry, and their aggression surprises me. I feel pulled in every direction by my emotions, sensory overload. I might combust. I try to problem solve and pacify them, while feeling raw and useless. Focus Evie.

I look up to see a man standing directly opposite me. He feels all encompassing. In one hand he is holding on to a large concrete grinder that clearly requires both hands. He stares, holding my gaze. I'm hit at once with the fullness of his energy. He is overwhelming. I want to collapse into these sensations, wrapping myself in him. The thought turns me into a little giggling girl, I can't stop smiling at him and a calm descends over me. Strangely I stand brazenly, towards him. A strength pours out of me and the woman inside me steps forward, claiming her space, meeting his sexual energy, showing that his manliness is met, equally. I want to step forward into the possibility of this moment. He reacts, moving towards me, responding to the sexual energy calling him.

I felt empowered and drunk by our connected experience and the world fell away. In one look, I was lost and found, in being caught in this very intimate space. I was looked upon as a woman by the strength of a man, of mutual attraction, of lust, longing to be explored, beyond our own abilities to comprehend what may be, of a love that could be written in the stars.

My dreamy self takes my romanticism to the next level. Is this what 'love at first sight' could feel like? Perhaps. I don't allow myself to consider that thought, dismissing it quickly.

Fuck, I'm in trouble.

Time disappears until I hear "hello, hello" and I'm snapped out of my fantasy. "I thought I lost you" the caller says. Instantly, I'm looking directly at this beautiful man in front of me, responding to the caller with "you have".

I turn away from him, breaking our connection. Why did I look away? He is real, he still watches me. The feel of him is intoxicating. I feel him exploring me with his eyes, caressing my skin, envisioning his hands on me, all from an electrifying moment of shared desire. I'm dazed. I feel like I'm overflowing with joy! My smile is unable to be contained, and yet, cold waves of fear shudder through my sweaty body. It's been seconds and feels like hours, is it him? Really him? Could love like this exist? For me?

As quickly as I felt him, it's gone again, blank. I walk, going through the motions, as autopilot has just taken over. All I can hear is the dial tone at the end of a call. Brain is yo-yo-ing. Millions of sensations jolt through my body, pumping fierce thoughts all jumbled within me. The room is spinning, nauseous, with vomiting close.

I shake myself, come on. Breathe in. I head back to the table, as people are leaving. I find it hard to pitch my ideas as a graphic designer and I hope that I haven't screwed this up as well, I feel numb. My business connection, Wanda ushers me away from the table and walks me to my car, stomach sinking even more with every step. Wanda looks at me puzzled.

"Are you okay?"

Obviously, I am not holding myself together as well as I thought. I reassure her saying there is a lot riding on this deal for me. It means not having to chase individual clients all the time. Wanda immediately encourages me, and I accept her feedback, despite nerves pumping in my veins, hopeful that I haven't screwed it up entirely.

I've lost complete feeling for what the business outcome is. I just search for him, not finding him in any direction. Devastated I avert my eyes, I stop looking, I hide within myself, embarrassed now, fear wins, I'm owned by my fear, how can I do this, I stop and look back, he's not there, I can't see him, so I allow fear to tear me apart on the inside, Mrs Jekyll and Mrs Hyde at once.

How am I equally excited and nervous about what just happened? What did I just miss? I'm broken out of my head by Wanda, saying that the team have chosen me, I got the contract!

I'm not even excited. My heart screams 'why didn't he speak to me?' Why did we freeze in that moment? I didn't want it to end. My thoughts do the dance between self-doubt and blame. My thoughts lie! Or was this the possibility of love burnt into my soul. Is this what it feels like?

'I can have it', comes from a tiny voice inside me. He burnt into my soul. Maybe love can exist for someone as broken as me.

I have felt something similar, to a lesser degree, once before in my life. I will never forget that either, even though this was hugely different. You see, I didn't run and hide from him. I stood in my power as a woman, a deeper layer of me came forward and I want to experience her myself, I felt worthy. I did not hide or feel less than. We stood together, sharing that space of emotion, within the purest nature of man and woman, human to human, stripped bare, raw and ripe, held completely in that space together. The chemistry of possibilities. The chemistry of my romantic mind running wild in the fields of a happy land that doesn't exist. We are mirrors to each other, calling forth each other to rise to our potential love. Maybe it was too much for both of us, or maybe it was just the chemistry initiating a primal response in my sex and it would fizzle quickly. Maybe, maybe, maybe…

If you have had to fight in this life, there are definitely a few hacks I have picked up along the way. Reading my situations and re-learning how to trust myself, trust that my feelings and thinking, was correct. Not borrowing others opinions, and how the world tells me I should be, I should be over it by now, I should not make other people uncomfortable, I should find a husband, I should take care of herself better, I should do this job, I should accept… Shoulds after more should! Most of these expectations were coming from me, not actually what others expect and think of me. It is not only what happened to me, it is what I had to become to survive. What I have come to learn to trust is my ability to sync with people, call it situational awareness or a good study of people's mannerisms, to understand how much I'm feeling and the knowledge that we mirror feelings. When you connect with someone it becomes reciprocal, we feel together, to a variety of degrees of course, same tone, different amplification. I was lost in the music of his eyes, lost in creating our own emotional tone, my desires driving the sense of what might be.

He's been with me ever since like he has curled up in my skin, keeping me simmering and I invited him in, wholly. I feel like he claimed me, like I am now his. I loved it, not owned in the sense of controlled, in the sense of freeing the woman within me by meeting my match. Freed by what came alive within me. Having all of me celebrated and desired, my strength as a woman in all my power, wanted, my wild woman met her warrior man and we stood toe to toe and it was electrifying. My skin feels alive, feels sensual with internal buzz fuelling the fire within. He burnt into me and I on him, which is why he's here, he's everywhere, each day I'm closer to him, each day I feel him, feel me. I hear his voice, soft and deep, nurturing me protecting me, I feel him lying stretched out next to me. His energy is all over me and I'm savouring every movement. He feels strong and tender, he feels like all I've ever known, he feels like home, my home. You know when you meet someone and click, you get a vibe and it's like you've been friends or lovers for years or even before, times a thousand. Your energies, presence, whatever you wish to call it, dance together and this leaves a residual effect. We did this. He and I did this to each other. As if after that moment we've been getting to know each other before words are even spoken. Every part of me drank him in and I was thirsty, unaware of my dehydration. Our energy swirled around me, touching parts of me that I never knew, the door has been opened, the cage cracked. I'm tempted and encouraged, caught by him and my fantasies that are being created. I'm telling myself that perhaps this helped me to open myself and my heart, learning to receive love and to give, love. Feeling what that desired part of me feels like, the awoken women who stood toe to toe.

I'm a straight up kind of person where if I am not into something, then, I'm out. Like everyone, life teaches me pleasure, sadness, joy, despair, loss, success, trauma. We open and close our hearts as we move through this life in love and fear. Fuck me if fear is ever going to own me again. Fear can and will show up and it will not own me or my choices. Life has taught me to work with my fears, be open to them, to evolve alongside my traumas to build and choose a better life for me. A life where I choose my own happiness and choosing things that scare me, that expose my vulnerabilities that teach me equally to love my light as much as my darkness. This is how I've learnt to get to the good stuff, the joy. I am a successful, emotionally intelligent woman, I think. I see strength in vulnerability and value these qualities significantly, hence why I try to show up in my authentic self as best as I can.

Maybe this is the first time I've been ready to meet this part of me. I feel I have this capacity to understand myself now. Sometimes, we are all mirrors being held up against each other, same, same but different story and then the world mirrors our internal selves. If you attune to someone, tap into their frequency, by simply paying attention and listening with your heart, then you are basically able to, if open and comfortable in your own skin, sync into their beat. This is like when we attempt to connect verbally, our bodies are also struggling to sync or tune in at the same time.

A connection is beyond words, you will feel someone with your eyes, so tune in. The sole reason your first two years of life are non-verbal, it teaches us to emotionally sync. Your sync ability is always on and working on your own beat enables you to connect with others. Some people are Apple, and some are Android. You are not meant to synchronise with the entire world. Same, same, and different. I'm dedicated to learning this and I practice on me. After continually practicing, looking into my own darkness, and coming out the other side, it has developed. I'm attempting to have a relationship with myself, learn about me, learn how I ride the waves of life. I understand I am a student of life itself because every time I feel like I'm getting somewhere, bam, a wave. He is my rogue wave, a gift. I experienced him and every part of me was turned up, tuned in, the volume was maxed out, a love at first sight kind of experience.

When I am emotionally invested, my own emotions are completely out of kilter and my beat becomes more of a thud than bounce. You could easily compare me to a swan most of the time. I glide gracefully around above the water and a random craziness occurs under the water, where all the shit goes down, I sink into the mess. We are all swans, all needing to survive. Sometimes we hide behind it. Sometimes we are aware of what we are doing and keeping our fears at bay while operating to ensure we don't confront or overcome them, a wonderful survival strategy... Some fears are real, some monsters are real, full stop.

For me, my fears spiralling about him are do I measure up, am I too broken, am I loveable, am I worthy to receive love? Loving myself, I know I must accept them as fears and move through the thoughts to become unstuck, because they are just thoughts, I give them power and I can take it away. Good fears have helped me survive and certain degrees of this is healthy, although my demons are cleverer and use them against me. I must overcome them by facing them within myself and building my courage. All of your painful monsters keep you on the sidelines of life! You've placed yourself on the bench of the game of life because you didn't comprehend you are the actual coach of your life. The realisation of the power lying within me, is what changed the trajectory of my life.

My brain has a patterned fear response, it will avoid pain and fear like the plague whereas your mind, AKA, the head coach, pushes you past those fears. I like to think as my mind and brain as two different parts of me. The coach is my mind, the part of me that believes in your abilities, the one who turns the light on in the dark, so to speak, who pushes you forward, this is the good commentary. The big moments in life where someone touches the corners of your soul, gently caressing you, kissing your most exposed raw, brightening the dimmest of corners of your mind. A place no-one has ever been before, not even you. He feels like home, a feeling I've not known, nor truly understood I was even missing. It's a strange sensation for someone to grab you so intimately and yet not even a word spoken, nor a touch, his eyes on you exploring you again and again, as if each glance is the soft touch of his lips on my skin. I close my eyes, he's there, standing opposite me, not touching me, yet I can feel the heat from his body rising my own temperature. I can feel the heat of his breath on my neck, pouring down my shoulders. I sense him reaching for me, and I yearn for his touch. I want to hold myself in his strength, holding his solid gaze, unwavering, while the tension rises, suspecting his own trepidation of the energy we created, frozen, savouring it. I now know that love is alive, it could exist for me. It's what I've dreamt of, I have been claimed, by the possibilities of love.

H I M | Four

She took my breath away immediately. I knew it was her; no one else could shake my core like she did. It's been months and those hips, swaying in front of me are instantly familiar. I recognise the curves of her and begin following her around the supermarket. I'm caught by her, wanting her, discovering her scent, experiencing her. Fuck, she's a very sexy woman. The feeling hits the pit of my stomach with the weight of being out of my depth. Okay, I want this. I can't let this opportunity pass me by. I'm going to get her number. She's walking between aisles in a world of her own. I'm breathless at her natural beauty that makes me pause, amazing blue eyes, lightly tanned skin, and a smile, wow, one she freely shares with people she passes.

I chuckle with the thought of her being a nice girl, someone Dad would have loved to see me with.

Shit.

I see her smile to herself and I feel the warmth of her coming towards me. I could watch her forever. I want to feel that smile for me, to experience her smiling at me like that. I just walk at her, kind of like a march, awkward as fuck. I physically cut her off amongst the pasta and without any real thought find myself scaring the shit out of her like a creep! I then reach out to touch her, like a creeper creep, what the actual fuck… I see her hand coming at me in slow motion. She went to grab my hand. I literally scared the shit out of the woman. My god. I want to steady her. I want to touch her. Pull back, be a man for fucks sake! Those eyes are on me, transfixed and I feel alive, she's gorgeous.

I blurt out my name and just like that, she tells me hers. Evie, Evie, Evie. I want to repeat her name, she is echoing around my brain. The supermarket and the world fall away and it's just us. I'm fixated on her, soaking in the feel of her right next to me, the intensity pumping through me, our chemistry surging through my blank mind as this incredible woman blatantly looks me over. I'm intoxicated. I turn towards the products on the shelves to regain some composure. Words are escaping me. She smells so good, dripping in the sweetness of vanilla and coffee. I'm lost and she speaks, thankfully, as nothing was coming out of me. Spag bol, she announces. I can do this. We talk but I can't look at her. I feel her looking at me. She is shaking, trembling as much as me, my hand automatically reaches out to steady her, she looks up to me, vulnerable and open, I want to hold her, to protect her, I say aloud from God knows where, "I have you." I go for my phone and just hand it to her. Mustering up as much composure as I can, I encourage Evie to return to her shopping and I would call her later. She looks at me directly and pauses before patiently saying "please." Definitely the sexiest thing a woman has ever said to me. I manage to stop at "I will" to prevent stupid from falling out of me. Walking away from her down the aisle, I feel her watching me. When I turn back to her, my suspicions are confirmed and immediately I feel exposed, like she's measuring me up, each step amazing foreplay. I turn and confirm again that her eyes on me and that she looks to be certainly enjoying herself. The horny teenager in me is stupidly happy and I manage a corny move pretending my hand is a phone, with complete regret as soon as my hand signals her. I turn a red shade of embarrassment and yet, paused by that smile she gave me, she beamed at me, etching the image of her into me. Who meets like this?

Does this even still happen, organically? This is what it feels like all the angst and anxiety, total excitement and excruciatingly frustrating at getting a number. Fuck, my brain is fried.

Being hit by this amazing sexy woman, she feels different, I feel different, I want to know all of her. Who is this woman? She is utterly mesmerising. I leave the supermarket without any shopping. I'm too wired by the bolts of chemistry firing on all cylinders and it's like the image of her eyes have burnt into me. I want to hold her. It feels right, maybe she can help bring some colour into this shamble of a world. The lump in my throat returns and I feel a pang of guilt. It's only been 3 months since Dad died. Should you really be chasing a woman?

Evie wouldn't want to know me if she knew what I did.

I start the car and drive around the corner to the beach. Calm your farm Sam. You just want to hold those hips, feel her sexiness, play in her garden, you can have fun. I immediately text her- great to see you again, coffee at the beach? Relaxed, informal, away from thousands of people, perfect. I hit send before I think too much about it. She replied straight away, and I'm relieved, okay, it is done until tomorrow.

I'm at the supermarket and starving, which is indeed a bad combination for me. I'm struggling to decide between curry or pasta, walking between this and that, slowly getting frustrated with myself. For a woman who's fairly intelligent, dinner can be a difficult choice, grand ideas often turning into quickies. I stop and turn towards the rice, slightly choking on my thought, right there, blocking my way, is him! I'm talking aloud to myself like the local crazy lady, again. I'm stuck, someone has paused the world, frozen in slow motion, lost in his eyes, my body rushing to catch up, my brain completely gone. He feels so nice, I want to soak him in. I reach for him. My hand moves towards him at the same time as he was also reaching for me. We pause before touching, the reality of the moment dawning on me.

I'm blank, completely blank.

My inner voice is screaming at me to speak. We both say our names awkwardly at the same time: "Evie," "Sam," with a smile and giggle. I can't breathe, I can't breathe, it's like my insides are lighting up like a Christmas tree. Part of me wants to beg him to avert his eyes just for a second so I can catch myself. It's like he hears me and looks towards the shelves.

"Spaghetti bolognese" I blurt out. I'd eventually decided on dinner. I calm down a little and banter ensues about ingredients, whether to mushroom or not and how with age, next day leftovers create the best sauce. I attempt to sneak a look at him, wanting to dive into his arms, soaking him into my skin, feeling immersed in him. Internally I'm pleased with myself: words are coming out and I'm resembling a normal human, I think. A glimpse of him and immediately I find myself caught again in his eyes, my mind is racing with a million thoughts of nothing, as I'm flooded with every hormone my body can muster! I reach out and his hand steadies me. He says, "I have you!"

There is so much going on and it's difficult to focus on anything, except for this amazing warmth I feel from this man, steadying me now in this moment. My body is trembling all over.

"Please give me your number, Evie."

Releasing this moment could be overwhelming for both of us, handing me his phone, I punch in my number and ring my phone, not quite believing my boldness while doing it.

"I'll let you complete your shopping and call you later."

I manage to say "Please."

He smiles, squeezes my hand and says, "I will."

And, like that, I watch him walk away. He's got his strut on and he is magnificent. A man swagger, not fast, not slow. He's well aware I am watching, completely awestruck. He reaches the end of the aisle, turns, confirming my eyes are what he felt on him. He puts his hand to his ear to gesture about calling and I giggle. I never giggle. He's embarrassed at the instant awkwardness and as quickly as it all happened it's over.

He is gone. My breathing is slowly returning to me. I place my hand on my chest, on my skin, lovingly caring for my heart, allowing the excitement to rise and fall and my heart to return to a normal beat. I'm still standing in front of the rice, I'm not sure how long I've been standing there. Within another 30 seconds, I'm daydreaming about our wedding day, and him entering me for the first time, again and again, only to be flooded by visceral sensations of the feel of those arms around me. I have no idea how long I was standing there for with a giant smile on my face, remembering his smell, imprinting it on my brain. My god, he smelt amazing, a mixture of sweat, dirt, timber, and him, soaking me in his want. I'm trying to picture every part of him, his dark blonde hair, the boy next door looks mixed with hot farmer. His strong shoulders, striking blue eyes, healthy, hardworking type, natural strength and never been through a gym door look, with a feel of 'I work with my body and will gladly work on yours.' My desire is having a great time exploring the potentials of this man. The thoughts of him working on me does things to my lady parts. Those powder blue eyes are intense, and kind, fierce in desire. I could lose myself in them easily. I'm smiling at my own internal dialogue while thoroughly enjoying a rebuttal of "too late, you are already lost in the desire of him!" He has a welcoming smile, the kind that immediately makes you feel at ease, at him, my god, my body is screaming! I'm hot all over, my legs are aching, I'm yearning for him. My soul is fighting to be free of my thoughts, my body recognises love. My body the truest of truth tellers.

I finish my shopping in a daze, an afterglow of the future glows that await me resting upon my face.

I look for him as I'm walking around, I look in the eyes of everyone I pass. No, no, no, no he is gone. In my car, I hear my phone, it is him!

'Evie, great to see you again, coffee at the beach in the morning, Shelly Beach? Sam.'

I can hardly contain my excitement as I respond. *'Sure, 8am at the Rocks café.'*

I lean back in my car seat and a scream falls out of me that scares the shit out of an old lady in the car next to me. I get out to check on her still unable to contain my happiness. I end up telling her all about Sam and what had happened. She grabs my hand looks me dead in the eye and says, "don't hold back girl. Love, loudly!"

I repeat back to her. "Love loudly."

She gives my hand a squeeze and off she goes on her merry way. I ponder - could it be this simple?

That night was a sleepless one. Scared I would miss my alarm, bouncing between a dream-like state of all the things we will do, and my wakeful fears of fucking it up. I'm desperate to see what this feels like! I want to chase these feelings as I feel so alive and amped, caught in the excitement of what this man could be to me. Everything feels like the switch is ON, all my senses are ON, hence the restless sleep. I'm high on hormones and adrenaline. I wonder what he would feel like naked next to me? What I will wear? It's only coffee, only coffee. It's only coffee for fuck sake.

At 1 am, I sit up and instigate a firm talking to myself with a warm milk, and funnily enough, it's no different from what I had been trying to tell myself earlier. It is only coffee you nut job! I need to stop fantasising about him, but my internal thoughts are screaming at me 'no you don't!' I'm in a fight with my own thinking, alternatively battling thoughts to run away, and soothing myself to accept the variety of emotions. Building up and over analysing these interactions are only going to continue making you the crazy arse chick, awake in the middle of the night, wired and desperate. My internal conversations slowly begin to subside to bring a slightly differ-ent perspective, one I can work with. I know. I won't be able to hold back my crazy completely tomorrow. I will need physical space, as the closed in feel of the supermarket was too overwhelming. I want to be alone with him, to feel him, to look at him, to allow time to get used to our energy together. It is truly indescribable! Our chemistry is so strong.

We should get takeaway coffees and find a private spot at the beach. I relax with this thought as it will mean I can just exist in his space and see what that feels like and we can evolve however we need to. I just want to look at him, to savour these moments of discovering him for the first time. I feel like I need an adjustment period to keep my crazy at bay. I mean, I couldn't form words the last time I stood in front of him. I want to be true to myself and part of that is my desire and I will not hide, perhaps I should curb it slightly, not hide. There is a fire ball of attraction between us and I hope there is more, the prospect of something special, equally frightening. I'm so caught up, faaaark. These feelings are new, and I want to allow them in, to experience them in a good way, even though they are equally terrifying and exhilarating. I want to embrace the chemistry of us, our desire. I feel it flowing out of him and onto me and I'm going to stand in the beauty that is the female desire and follow my souls lead.

I wake startled by my alarm screaming at me. I speak aloud, "soul lead, trust yourself." Let my soul lead via my body. I laugh a little at how crazy I am, here's classic crazy woman phenomena occurring!

And it feels fantastic.

The romantic in me reassures, 'if it is meant to be, it will be.' I need to trust people are put in my way for a reason. I look at my body in the mirror. I want to feel his hands on me, the sensation of his entire body, washed over me, stretched out touching my everything, holding the centre of my womanly gifts. These thoughts make me feel sexy, different. I feel wanted. I'm surrendering to these feelings while imagining his hands tip toeing across my neck, tracing my bends and folds, shoulders, my back, the feel of his manhood. I ease the tension by making love with myself. I'm lost for a moment and relieved that the edge has been taken off, all the while knowing my daydreams are nothing in comparison to him and our potential.

Driving to the Rock's cafe, I'm okay. Kind of calm, singing along to whatever song is on the radio. I find a park easily enough, jump out and there he is out the front, those eyes on me. I smile nervously and walk over, feeling my legs shaking with every step towards him, my thighs quivering and oh my god, Evie, get a hold of yourself. My internal self begins scream- ing. I take a deep breath, allowing the waves of excitement and nerves to pulse out through my body, sensing the anticipation of his closeness. I stop resisting, allowing my body to feel encouraged to embrace these sensa- tions. Permission to feel. My own desire finds expression in my lady parts, my body is calling to him and I'm allowing myself to do so. I try to feel into my heightened senses calling to him. I take another deep breath and allow my body to feel encouraged, to embrace these sensations rising within me, to go with the waves. I need to trust my heart and body as they are both screaming loudly for me to chase these feelings and see where they could take us, to roll with the waves, the rising sensations in acceptance.

I've reached him with a smile, unsure how to act. Sam says, 'good morn- ing' and his hand slides down my forearm to take my hand, causing a warm tingling throughout my body. I can feel that he's not entirely sure about doing it and follows through anyway. My body is screaming you have my full permission. Can he hear it? It feels so sexy, and I can't stop "oh my God" from falling out of my mouth at the level of intimacy in his touch. He blushes and nods towards the beach. "Takeaway?"

"That's precisely what I was thinking."

He urges me to order first and is ever so polite to the barista. He hasn't let go of my hand, in a sweet and comfortable way, despite the intensity of our heated chemistry in the air and overflowing within me.

We are both aware of our heat and, the electricity around us. The young girl behind the counter visibly reacts to us, blushing the entire time she is serving us.

It is comforting to see his nerves as well, while I'm also trying to support me. My heart is beating so loudly I worry that the entire cafe can hear the solid thump, thump. I wonder if Sam can feel my heart calling to him, being this close to me. I breathe into my heart, allowing myself space to encourage me to appreciate this very moment right now. His hand is steadying me.

I feel my thoughts beginning to race, with fear cascading over me. "He is too good for you…" screams my mind. I decide to remind myself that my crazy thoughts are like TV commercials and I'm going to let them roll on by. I am not engaging them, just letting them happen so I can allow these feelings for Sam to grow inside me without colouring the feelings with my old fears. I'm basically forcing my feet to stay on the ground and in this moment with Sam.

I am enough. Stay with what your body wants, Evie. Stay here, in this moment. I glance down and realise I'm holding his hand very close to me, standing waiting. His hand is next to my thigh and both of my hands are on his. He feels so familiar, safe, and, wow, he is soothing my inner crazy.

We say nothing beyond the niceties of please and thank you while in the café. There is a little walkway outside leading to a seat overlooking the beach, a secret only known to the locals.

We sit still for a few moments in silence like we are tuning in to our music, our beat, to each other. We are close on the seat, not touching, yet close enough to feel one another. Our souls are dancing around us, as we feel into the space and energy. The ocean is calm, shinning with the bluest of blue. It's a soft winters day, and unseasonably warm with the sun shining down on us. He feels homely and I smile at the feeling that we are simply soaking in each other. I close my eyes and tilt my face towards the sun, inviting her warmth into my body. I feel him looking at me and I enjoy it and allow it, relishing the feel of his eyes on me.

Opening my eyes to look to him, he smiles.

"Evie, you love the beach, hey?"

I pause to feel the way Sam says my name, how it rolls off his tongue and through those lips, watching them for a moment before realising I needed to respond to him. I giggle and say a hurried "yes, yes I do Sam."

Pausing after saying his name, I want to say it again and again. We begin the small talk, testing the feel of each other out, all about the ocean, our love of the water, we laugh about my inability to master fishing or surfing and finding a shared love of ocean swimming.

Sam asked why I left the city and this question presented a choice that I had not even considered. I breathed in and out carefully, and as it felt right and natural, I opened up and shared with Sam, that in the city bad things had happened to me. I moved here because I needed space, physically and also to connect with this every day, gesturing to the ocean.

My vulnerability shared, Sam looks out to the ocean and says quietly, "sometimes it's places that help us". We both seem to drift into our own worlds and it actually feels important.

I remember the first time I sank my bruised heart into that ocean and felt comfort, felt like I would be okay, and I was. I am still holding my breath concerned about how vulnerable I have been. Sam sips on his coffee and says that he "feels like that at the farm". Our eyes lock in a softer way, it feels different, kinder for me and, wow, the realising that he could be more, beyond our chemistry, he could be…

"Sam, tell me about the farm…" I listen. He talks of rolling hills, his house, situated in the valley, while his parents are on the other side of the farm. He jokes in a big brother teasing way about his sister's house being still in the works. Ruby, his sister, loves the city and moved many years ago for university and stayed. Clearly, they are all immensely proud of her accomplishments and he boasts about her being a successful law-yer, which is lovely to hear, and it feels like they have a genuine loving relationship. Sam describes his mum as the country mother, the CWA mum, personified, proudly telling me all about her community work, and how growing up she was always raising money for this or that and doing the school bake sale, a clear leader of the mother's club. His dad, Robert, a working man, sun-up to sun-down kind of man, always willing to lend a hand and to give someone a go. The farm was his grandfathers, passed down to his father. Sam's dad always pushed his kids to dream bigger than farming, as it is such a hard life, backbreaking work, reliant on weather, markets, and other outside factors. Without the 'lucky' breaks the farm had, perhaps things would have been hugely different for all of them.

Sam shares that his dreams are to return to the farm and combine his building business with the farm, hoping the farm can stay in the family. Sam pauses for a moment lost in his thoughts. I'm guessing that he feels the pressure to do both. The conversation moves to my background and family, my older sisters who are much older than me and two younger brothers in New Zealand who I see a few times a year. My parents were not together when they had me and thankfully, they ended up developing a sort of friendship over the years. I let Sam know I am fairly sure I am a one-night surprise for them both. Sometimes I feel ashamed to tell people this but right now with Sam, I don't. I am much closer with my brothers even though they are across the ditch. When they do visit, they cause a little havoc up and down the coast, completely harmless at 19 and 21 years old. It's nice to feel like a family when they are here, we cook together, beach together, board game nights, we just spent time together and its nice.

"I feel very safe and loved when they are here."

I pause in my own reflections, reliving the last time Teddy and Cam visited. Our conversation finds more depth and meaning, it feels surreal and normal as we begin to talk of our values and beliefs while moving from sitting at the beach, to a stroll. He again reaches for my hand, running his fingers down my forearm with the lightest of touch, this time asking permission. I respond with a nod of encouragement. The heat from his fingertips, tracing my skin, the smallest of tastes of his touch. My forearm tingles in the aftermath of his touch.

We end up grabbing something to eat back at the café.

He feels so comfortable, it's very natural. His voice is deeper than I remembered, it's slow and considered. I watch his hands they have seen hard work. There's strength and resolve in them. His smile is, soft and somewhat strained, maybe. I think I can see pain in him, his eyes are as blue as the ocean is today, with a hint of greyness. I know he's younger than me, I think he knows too. He's very polite with everyone around us, we are carefully testing each other, both equally wanting to be liked. Thankfully, we have very similar values. His appeal is ever increasing. He is impressive and the way he talks of his family, makes my ovaries sing.

Part of me is not sure this is even real. Obviously, he's a good man, so why is he here with me?

While listening to each other we are searching beyond the spoken word, a conversation is occurring below the surface. We are dipping our toes into the space being created between us. All the while we are exploring each other, his eyes are in my soul, he feels like he is peeling away layers of me, holding me close, feeling every inch of me, igniting parts of me, discovering me, as am I him. Sam speaks and I'm watching his lips, his tongue, the way he moves, transfixed. He feels me doing it, and I'm wondering how those lips feel. We both blush upon coming back to reality of the café it's as if he's reading my lustful thoughts. Those eyes are hitting me in my depths. I can see and feel him searching within me, we both are, each time he gazes into my eyes with intent it's like he is diving deeper into me, his eyes peeling back the layers within me, searching.

Seeking out privacy we head back to the beach again, neither wanting our date to end. We go for another walk on the sand, eventually finding a spot to sit, settling in side by side. I turn to look at him, he smiles, and I can see he's nervous too, his lips quivering as he says, "You overwhelm me."

"I feel it too. You fascinate me. I had hoped to see you again. I was caught by you, frozen. I have never experienced a moment like that you drew me in, I could feel you, I was fixated by your desire, and I wanted you, I want you now, it's more than that, I don't fucking know. I'm not really sure what is happening to me." I blurt out. Sam's bottom lip is uncontrollably trembling now with emotional vulnerability and I'm scared of his reaction.

Sam expresses the same confusion and his frustration seems equal to mine. "I was also paralysed by you. I've been searching for you every day since! I hoped it wasn't over, maybe it was wishful thinking, who knows. Then when I saw you in the supermarket, all caught up in what you were doing, talking to yourself, I knew it was now or never. I stalked you down a few aisles, composed myself, and you know the rest. This just feels so easy, nerve racking, yet I want to us to continue getting to know each other."

I take a deep breath my mind spinning, not sure he just said those things. I manage to say a shaky "please."

Collecting myself, I take the same risk to expose my emotional naked-ness, sharing what he did to me that day. "I looked for you too, I went back there three times that week. I felt stupid for not talking to you. Our intensity overwhelms me too, you feel lovely. I didn't know I could feel this and feel stupid saying it because I just met you, I desire you and feel our attraction developing and I want to know more, I want more." My face flares red at this level of honesty. I'm trying not to look him in the eye, did I really just say that? Just roll with it, I tell myself. Don't hold back. Rolling with my inner turmoil. "I clearly like the feel of you and I'm also scared and want to run from you, even though you feel ever so safe." "This is new ground for me, and I want to get to know you. Just to be clear, so you know where I am coming from, I do want something real, I want love in my life and I'm not here for a fling. I want to discover the possibilities of what we may have, whatever that turns out to be. I made a commitment to chase things that make me feel good, even if they scare the shit out of me. I do feel like there is something big between us and I want find out more and I am here with all my crazy and all that I am."

He stops me. "Evie, I am here honestly, too."

I tell him that I promised myself today that I was going to show up without bullshit fears, of wanting to be liked. "I like you I want to get to know you and I want to honestly share what I am feeling. I feel compelled to tell you, even if that scares you away, I get I am being pretty full on." As I'm saying this, I can see his expression change and his body language pulling away.

I attempt to reassure him. "I didn't think it would happen on our first date although I am happy it did, and you now know what my expectations are."

He turns to me, pauses in anticipation. "Evie, I want to taste you, I want to hold those lips with mine, now…"

Bam, I'm breathless. The sexual tension between us skyrockets, stunning me into silence. I'm shaking, taken aback by his level of intimacy. He notices, the intensity continuing to rise between us. His restraint is powerful. He holds my hand up towards his chest, for a moment, getting lost in those blue eyes, the intensity of his gaze, our closeness, his presence slowly washing all over me, his scent swirling around me, gently caressing my skin, claiming me. His heartbeat pounds through my hand, as I turn and spread my fingers on his chest. He's still touching my hand. We are so close, it is electrifying. He interlaces our fingers and stands, pulling me slowly up towards his body. I want those lips to pour over me right now in kisses.

He turns and begins walking and I'm desperately trying to breathe. I think we both are! I'm letting my body shake, allowing him to see the impact he is having on me and spending the sexual energy between us. I can feel us both attempting to steady each other after our vulnerability and the power of dipping our toes in each other's desires, our wild selves us. The little girl inside me is crying with joy because she just literally fell in love with her man.

H I M | Six

I've been here since 7am. I've scoped out the place, gone for a walk and found a spot we could sit and get to know each other, while I fantasize about touching every part of her with my tongue.

The early mark means I'm here first, waiting and desperately trying not to sweat too much. Fuck, I'm nervous, the sweat pours out of me. She will arrive to me sitting in a puddle. Fuck, get control mate. I give up on trying to feel comfortable and go with nervously controlled, well that is what I tell myself over and over, again and again until I see her. Out the front of the café, I'm pacing, feeling completely out of my depth here, and then she is here, stepping out of the car. I'm immediately breathless, she's got that body in jeans and a tank, letting me see all of those curves walking towards me. I am paralysed by her swinging hips, panic rising the closer she gets. Fuck, that smile, she's indescribable. Fuck, why is she here with me? Words fail me, again. Evie says good morning. I move my lips, but nothing comes out. Reaching for her hand, I, miss and touch her forearm, so I slide my hand down the inside of her hand, staring blankly at her the entire time. She looks up at me with those eyes and 'oh my god' falls out of her mouth, giving me some courage that we are both nervous. Okay, getting my shit together. The longer I feel her skin, touch her hand, the calmer I feel. My mind is slowing, and I can focus, suggesting coffee at the beach. Space. I need space with her. I need to get used to this feeling. I'm focused on obtaining coffee and getting her on my own. I continue to hold her hand and she holds my hand so close to her body, sandwiched between both of her hands. It feels intimate, her delicate fingers running up and down my much bigger hands. They must feel so rough against her soft fragile hands. It's holding me in a trance, watching her hold my hand, ever so lovingly. Observing her gently touching me, feels dreamlike. I'm sure it's happening but not and it also feels like the most normal thing. I guide her out of the shop towards the seat I staked out earlier. It's private even though it is close to town. As soon as we sit, the normalcy of the moment is gone. The overwhelming attraction and desire builds instantly when Evie sits turns her body towards the sun and tilts her face up, and I can see all of her body. My eyes trace her neck, over her breasts, and return to her face. She is smiling at the feel of the sun, I think. She happily explains to me how the sun feels, 'on her'.

She talks a bit strangely, but I think I understand she feels comfort from the sun and like it's good for her health wise. She talks of golden hour, and I ponder how that is also my favourite time for the day, when all the work is done and it's a time when Dad and I would have a quiet moment. There is nothing like the colours of the sky at the farm. I'm sharing this with Evie and it's comforting how easy she is to talk to. We both look at each other in a long pause, without words, yet this feeling I have with her, it's so strange to explain, like kind of coming home?

No, no that's not it.

I've never described a sunset in the way I just did to her, and yet it is how I feel about them. I look at Evie and ask her to truly tell me about herself. I'm still not sure what is happening nor what truly means, but Evie, takes a deep breath, looks at me and responds with okay. She begins with the ocean and how she loves the way the water makes her feel. She's so intense and open. It's refreshing but I'm not sure I can keep up, feeling a bit puzzled. Evie then tells me about her family. - She's close with her brothers from New Zealand - and kind of skims over her parents. She tells me about the child she was, a bit of a dreamer, wanting to be a marine biologist. How her dream didn't work out, life threw her some curve balls. She's worked hard on herself to overcome these challenges, she's very purposeful in her life and wants to make sure she is contributing to the world, to bring a sense of meaning in what she is doing.

We are very different.

Our conversation is very intimate, she's truly showing me who she is, her hopes and goals. I feel challenged by her, so I match it, telling her all about Ruby, Mum and Dad. Our conversation errs on the side of positivity and I don't want to share with her about Dad. I don't want to ruin the mood. I know I choose to leave out Dad and that he is gone, maybe I am practicing a bit of denial? How do you even say that? I don't want her to know, anyway. I share with Evie my dreams of the family farm and my building business and being able to combine the two businesses. Truly my heart is in the farm.

It is so bizarre that I am actually sorting out my life while talking to her. I am figuring out what I genuinely care about and value. My family legacy feels so important now and I want to make Dad proud of me. I do know that. I haven't shared this dream with anyone yet, well except Dad. We had been planning this for years.

We talk and talk, and she asks loads of questions which is great as it helps me to consider what my next move is and what is important to me right now. I feel like I know her, I feel like I'm talking to an old friend I haven't seen in years. Every now and then she takes a breath in, smiles to herself and refocuses on our conversations. There is so much about her that I like and so much that confuses the fuck out of me, and yet I want more of this. She is intriguing, she has big dreams too. Big aspirations for her business to make an impact, and although what we do is polar opposite, we find commonalities and time to listen. It has been such a long time since I have had a conversation that flows in this way. When she laughs, she curls her toes in the sand. We are both taking each other in, moment to moment. I notice her watching my mouth, how she plays with her hair, how she takes the time to consider my questions. She doesn't jump in, she slows down and takes time to respond thoughtfully, well, at least, that is what I am learning of her. I've watching those hips so closely. They're calling to me, I want to taste what's in between them. I'm having waves of pure desire and need, amid beginning to realise she could be the coolest chick I've ever met. The thought of Dad really liking her, too, brings an uncomfortable space. I need to move, hastily suggesting lunch. The contemplation of Dad is impeding on what's happening. I'm uncomfortable and dread is building in me. I need to move and still want to get to know her, I don't want this to end, I don't want her to know about Dad. I don't want her to look at me differently. The guilt rises in me from my pain and my attempts to shut it out. We have talked for hours and it feels nice to be with her. I want to stay in this space with her. She is so deeply passionate about so many things and doing things with meaning is important to her. There is so much I don't understand, and I'm intrigued. I think she's been hurt, there feels like something is big there, she said she has been through something and struggled with processing what happened to her. She also said she found her way on her own, my God, she feels strong and capable. It scares me equally, making me want to hold her, protect her. I'm ashamed of hiding my own pain, pushing it away and down, refocusing on her. We eat lunch and it feels natural. We're still learning and testing each other out. She feels intense, the way she moves gliding those hips in front of me, seductively. She doesn't see me as a tragedy. Even though I'm talking away with Evie, I'm not even sure what I'm talking about. Her eyes are focused on my lips. I can see what she's thinking about. I deliberately slow my talking and still she's watching my lips, my shoulders. She is sizing me up. I've never had a woman be so publicly direct, and open with her flirtations. She's touching her lips and clearly considering what mine would feel like. I edge a little closer to her. She blushes. I can't help myself and I ask what those lips would feel like. She looks directly at me, holding my gaze and suddenly, I'm blushing, and she is smiling. My reaction to her is so unusual for me, and I like it.

I want more of her, to know her.

We seek out the privacy of the beach again.

My mind is racing. I feel excited and want more of her, I want to know her. The way she watches me is so intoxicating. I want to take my time with her. It is clear to me now I like her and find her truly captivating. Everything is building, the intensity alongside my realisation has me both wanting to experience her while feeling daunted.

We sit and I tell her, it just falls out of me. I have this need to be straight up with her. To my shock I actually tell her I am mesmerised by her. Fuck, words are cascading out of my mouth and I have no ability to stop. What a dick. This is not me. I've never been so forthright before and it feels very fucking uncomfortable. Her closeness, being in my space, every breath. I breathe her in, she smells like a mixture of beach and, sweat, with our chemistry filling the air. I could touch her, she is so close, I could hold those hips while pressing her entire body against me, in one swoop, I'm sure of it.

Evie breathes a long slow breath, looks at me and utters the sexiest response. It curls my insides. 'Please.' Simply exquisite, I can't hide my desire. She tells me we clearly both are coming from the same place, except she is talking about attraction developing. Okay, fuck, listen. The way she moves her mouth, as her tongue curls, I'm brought back to her immediately when her body shifts. I scare the shit out of her, fuck, out of her...? Jesus, I don't want to be hurt either, I interject, I am here genuinely too. I like her honesty, she is keeping me on my toes. I hope, I can keep up. She's overwhelming, her fears, her expectations, fuck this is too much, wait is this what I want? How did we get here?

I trace the curve of her neck to the rise of her breast, I can't stop myself, golden tan. I move closer, wondering how far that tan goes, I glance up to her eyes and back to her breast, wanting to wrap my lips around her nipples, tugging slightly. I want to tell her how I need to taste her, those lips, dive into her and feel all of her from the inside, it is thrilling. Watching her feel my words, space freezing around us as she moves closer. I want to keep this going, I move closer and force my cock down, grabbing her hand, pausing. Attempting to compose myself, controlled, standing up and pulling up her up close to me. The anticipation is written all over her face, she touches my heart uncontrollably beating, fuck, I turn us both to survive the moment, head spinning, heart thumbing, sweating and dizzy. I think I just learnt what bewildered feels like.

What the fuck! I want more of this. Not wanting this to end, I suggest dinner the following night. That was amazing. I'm hoping it's not too soon, that I'm not too eager. She agrees and just like that, my head stops spinning. I'm not sure what has happened, I can't get the feel of her body out of my head. I'm pumped and shitting myself at the same time and happy, for the first time in a long time, happy, even before Dad.

The pang of shame rises in me. I didn't tell her. I pretended Dad's still here. I get a flash of Dad, the smell of diesel, the stench of sweat, that sickly smell, the dogs fearful barking, his anguish and my clear realisation of what I had to do for Dad, rapidly bringing the cold sweat of despair. The dread in knowing what was needed, I can't do the right thing, is bouncing around my thoughts. Another punch of emotion, the stinging of pain, trying to pour out of me, what the fuck, this is fucked, desperately trying to push it away, fucking pull it together, saying it out loud to myself, through gritted teeth, strained muscles, all of that pain swallowed down deep. I literally drag myself back to reality, what the fuck was that? This mass of emotion, forcibly telling myself to leave it in the past, let it go, it's time to move forward. Move on, move on dickhead, I repeat aloud.

After getting home, Harold is barking and jumping around like a crazy person. Harold doesn't know he is a dog, mostly human, that dog. He needs exercise, so we go for a run and it helps me to pull my shit together and plan how the date will go tomorrow. I am surprised by how much I like Evie, while reminding myself that I am not looking for anything serious, despite her being utterly alluring.

H E R | Seven

I think you need some background. You see, although I've loved in life, I've not loved loudly. I have never explored the love in my heart, this gift that exists within me. I was limited by self-preservation and the belief that love did not exist for me. I have felt a tender hand and not so; trauma locked away my heart and me with it, caged. My love life since then has been something of a silent war zone with a dictator in charge. I've had myself on the bench when it comes to love, basically. My history has meant that I had to learn to stand up for myself; fight in ways that are smart and that keep me safe, that meant I never put myself out there to be in a vulnerable position, basically keeping me benched. It was safer that way and I didn't have to be confronted by my horror story. I let hurt win, I let the pain of what happened to me dictate my life, I did my best to get through. Even though then I didn't even know what my best could look like! You see, surviving the unthinkable means letting pain and fear control me in every way, ruling my world without consciously knowing it. Truly I was just surviving. I knew there was something wrong with me, and because everyone kept telling me, I knew it must be true.

I closed myself off to all the possibilities of life, including that I was worthy of being loved. In order to block my pain, I inadvertently blocked out every emotion and everyone. I spent so long trying to not be too damaged that I became damaged, by believing there was something wrong with me. Somewhere in my healing, I unwittingly decided that I was too damaged to be loved, that I couldn't put anyone through my shit. My traumas have meant I had to learn to survive and predict my world, and even though I crave intimacy, I am petrified of it at the same time. No-one was ever going to get close to me. This was my survival tactic, my way to cope in the world. Trying to predict people's behaviour and not putting myself into situations that I couldn't control is how I survived. To achieve this, I learnt about people to better manage my interactions. I became hard and cold towards the world as I needed to be someone people couldn't mess with anymore. I had to turn and face the danger, fight, walk straight towards it and get my power back which has helped me get out of some scary situations while aiding in healing my horrors. This also meant I discovered how lost I had become, how scared I was, and that I as a person am fluid, not rigid, that life is the ebb and flow. It took a lot of running at first and freezing to learn to retrain myself in those situations and feel my own fears so as they became a strength, to use my fear and throw it back at what's scaring me to walk into my fears and rise above.

In mastering my environments, predicting when I need to be scared and when not, working out what was logical and rational. I became the manager of my fear. Monsters are real. I was no longer going to be controlled by fear or people who hurt me.

It is wholly exhausting living with trauma, mentally, physically and emotionally. They all work together in overdrive, so I had to have a relationship with my triggers, a relationship with a solid understanding that I am working through. Trying not to make sense, trying to just accept me for me and to live authentically as best as I can, for my survival, trusting if things are showing up, I must listen and allow. To be fiercely me, switching out of fearful survival mode, I was actively choosing my happiness mode, with limited protection detail, because of life's ups and downs. I can and have found such love in the depths of me and what I am capable of and the realisation of wanting to one day share the love inside me, before I was put in a cage.

I am not caged anymore.

This led me to learn to soften myself. Funny enough, one of the ways I did this was to practice smiling more, as I was so awfully hardened and closed as a person. Surviving is equally hard, and I found my hearts strength and who I could be before she was taken from me.

I am only just now learning the possibilities of my heart, of the love that exists, already within me. I have not ever allowed myself to completely understand this love. You see, my heart, was locked away a long time ago, along with who I was meant to be, it was all taken from me. Monsters locked me away and my sense of self followed soon after, and I stopped functioning in life. I didn't live nor know how to thrive, until recently. You don't know what you don't know.

Opening my heart and self to softening has enabled joy to show up, for love to be felt from within. I fell in love with myself and I so appreciate her and all the lived parts of me. I do understand that my heart is my way forward to evolve and be the woman I was always destined to be, and hopefully, if I am lucky enough, to know love. I know it's mind-blowing and I'm yet to fully explore or surrender to my love and discover the love of another. You see, while my experiences in life have made me into this person now, I don't believe I have ever been broken. I refuse to break but my god, I have bent. This is my inner bent heart, my love of real things, my body and soul being ignited by the desire of a man, attraction, all the while I'm attempting to allow space within my hurt heart for something new to grow and for me to learn love. This is not just any man, nor is he a fucking warrior, he's an ordinary man with good values, built for me, I hope, and I him, the soul's recognition of love's potential.

This is not a glance across the room kind of moment. It's a stop you in your tracks love at first sight, showered in chemistry and sprinkled possibilities. Your body ready to explode like a firecracker, with heat firing in all corners of you. I would not have been able to love him previously, as I was locked in fear. I had to learn that fear is a beautiful thing when I embrace all the parts of me, not running nor pushing it down deep inside me. I didn't want to be stuck in my traumas anymore. I had to face these otherwise being 'bent' was going to become 'broken'. I was so very sick, so very tired of fighting. I found myself rising in my own darkness, learning to just allow myself to feel, to trust me to swim in the ocean of life. Truly deep down, I believe I took back my life through small moments of bliss, like swimming in Mother Nature's ocean. That one thing for me that made me feel free from my horrors every day. The ocean, beautiful and dark, embraces her storms and rolls with them, her power shining bright in storm and light, she shares her magnificence, so I learnt to tread water in my stormy darkness, followed by swimming in the sunshine. I allowed and learnt to love those parts of me too, accepting my fears and my pain as real. Then I managed to stand up and get the hell out of my own way.

I learnt new ways to tread water, not judging my screams, just by rolling with myself daily not looking for a reason or label. I felt and accepted my feelings and found my emotional expression could be whatever it needed to be. I was expressing my emotions and the storms within began to subside.

The treading of water taught me so much about my storm, how to read what was happening for me internally and what my fear was thinking. Experiencing the storm inside me from a perspective of kindness and softness led me to a tenderness from the fight within, that nurtured my rage, felt my sobs. I felt my overactive and fearful mind quieten, as I stopped trying to dissect what happened to me and let it be viscerally processed, while learning what swimming looked like. I stopped fighting with myself and my demons. I accepted, cried, accepted and raged some more with a tender heart, allowing space for my demons to exist and my irrational fears to dissolve and the things I should be fearful of stayed and yet didn't control me anymore. I understand that fear has a value we need it to survive. There are things I should be afraid of and things that are there because I am afraid, retrospectively defined by my past and my traumas. I needed to distinguish what was real fear, and what was preventing me from living my life. I practiced trusting myself, realising that within me was all I needed. I found that everything is within my power and I can also get out of my own way.

Being too scared to go down my dark tunnels meant that my life was on rinse and repeat! The same merry-go-round every day, so I decided: life must be more than this. I planted my feet on the ground and began with accepting and allowing whatever to come forth without judgement or expectation. Only softness could live in my responses, so if I felt like crying I would. If I was scared, I trembled and encouraged my body to express it. I cried a lot, like truckloads of tears, mostly exhausted, mostly in the dark and often ending in exhausted sleep. I screamed, I shake, I beg, I still do. I process.

My body releases for as long as it needs to, and I don't judge her. I am grateful for my body's expression. From deep within me, my all my power came back, replenished, a new beginning for me. The way my body releases scares me at times, with trembling continuously, shaking in my bones that creates that dull ache, that continues physical pain, convulsing out of my body. At times I didn't know if I could go on, although I did believe that forward was the only way, backwards was not in me. Moving forward, I felt a building strength in me. I could feel the mountain moving, but I could trust myself to live through it. I am not going backwards, so, I shake, pain burns into me. I'm bending, not broken, all things that provided a glimmer to go on, to choose me, no longer letting monsters in. I continue to express my feelings without judgement, if I am lonely, I let loneliness in, if I froze in the moment, shutting out the world. If I have a pang of emotion, I accept it and just allow my body to express it however it wants. Allowing and accepting with kindness became a daily focus. Even if accepting was screaming my house down, I learnt to listen, not to judge. Over time this listening to myself and allowing space for whatever expression soon developed into softer, less pained expression. I guess I stopped getting so out of control in trying to be in control of my darkness, that it allowed me to gain back my control. I went from expressing rage by screaming, to being able to just feel, note it to myself, combine my body and the feeling, the rawness of healing, a messy, exposed, red raw fight to release and trust.

My internal volcano became a mountain followed by a hill. The opening and closing of my heart enabled the true horrors of my pain to show up. Please understand my pain is mine, it belongs to me and my heart's strength is releasing and holding on to some of that pain in order for me to find my way back to me. It is a relationship with myself, not an end, not a label, I need an understanding of who I am, being open to me, I couldn't get over it, I couldn't get it out of my head, I have learnt for me that is impossible. Some pain is meant to be remembered, held on to or simply exist in the depths of your darkness, it's not necessarily meant to be dissected. I understand the stripping back of a person, of the slow unravelling, it happened to me, first by others now by my choosing. My bent pieces have lived and mended and lived again. The heavy pounding of the darkness, on my chest, the tricks my fears play to on me, to keep me locked away, protected, my nights of shuddering, begging for the waves of ugliness to pass, for self-hatred to swallow me whole, for someone to save me, for it all to stop, for the self-loathing, the torment, the tearful exhausted sleep to engulf me, awake flashbacks and surrender to the empty night, repeat. Finding hope in the dark, then awakened monsters again, my darkness knows me, understand me, giving up, cuddling my insides, darkness wins. It's mine, not anyone else's. No one can take it, nor save me from it. I live, I rise, fuck you, I know my monsters and I control my internal self now.

I understand making meaning on all levels of heart, mind and body. I have battled and learnt to embrace and love my darkness as much as my light, I know their ways. I am blessed to understand my bodies expression of that darkness, the shudders, the heaviness, the dread, it is how I become, feel, and show up for me. I know my pain, my monsters, I've learnt to free them, trust in myself to visit those dark places and return to me. Each day I take back my life from the monsters that had taken it from me. The more I accept me for who I am, the more the judgement leaves me. I argue less with myself on who I should or should not be, and I've never felt happier nor freer in my life. It doesn't mean I haven't revisited my dark places, or they don't occasionally sneak up on me with ferocity. Instead, it means I now allow and accept a different response, one of self-trust and belief in me to show up for myself. This is what led me to my happy, to my chosen life.

Despite this internal world that exists for me, I live also in a world of confidence and strength, a hard shell. Well let's be honest, I'm a fucking smart warrior woman. I've been tested, and I've shown up for myself. Some people are lucky to find their love within and not know horrors. If truth be told, we all have a horror show in the background these days. Finding love helps us to have an anchor in this world. You see, I had to be my own anchor, drawing strength from within, not from the love of another. That 'you need to love yourself first' bullshit is true. When you have a solid foundation to start from, it makes a huge fucking difference. That core strength that rises in you to overcome any challenge success-fully. It's that feeling of invincibility, like a honeymoon period of a rela-tionship where you believe you can achieve and overcome anything. It is a foundation within us, I have all that I need within me, my belief needed to be reinforced continually. I had to show up and find this within me, as I didn't have any other choice, than to choose me and believe that I could be that for myself. I chose to begin living and creating my own version of happy and now with this man walking into my life, my world is shaking, my foundation scared, my belief in my sense of self is afraid. All that I've dreamed of is in front of me, maybe love could be real for me?

I did believe for a long time that I was too bent, too damaged and com-pletely unlovable. I discovered how wrong I was through self-love and taking a risk to trust myself. I know that my traumas will come out, I understand that my brain and fears will work hard to sabotage this, which is why I'm trusting my inner self now with my darkness, to help me be grounded. To help me to stay in my authentic self, to feel out of control and free to still show up, to help me to learn to love like a goddess in my truth. I am love and I want to share it. Holy shit, perhaps I should even drip feed you on my crazy. Please, let me not be so damaged for love.

H I M | Eight

Driving to Evie's, my hands are shaking. It dawns on me that in my haste to get ready, I choose the shirt I wore for Dad's funeral. It's been a while and it's not that bad, I guess, but I ask myself should I be wearing it? Is this a reminder that I shouldn't be?

Fuck, it's a shirt for fuck's sake. I'm struggling to make decisions and knowing what the fuck to do lately. I'm all over the shop. I'm not so sure it's a good idea to have dinner so soon.

She's got this spell over me. Well, truly, if I'm honest with myself, I like her and would do just about anything to bury myself deep in her. Fuck, buried, fuck. My thoughts are all over the place, going from Evie to Dad. I want Dad out of my mind, I just want to forget it all. I can't cope, automatically regretting my thoughts and feeling like I'm betraying Dad. Guilt punches me square in the chest, leaving me breathless. I want to be close to her, I want more time, I want to break away from my fucking shit life. I'm fucking useless. Why would she even like me? If she only knew I killed my Dad.

I pull the car over. Get control, Sam! Composing myself, I wonder what the hell is wrong with me? This thinking is stupid, it's just a date. Frozen in my seat, gripping the steering wheel, wanting to break it off and throw the damn thing down the street. The pressure continues to build. Tightening my fists, forcing myself to get it together, I force control to return. This is not you, STOP. Go have your date and see what happens. I allow a moment to dream of her creasing me with those hips. "Right, here we go." Adjusting myself and moving the car towards Evie's again. Just like that those thoughts are gone, perspective has arrived.

Standing at her front door, I hear soft music and Evie humming. The house has a wide hallway, with soft lighting all the way along. A giant staghorn is growing on the wall next to the front door. It's an older home, in a nice area. I knock on the door, looking toward the end of the hallway. All my senses alive with the smells and allure of her. I'm caught in her trap. She's dancing. Seeing her body swaying in front of me, speaks volumes to my fantasies, of her nakedness and my willingness to be at her mercy. It feels wonderfully warm inside. I want to please her. My cock attempts to sway with her hips. I can't take my eyes off her. From hips to breast, to thighs, I'm mesmerized and settling into the feel of it, moving towards her desire. She arrives in front of me and I can't help but continue to take my time with her, teasing the space between us, my gaze exploring her inch by inch, until I reach those eyes, piercing me with want. She touches me and leans in to kiss my cheek. As she holds her presence close, the scent of her desire mixed with sweet vanilla drawing me in. She thanks me for the flowers, slipping them out of my hand as she invites me in. Words have left me. Autopilot has taken over, following only my primal instincts, because on one side is overwhelming desire and sheer terror on the other. Her house has so many pictures of her ocean, of her family, it feels comfortable and homely, a place lived in. I'm following her around like a puppy, lapping up her every word, although I have no idea what we are talking about. Being in her space, this close to her, fixated on her body and her openly letting me, I'm struggling to keep my shit together. I comment on her photos and try to play it cool, not wanting her to know how much I like her. Suddenly, I want her to be impressed by me.

We leave and head to the restaurant and it is awkwardly comfortable.

By the time we arrive, I'm feeling more in control. Evie's home felt good but so fucking real, maybe too real. I want to know her more. She feels special, different. Maybe I'm different? Rebutting thoughts cross my mind while the waiter describes the specials.

I ask if she would like to share and she agrees. Surprise her, she says. Fuck, surprise her? I hope she doesn't complain, shit, okay. I choose, three different dishes, eager to impress.

Straight away she asks what makes me feel alive. I'm taken aback by the questions, and I really like it. There's a lot happening at once.

All I can think about is the farm, working with Dad. My thoughts race, and I manage to tell her about the last time Dad and I worked together, how I had been helping him with fencing, how like old times we raced back to the shed on the motor bikes. The proud moment of me winning and the truth is that Dad hasn't been able to beat me since I was 15 years old, despite his gallant efforts. How we would always share a beer after a hard day and even though we didn't often talk much, we could enjoy the silence of the farm together. I smile sharing my experience with Evie, while that lump rises in my throat, the acknowledgement of what I have lost. I look to Evie, quickly asking her the same question, trying to concentrate on her response. She describes the feel of a sun setting at the beach, the colours, and how the beauty in a simple moment can take her breath away. How she can feel so much contentment in a moment like that, small things. I ask when the last time was, that she did that, and she smiles. Tuesday. She feels open and honest and I ask how she is single. Why has nobody swept her off her feet?

Our food arrives and I can see she's struggling with my question, I tell her not to worry, realising I've stumbled into a difficult question. "Let's eat."

Evie looks up at me, holding my gaze. Instantly, I feel uneasy. She waits for the waiter to finish before speaking.

"I was closed off to love by fear and pain. I have spent a long time working on myself and feel that I am ready to meet someone special."

Words escape me her level of honesty, and all I have is "thank you for telling me." She sizes me up and continues.

"We all have a story Sam, one that we are trying to survive. I have one and I think you do too, that's life these days. Pain is a high probability."

Okay I think to myself, man up. "Evie, that is true, and I do. Have a story, that is, and I am also not sure on what I am looking for here with you."

Evie talks about the sweetness of life, and the sour, like our food in front of us. It was, a nice redirect or that was too much, either way, I'm left unsure she heard what I said. After some more small talk eases the pressure, I build enough courage to ask her about feeling alive and how I liked the question. Evie says she wants to get to know the man I am. As the words come out of her mouth, the lump in my throat returns, sweaty palms, anxious. She will discover I am definitely not a good one.

Evie talks so differently to anyone I have ever met. She is up front and not at all what I am used to. Under all of that she also has a quick wit, sparking banter as if fresh from the farm. She feels like home, family banter that used to exist in the kitchen at Mum and Dads. I force my mind back to Evie. It is so erotic the way she watches me. I find myself reaching for her skin, safely landing on her hand and gliding my fingers over hers, showing her how I am going to take my time.

To break the intensity, I ask what she does to relax. The usual: cooking, reading, beach, swimming, loving baths. She tells me that one day to have a bath outside and talks about how she would love a bath under the stars, a his and hers with hot water, for continuous topping up. I interject. What about a shared bath?

"No," she firmly says. "Two separate; perhaps sharing at times" with a wink. She brings lightness to the moment, even though that was a bit of a random response. I feel encouraged and ask her about her dream home. She hesitates and, again, becomes fierce in her eye to eye connection with me, like she is deciding how much to trust me. It is the strangest feeling, both arousing and frightening. She mumbles, fumbling over her words. "I don't know, something created for a family with my loved ones."

It's nice to see her nervous. I watch her intently and, there it is, she looks down and away. She's vulnerable. I desperately want to go to her aid, I need to protect her, to hold her, I want to know what she's made of.

Abruptly, she suggests a walk. I'm somewhat relieved to experience her privately and don't want the evening to end. I want to kiss her, to hold that body against mine tightly. The darkness of the night and the lack of people help to alleviate the uncomfortable space between us. I can feel her trembling and I automatically switch to protection mode. I notice I become more solid for her, I want to be strong for her, I want her to trust me.

What am I thinking, where is this coming from?

She stops and leans against the walkway her perfume lingers. I'm going to kiss her.

Evie grabs my hand and places it over her breast, what the... I'm completely frozen. Deer caught in the headlights. I feel like a horny teenager. My mouth gapes open. This feels great and it's happening to me! Suddenly, as if out of nowhere, I feel this thud, again and again, pumping against her rib cage. I am hit by my own wave of emotion and my pulse quickens. I move quickly to hide my overwhelm from her, and so I lean in to kiss her, slowly. I can breathe, focus on her, taming me. She tastes sweet and soft. I play with her, discovering her lips, drawing her into me hard. The push, pull dynamic, is pure bliss building within me, together with Evie in my arms. I deepen our kiss and reach for her breast to feel her skin respond to me. I'm hit by another wave.

Fuck, I feel exposed.

I push down hard on my sadness, on my fucking emotion. "Be a man!" reverberates around my brain. I can't stop. I pull her closer to disguise my emotion. I pull back and feel more of it coming. I move us apart and cool our temperature, focusing on her while a few tears claw their way out of me. I move back and away, manoeuvring Evie towards the car, in dreaded silence, trying to keep my shit together. She's too much, I can't deal with feeling this, I can't be the man she talked about. I don't want this. It's too much. If she knew I'm fucking weak as piss. If she knew me really, she would never have let me kiss her. I'm ashamed.

H E R | Nine

I've been ready for a while now. I hear him at the door and walk down the hallway, open and full of golden ginger light from the setting sun. As I gesture for him to come in, his eyes hit me like a rogue wave, even though I am swimming, fighting to keep my head above the currents of my emotions. I knew he was coming and, yet, his surprise pumps through me, the way my body reacts to him, like I didn't see him coming full in his desire and the energy of our aloneness. I feel his eyes trace my body as I walk towards him. He doesn't move, captured by my hips. I'm caught in his excitement of my body. As a curvy woman who's had body issues, the sensation of a man so openly aroused by the swing of my hips only strengthens my own love for the feeling of my womanliness. I feel sexy in his presence.

Standing in the doorway, he takes me all in while drawing breath and running his fingers through his hair. I feel like his lips have gently passed over every inch of my body, covering me in goosebumps. My god, he smells amazing. I wait for his eyes to get back to mine. He takes his time, the space is electrified, and I am patient. I nervously place my hand on his stomach, kissing him on the cheek, holding our closeness ever so lightly. I pause to take a deep breath of him, thanking him for the daisies and inviting him in, to all of me. I have to turn away to catch my breath. My heart is attempting to steady her drum. She's been beating with emotion, drumming loudly, showing me the way forward. I internally acknowledge her, my heart, the centre of my soul, lovingly appreciating the beating of my drum, welcomed throughout my body, welcoming how he feels in me.

God, I really want to invite him into all of me.

Walking back to the kitchen, he's behind me. I know exactly where his eyes are. I can feel the heat of him, drawing on all of my willpower to not turn and devour the man. My mind silently reminds me to taste every moment, make it last, holding him tightly in the softened beat of my drumming heart. I am enjoying these feelings right now, encouraging myself to feel him in this space. We make small talk, clearly struggling with the chemistry and privacy of my home that is engulfing us.

Okay, I'm ready, and he's a gentleman all the way, doors opened. Wow, he loved watching me get into his four-wheel drive. We get there and he's already made the table reservation.

We talk, enjoying each other. I love the way words roll out of his mouth. He is watching me watching his lips.

He's holding my hand over the table, occasionally ever so lightly gliding one finger over my fingers, the sensation of his smallest touch leaving residual heat long after his finger is gone. We have flow, it feels easy, natural, my God do I know you? have you been here this entire time? These thoughts are running on a loop in the recess of my mind.

The night is clear and after dinner I suggest we stroll along the boardwalk that stretches along the coastline. We walk slowly in silence, comfortable and playful without words. Lost in thoughts, I wonder if we are both in shock from our intensity and are slowly absorbing the chemistry of our experience, washing off the shock as we go. I can feel him in the dark, like a solid support, as we approach a part of the walk that is dimly lit over the water. I stop and lean against the railings facing the ocean. I feel our nerves rise in the anticipation of our togetherness and our aloneness. I want him to know what he's doing to me. I want him to experience what's happening on the inside of me. I smile at him, unsure and do it anyway, pulling his hand to my chest. I'm not sure of what I'm doing, shaking and feeling quite exposed, as I open his hand, placing his palm on my chest, hoping he can feel my beating heart on my bare skin. I'm instantly over-come by his hand on my chest and, regretting the level of intimacy.

"Sam, I want you to feel what you are doing to me."

I search his face in the dark, looking for the recognition when he feels my heart pounding under his hand. He moves closer to me and I'm gasping for air, we are so close, his lips are within reach, right there. He's got such restraint, and all I want is for him to devour me. His hand holds my face, pressing his firm body against me. I can feel all of him as he tilts my head, gently brushing his lips against me, playing with the feel of me, slowing me down, drawing me further in to the moment, into the feel of him. I feel everything at once, his body, strong, pressed against me, my legs like jelly, his chest, his manhood, his hands, those lips, his smell, while all of me is melting completely in his perfect kiss. I'm yearning for more, as our lips establish a tempo all their own. Slow and peppered, patient, he feels my desire, my hands on him. The kiss deepens, as does his hold on me, with his hand returning to my chest, search-ing for my heartbeat. It's only milliseconds before he responds to the feel of my pounding drum heart, returning his hands to my hips, slowing our kiss, holding me closely. He releases me, both of us trying to compose ourselves after dipping our toes into the vastness of the ocean.

Shock descends upon us both. He relaxes his grip on me and stares at me, in the darkness, I can't tell if he's searching for something. His shining eyes light up while he confidently holds my face, smiling into my soul while brushes his lips against mine, ever so softly, as we walk silently to his car. A calm descends on us, a knowing, perhaps, that this was big. He felt amazing. I can feel the firmness of him tasting me so deeply and fear is peaking behind the dark night. He puts his arm around me, does he sense me? We feel bewildered, I think. I feel bewildered. I want him to lay with me, to just lay in each other's skin to expose all those parts of us that need to be nurtured before he owns me. I'm dreaming of this when I see we are out the front of my house. He gets out to open the door for me. I don't want the night to finish, autopilot takes over. I open the door and he's still holding my hand. My mind is racing, what do I say? Should I say, 'would you like to come in for coffee?' Who has coffee at night, anyway? Fuck, what's next? Fuck, panic and overthinking rampant!

I stop and turn to him and he kisses my hand, "Goodnight, Evie." He doesn't even really look at me, then turns and walks to his car, not even waiting for me to respond. I'm speechless, he's halfway into his car when I somehow manage to say "see-ya." I stand at the door, knowing that was vastly different, tears flowing.

I felt the rip, kind of like the connection was being torn from me, what happened? Is this in my head? What did I do? This hurts, I'm hurt. I make it to the bottom of my shower to allow the water to comfort me. While my tears flow, the tormenting thoughts engulf me. The torrent of my fears and monsters roll on by with their most agonising memories, the reruns of my harrowing hurts confirming why I'm unworthy of love and on why I am so damaged, how I fuck everything up and the final twist of the knife. Sam was lucky to escape me. I'm somewhat grateful for the worst of demons for staying in the background smirking at pathetic me, which helps me to convince myself of the lie, that I'm reading way too much into this, long enough for my tearful cries to become exhausted, sleep, swallowed by my darkness creeping over me to offer comfort and safety.

Sunday morning, after tossing and turning all night, bouncing between confusion and reassuring myself that it's okay, and it was just an awkward space, even though I know it wasn't just an awkward space, it felt torn away when he didn't look at me in the eye, I was so caught up in the feel of him, the feeling of safety, of skipping off to the rest of our lives.

Fuck me, I will not let anyone make me feel this again, repeats in my thoughts, complete fear-based thinking trying to make me avoid the pain closing in on me. I am unlovable.

The next few days I'm every emotion: mostly stunned with an enormous number of tears. I have some understanding of what I need to do, by allowing my pain to wash over me, attempting to go through the motions of my fear and not let fear own me. I can't be triggered again, I will not allow this to dictate a full-blown crisis, reminding myself to be authentically me. At the same time, allowing it to feel big, because clearly, I am so wrong and read our chemistry wrong, didn't I? Luckily, I can work from home and have some degree of function, I feel like my inside are red raw, like meat that's been tenderised. I'm somewhat proud that I've only sent two unanswered text messages: a timid 'a good morning,' and panicked 'are you ok?' Considering the number of thoughts telling me to track him down, and the thousand times I didn't press send only, to find defeat and my wounded heart.

Last night I convinced myself to call, I didn't leave a message because I'm a fool, a fucking fool.

I'm angry because I uncovered hope, I felt the possibility of love, an actual love that could exist for me, the kind that we all dream about and never really believe in, you know 'that kind of love'. My thoughts are battling between 'could this love exist?' and that I am entirely unlovable. I had bouts of giving up on that possibility and now I have experienced a possibility that gave me hope. My hope feels like it's been ripped away, part of my heart is screaming you were better off when you didn't believe in the likelihood of love, when you hadn't truly experienced a felt moment. A flash of pure connection of heart to heart, finding a synced beat, my body confirms his feel to me, feeling him in all of my corners as my grief is screaming from my pain, one instant feeling like your souls accepted and nurtured, is enough.

I heard and felt him loud and clear: fuck off. What the fuck happened?

I feel cut off, I feel exposed and stupid because he is just gone. That was a once in a lifetime kiss, I allowed myself to dream big, everything was going so well, I was too much, I know, too much, too desperate. I keep going over it, grappling with what's happened. I had shed my skin and allowed myself to show up in the possibility of love and now after working through the rejection and hurt of being cut off like that, I will start to feel my way back to me.

He had to have realised this was more. I mean, we talked about it, didn't we? I haven't become a shadow of myself that doesn't leave her house and mourns for months on end. I didn't give him my power. I have worked and functioned, spent time in my sun and by the water healing with Mother Nature, the one constant in my life. I've worked with my torment, allowed space to express the pain, confusion and loss.

Sam felt so real, I truly thought he was in it with me so he must be in a coma somewhere, rather than blanking me. Anything other than to feel the shame of his rejection, was it just bullshit? Was he playing with me?

No, I like you but… No, you're a fucking nut job and here is a restraining order, nothing, cut off entirely, it must be something else. I'm confused on what I should trust, at night I ache for his touch and then sadness consumes me. My heart cries deeply at being too much and my vulnerable self at being not what he wanted. I take a deep breath. "Evie," I say aloud, knowing my monsters don't like it when I say things aloud, "remember the woman you are." Trust yourself. The fear voice snarls in the background with an 'I told you so,' is my brain trying to release the fear, so I crawl back into the darkness, give up the battle for now and allow my monsters to run wild around me without resistance. The succession of thoughts proceeds: 'you're not good enough, too damaged, too confident, too emotional, too independent, too strong, too intense too…too!' All my fears as to why I'm so unlovable run on repeat in my brain. I don't fight these feelings, I don't argue, I don't justify, I just allow them to roll on by. I sob and surrender to my pains.

One thing I know in my heart is that I will not allow fear to dominate my life. Pain will be expressed so that fear doesn't hang around because I am hurt. I have fought hard in my life and pain is to be acknowledged and needs an outlet, otherwise fear sets up house in my thoughts. I will not retreat into closing myself off to life. This will not reinforce a cascade of what's wrong with me, I focus on coming back to me. I allow myself to experience my pain while being gentle to myself, permitting me to fall apart, to be comforted, feeling in the silence, the big hole of unanswered. I bring kindness to myself and what my heart feels. I am proud that I showed up and that I put myself out there to the possibility of love, these thoughts giving rise to a shift from within me. A slight softening.

H I M | Ten

Evie's tormenting me. I wanted to see her, touch her. She's haunting me, the feeling of her under my hands, the sweet taste of those full lips, my rising desire at the thoughts of her, her heart. She is truly just her, without the bullshit as she had said.

Confident, yet I see a genuine vulnerability in her that felt nice. It feels terrific to hold her, to be the man she needs. I want to be that, but at the same time I don't think I can be. Tattered and tormented, no one understands. I have no-one to talk to. Dad's gone, and I am fucking losing it. I can't focus on work. What has she done to me? I want to see her, I want to be near her, to be close to the feel of her. What would I say?

I am an arsehole, I just cut her off. I have responded. I just haven't pushed the send button.

She wants the forever, I can see it in her eyes, the whole 9 yards and I can't keep my shit together for one kiss, a fucking amazing kiss. She's too much, she has something over me, or maybe it's because of Dad that I'm acting crazy, it has all caught up with me. I can't contain my emotions, I'm a fruit basket. I found myself at her house again yesterday. I am a stalker. I am so shut off from myself, I have no idea what I want. I didn't even realise that I'd driven to her house, in the complete wrong direction, for an hour, until driving down her street it dawned on me and I ran from my shame. I'm shaking a lot these days, driving past her house, crying. Who is this guy? I don't even recognise myself. The last week has been horrible. Bouncing between absolute arsehole and babbling in my tears. I know this is probably okay considering my losses, I guess, both Dad and Evie. Something has short circuited in my brain. I'm a fucking broken man. People are noticing, particularly my offsider, poor kid is taking a lot of shit from me. He looked like he was going to cry today when I yelled. Thankfully from somewhere deep within me, I realised and apologised. Gave us both the rest of the day off, fuck. I'm pushing so hard and I can't believe a woman has done this to me. I'm paralysed by her, by my emotions. She opened a door that was bolted closed! None of this is making sense, in my mind, not her, not anything, the last 6 months.

Fuck, it all feels like an avalanche I can't escape that keeps hitting me. It's not the first time I have driven past Evie's home. It is, however, the first time that I've stopped, and I just can't leave. I sit staring for 2 hours out the window, not knowing if she is coming home or if I'll get out of the car, glued to my seat, stuck in desperation to change how I feel, anything other than this. I need to not be that guy that does this, I am not this man.

A car pauses in the middle of the road; I know it's her. I get out. I want her to see me, a stand-off clearly. I need to feel her, I'm frantic. She drives towards me, not making eye contact. I want her to look at me. My thoughts beg her to look at me. She drives into the garage, gets out and I see those eyes, piercing my heart. The pain in them, fuck, I see how I hurt her. I'm a bastard. What am I doing? Her pain hits me solid in the chest. I've no words, nothing is coming out. I inhale deeply, composing myself, scared to death I'll make things worse. Her eyes pierce directly through to my shame. I can't tolerate her pain, I want to fix it, I want to hold her, I want...

I ask her to hear me out and then tell her that she scared the shit out of me, and I freaked out. It's like I'm watching myself saying all of these things to her and the words continue to dribble out of my mouth. I'm all in now, what more can I lose? I'm trying to explain something that makes no sense to me. What is she doing to me? I'm left with 'fuck, Evie' in all of that. It's the truest reflection of things and that they are just fucked. It enables my panic to subside, my god, it was as real for her as it is for me, fuck it's all too much.

I'm trying to tell her what I want, like I have the right to do so. Fuck, I don't even know what I want. Words again fail me. All I can see is her pain and that I caused it. There is too much emotion. I just met her, and I tell her immediately I can't be with her, fuck, I can't hurt her, what am I saying? I'm not the man you need. I'm so conflicted by our situation, by what is going on, in desperation I ask her what I should do? Then from nowhere, from sheer frustration at myself, like I'm talking through my feelings in front of her, having the conversation I should have had by myself, and surprising even myself, explodes: "I didn't realise this could be love."

I'm stunned by my announcement. Shock descends on the babbling idiot while he attempts to take back the comment. Fuck, get out, just get out. My feet are stuck to the ground like concrete, not budging. I return to my ole faithful response, "fuck, Evie." I don't have answers. I have no fucking clue what I am doing, I just can't feel this anymore. I manage to stop, forcing the verbal diarrhoea to stop, just stop speaking. My eyes are pleading with Evie to say something, desperately hoping she will ease the blow.

Evie looks at me, eyes ablaze. I'm not sure what she's feeling, but she is scarily composed now. It's clear I have ruined any opportunity I may have had with her. She is direct and cold. Sort your shit out. She's ready to meet someone.

I think I have really fucked this up, again.

She moves to walk past me, putting her back to me. I don't know what comes over me, but I reach for her, and she responds with her body arching under my hands, the feel of her against me, those hips fitting in my hands perfectly. I want to see her, so I turn her around. She's in pain, and on her face is written what I have inflicted upon her. The moment is gone, replaced with the shame of what I have caused to Evie. I step back, in shock at myself and at the pain of how I hurt Evie, as she pushes the garage door closed. She ends by saying "I want you too, but all of you, not just a moment of you."

I hear her sobs as the door rolls down to the ground.

I'm sorry. I muster up another apology. I'm sorry. I'm not sure if she heard or even if it is any consolation for the fucking coward I am. I stand in Evie's driveway for a long time, frozen in disbelief. Tears tumbling out of me, for Evie, for Dad, for Mum, my sister, for everyone, then cry in my car for another hour or so. I know she's inside in pain, as am I. I caused this, my thoughts are empty except for hatred and shame. I'm a zombie, dead on the inside, fucking everything up as I go. The days that follow seem to occur with autopilot, frozen by how much I have hurt everyone and my own guilt.

Ruby, my sister, has perfect timing, arriving at home when I do. I can't pretend anymore that things are okay. I'm fucking empty. There is nothing left at all and I can't hide the volcano inside, it's all gone to shit. If Dad could see this weak man in front of him, he'd be ashamed.

Ruby is on to it instantly and she won't leave well enough alone. I know that no matter how dismissive or rude I become she won't let up. I snap at her in a way that sends her a message to back off, its none of her fucking business. I know I'm a bastard to her now too as she leaves, slamming my door. Fuck, I know I must pull my shit together, but how?

I go for a run to clear my head and because Harold the dog won't leave me alone. We run for as long and as hard as I can. The sweat hides by tears and frustration at what is happening to me. I hit the foreshore and head down to run in the sand and push myself to almost vomiting. I want this out of me, I want rid of the pain, I want to be free from these feelings of Dad, from Evie, from being so weak. My body is burning. Pain pulsates and weakness everywhere. I collapse, exhausted, spent, fucked.

Another week passes, and the weather is really starting to warm up again. I'm feeling stronger, getting back to my own rhythm.

I decide that enough is enough and dress up today, a lovely summer dress, feeling good in my skin, a little shaky yet strong, bringing forth my anchor, my internal power reminding me of the woman I am. Encouraging myself to stand up after falling down, to let life in again. I'm feeling like I'm taking my body back after giving it away. I feel like the emotions expressed are gifting me my mind back, my control to stand strong in my skin. I am taking back what I had given to him. In the dark of the night I nurture, holding and allowing my body to be loved by me, nourishing her with kindness.

Driving home from work, I turn into my street and I see immediately, a car. I know it's his car, out the front of my house. Heat rises from my body, instantly reacting with desire.

'FUCK.'

I thought I had come so far.

'FUCK.'

I was delusional to think my womanly parts wouldn't scream for him. My mind is confused, angry and hopeful. I brake in the middle of the street, not knowing what to do. Can I reverse? Shit, I see him get out of the car, fuck. I drive towards him, shaking. This is a standoff. I can't look at him. I drive into the garage with tears and a solid lump in my throat rising. Internally, I'm pleading, please don't cry in front of him. He's there as I open my car door, my whole being shuddering.

"Evie, please, will you hear me out?"

I'm confused, I'm hurt, I fight the tears coming, even my breathing is shaking, heart slamming into my rib cage, waves of shock running through my veins. Coaching myself, I swallow harshly, don't be weak, I don't want him to see my pain, he can't see how hurt I am, Evie, pull it together.

Too late. The flood gates open, I'm crying now, without words, just tears streaming down my face, a silent cry in complete turmoil expressed. Listen.

"Okay." I mutter, standing mostly frozen right where I am. He moves towards me and I take a step back. He is in between me and the door to the inside of the house. He looks around, there is no one else around.

"Evie, you scare the shit out of me, my life is different. That kiss, you, it's all too much, it was too fucking intense, I can't, I'm not there, there is too much emotion, I'm not there, I can't do that much emotion, you are very intense, I'm not ready to settle down. I can't be who you need me to be, I'm not ready for this."

He goes on rambling a little, he's confused, he's had to fight himself to stay away, to end this, to not respond. I'm angry, not at him, but at myself. I can recognise the panic and fear in him, which makes me even more angry as it's clear that it's winning in this very moment. My rational fucking mind brings fucking logic to the situation. The woman in me who can't bear to see anyone in pain, gives rise to a kindness towards Sam, one that I really don't want to have for him.

Sam's continuing. "Evie, it's too much, I can't get you out of my head, I don't know what to do, there's so much you don't know."

My tears are well and truly dried up now, I'm mad. I can feel the sensation of anger rising in my body, like a wave from the pit of my stomach. I'm flushed, my body starting to tighten, and freeze. He says he's sorry that he hurt me, that this type of relationship is new for him, we had chemistry and a lot of it. He says he didn't realise that it was love, then he's stumbling over his words trying to take them back, my emotions are starting to rise again, he's now saying he didn't mean love, strong feelings and he ends with "fuck, Evie."

I see the battle, plain as Jane. It's not up to me to fix this or make it okay: it's his fight. I'm silent, in the depths of my own shock, dumbfounded and he's fumbling around, begging me to say something. He goes on, he felt alive, our potential and continues to repeat "I don't know what I want."

He's sat out the front of my house twice before, like a fucking stalker and drove away. Today, he couldn't drive away.

"Please say something, Evie."

This is the first time I am actually able to look at him. I'm cold and disconnected. I need to be cold to survive this conversation, to survive what I'm saying and accept that it was me, that I am damaged. I can feel it, I can see he's stuck. I can see he is having an epic panic attack, but I'm still hurting. I'm so angry, at myself for understanding his point of view and that I can't fix this and at him for laying this on me.

I take a deep breath and see the hurt in his eyes, gathering all my courage to be able to respond with kindness. I know how fear fucks with you. "You need to figure that out for yourself, I can't help, I don't have the answers, you have to decide what you want. I know what I want and it's a fucking fairy-tale, is that you? I don't know, but I do know it will be with someone who is equally in it with me, in fear and love. I owe you thanks for helping me to see that is a possibility, when you figure out what you want, let me know."

I attempt to walk past him, knowing I am going to have a meltdown, turning my back to shimmy past. His hands find my hips, and our chemistry overwhelms us both. I'm caught in the moment and my body betrays me. Feeling him behind me, my back arches and leans into him. The sensation of him against me feels excitingly safe. What are we doing? Lost in how he feels against me, hands on me, he moves to turn me, "stop, please stop, don't do this to me."

Tears are falling down my face in a steady stream and I'm sobbing now. I'm begging him, please. He says "Evie, I want you, I need you."

I look into his eyes. He recognises my pain, the hurt on my face and steps back, apologising. I hide my face and walk towards the door, the tear between us feels physically painful. He looks defeated, sad. I manage to blurt out, "I want you too, but I want all of you, not a moment of you, figure out what you want."

I push the button for the garage door, as he steps back and mouths the words "I'm sorry."

I walk inside, straight to my bed, in sobs as my heart ache pours out of me again. I felt the goodbye, our bond broken from whatever we could have been. I don't move from my bed until the next day, realising only in the morning that I left the shopping on the bench, and now have to work on an empty stomach, even though I'm not feeling hungry. I'm in shock again, going through the motions of the day, just functioning. Being exceptional was never going to happen today. The little girl inside me who dreamed of one day finding her knight, found him and she's too much, he's not ready, you're too much. Under my surface I am a mess. How is it that he didn't recognise love, that he thought chemistry could do that? The little girl simply adds maybe he knows we could be more and that is his fear. She still defends him. I hush her with a huge pang of pain. The demons in the background are smug fuckers, they are happy. Life proved yet again that I am damaged, I am unlovable, they win again. How could he not know those feelings don't happen every day? Yes, a spark can happen, but that was a fucking tidal wave. It's not a glance across a bar, it's an earth stopping moment of mutual attraction. Hope rising out of me from somewhere. The fire roared, the trembling inside and out, that's fucking next level. The complete body, mind and soul overwhelmed me, the felt feelings. I'm so weary. I'm still fighting trying to believe I am okay. I can be wanted. I am proud of this warrior woman who showed up. I'm making millions of different arguments in my head tearing myself apart and slowly realising I'm leading the charge in my own thoughts, so I step out. I allow them to continue without being hooked in, no debating them, no arguing. I don't get involved in my fear chatter.

I truly thought that finally, I had found something meaningful and I was willing to step into the woman I am, to trust me on a new level, to love the woman who faced those fears and did it anyway. For someone who had been switched off to the magic of love, this pains me so, there is a tremendous amount of truth to the saying ignorance being bliss. I was enjoying the process of us evolving. I feel like I've said goodbye to what may have been, while lying to myself that the scar on my heart is not too major. When someone doesn't want to love you, a fight ensues for you to crawl your way back from your belief that you are unlovable. It marks you, carves into your soul. Undoubtedly, bent today, 'but never broken,' whispers my heart.

As my own boss, I kindly give myself the rest of the week to work from home. I shower with not as many tears as yesterday, visualising my pains dripping off me down the shower drain. Reminding myself I am stronger than this, I picture little Evie and hold her hurt parts, encouraging her to hope for the future. I let her out in the shower, feeling calmer although my eyes are stinging from all the tears I shed, the acceptance again of losing him or never having him. Desperately resisting the "you're pathetic" chant from stepping up to the plate. I have answers now and moving on seems easier.

I look down at my nakedness, holding my curves and closing my stinging eyes. Straight away I'm picturing his hands on me, my body against his, his touch, feeling him. I'm overcome, out loud, I beg my body, 'please,' in an attempt to resist the sensations of him. Then with my body still feeling connected to him, pushing me, I say aloud to myself "it's not over." My hearts' message to me. My hands are shaking, I'm flushed, I try to push it away and fuck I'm starting to panic, battling myself, I breathe and try to release, but it's too late, panic sets in. It registers that I'm having a panic attack and I start shaking my hands more, trying to encourage the panic to be spent, releasing my fears, the hormones surging in my body, tremors taking control of my body. I allow and embrace the shaking, setting the energy behind my emotions free, without argument, and kindly coaching myself through, without judgement and thanking my body, nurturing her to release the emotion, knowing my body is screaming loudly at me now and I must spend the trapped energy. Using breathing and physical movement is the key for me and as soon as I can move, I start to feel better, quickly. Soften, Evie, this is big for you. Don't work yourself, allow space to feel or your body will scream again when you're not listening to our inner world.

I know how to manage panic, anxiety, and not fight myself. Clearly, I was trying to convince myself to think my feelings, a common habit of mine, rather than to just feel them. I've been standing on these two feet for 35 years! I've survived a lot of storms. Evie, remember, my internal self, reminding me to calm. I reach down deep into the part of me that knows what I need to do, slowly curling into a little ball and holding myself. Nourishing my hurts, acknowledging the pain swirling around my skin, softening in thought and touch towards myself. Giving myself permission to feel overwhelmed and I need to stop attempting to think my way out and just feel.

I go for a walk, fast, then slow, then fast, then slow, burning off those stress hormones that I've just released from my panic attack of anxiety.

Everyone has a painful story, and, well, I'm not going to spend my life looking in the rear vision mirror, I've done that before.

I'm grateful when the weekend arrives. Feeling renewed, I head to the beach. Although still fragile, the sun is out and warm enough for swimming. I am going to place my feet in the sand, exposing my body to the sun for some mother nature loving. I head to the local's beach, as it's always deserted there and a great spot for me to feel alone with Mother Nature healing my body and soul. Pausing in the dunes, the water rolling on the shore, small waves, the sound of a slight crash as the waves roll up the sand, crystal clear waters. The warmth of the sun on my body, penetrating my soul, instantly eases my thoughts. I've arrived at my happy place. I feel like a vampire sucking in all the goodness, sun, sand and water. A dip in the water, she's fresh and immediately I'm alive. It's truly refreshing. I'm covered in goosebumps outside and a smile on the inside, one only Mother Nature can give you. After a few hours of soaking in the sun, I'm not ready to leave my ocean yet, so I walk up to the local milk bar that also moonlights in coffee, to enjoy more time at the beach in this beautiful sun as it's all the medicine I need. Strolling along in my own thoughts towards the shops a few streets back from the beach, it crosses my mind that I have not told anyone at all about Sam. Initially I wanted him for myself and I wasn't ready to share him, not really having the time to even consider telling anyone. I ponder what Teddy and Cam would say, even though I'm not sure I want anyone to know. I arrive at the road in front of the shop, deep in thought, and I see everyone and their dog, have the same coffee idea as me. It's crazy full. Walking across the road and I feel it straight away, with his eyes on me, I know it's Sam. I'm arguing with myself: Don't look for him. Do not avert your eyes from the shop door, Evie! I forcefully talk to myself, attempting to will my own will away and clearly failing again. Smiling slightly at myself, I look around, making eye contact. I smile. Fuck, he's sitting with two women. I nod and say hello, like a cornered puppy that gives a little hello bark while creeping backwards into the corner, knowing there is no other way out. I keep moving. I'm quite sure he said nothing in response. I made it into the shop and for fucks sake, I haven't seen the man in 35 years now he's where's fucking Wally! Everywhere. I'm relieved when a familiar face bounces over to me, connecting with some small talk, a slight banter, easing my emotional need to scream at the universe. I'm the fucking swan, again. Involved in the conversation and fucking epically screaming on the inside, panic shifting quickly to hurt, to stop this thinking, or I will cry, to willing to promise just about anything for another moment with him.

I take a deep breath and move towards the window, only to see a very heated discussion at his table. I feel like I am imposing. I retreat to the opposite side of the café, pretending to be out of the way of the crowd while I wait for my flat white. A good old pep talk begins despite my bargaining with God, Buddha, whoever will listen, for him to choose me. I admit defeat and prepare my walk of shame. Shoulders back, eyes forward, walk immediately to the ocean. Do not stop, do not collect $200.00. Place your entire body in mother nature and let this scream out of your body into the love of the ocean. I grab my coffee and proceed with a purpose. I think both of us need to evacuate these horrible feelings. I can feel them all looking at me. I have to run. I cross the road and let myself go, I run. I don't care how it looks. I don't care if he sees that I am hurt. I flee the situation, leaving my dignity along the way. A big wave of emotion is barrelling down the street after me. I kick off my shoes, plant my coffee in the sand to insulate, smiling at my forethought, and launch myself at that ocean. Part of me is screaming - when did you become this woman? When did you allow a man to do this to you? I'm so frustrated with myself, it's echoing around my head, tears are beginning, and the scream is tearing its way out of me. I just make it into the shallows when my screams are consumed by a mouthful of seawater, pained. For a while, I stay on my knees, being thrown around by the waves and I don't care. The ocean is battering my body and each time I get up on my knees again, aided by the roll of the water. After the scream is out of my body, I stand and walk further into her, I want to feel the ocean swallow me whole and shut out the world. I swim over the rocks allowing each wave to submerge me, my tears being washed away. My body is lulled in each wave, the chill in the water soothing the heat of my pain in my heart. I feel her slowly putting me back together, feeling like I've expressed my hurts and in need of the soothing sun to warm my body, to nurture her, I begin to swim to shore. I'm slapped back into reality because he is sitting near my blanket.

FUCK, FUCK, FUCK.

H I M | Twelve

Mum rings: "I'm on my way. Be ready to go out in 15 minutes." Click. All I can hear is the dial tone, what the? I expected a call today after Ruby was here yesterday, and I was not the best company. Actually, I was an arsehole. Well it is none of their business. I can see I'm being a dick.

Going for the run last night has cleared away a bit of my stupid, even though I can't seem to stop the train wreck. I shower, and Evie haunts me, my cock aching. I get my shit together, just as I hear the toot from Mums car. Halfway down the stairs I realise just how much of an ambush this is as Ruby is in the front seat, fuck. It's now 6 months since we lost Dad and it's been tough for everyone. To say Mum and Ruby have struggled is an understatement. It's a mess, just a fucking shit storm I'd like to think I've managed to keep my shit storm at bay and take care of the farm, my business and the two of them as best as I can. The toll of losing Dad has aged Mum. She has sadness in her eyes now and struggles with loneliness. She was with Dad since she was 16 years old. A lifetime of loving each other, gone in a flash, just gone. She has to also look at me, the spitting image of him, and the one who killed him.

They are my responsibility now, and I am not going to take shit if this turns into a family fucking ambush. I'm outnumbered now, a painful jab from the loss of Dad, hits me in the chest like a fucking brick. I'm so fucking angry all the time and I don't want anyone near me.

I jump in the back. Mum's chatting away, driving us down the coast. I realise, we are heading towards Evie's and I'm trying to keep my shit together, why am I so fucking emotional suddenly? The weight, like a ball and chain, forcing the weight of it all backdown, how can this be happening to me? They probably think this is about Dad and, well, it's not. I don't want to hurt Mum because it's not. Fuck, they are going to want to talk and talk and talk, bloody women. Honestly, I'm so fucked up, who knows what's going on. Ruby and Mum are the gold standards of farmer's wives gossip heads! The harmless kind, but when they get on to something, pray not to be the target. They are relentless when they sniff something out, and clearly, they already think they are onto something with me. It is kind of nice that they are resuming their harassing of the men in the family ways. It actually feels nice, horribly, gut-wrenchingly, nice.

My focus returns to the conversation. Mum's banging on about chocolate eclairs, Dad's favourite. She's heard this place makes the best on the coast. This is something Dad would have done, kidnapped you for an adventure to a random bakery to test out the delights, at times causing more haphazard adventures. It's nice to remember those trips, a genuinely addicted man to his sweet bakery treats. Even though he really was more addicted to adventuring as a family, from cheese factories to country bakeries. Often the escapades resulted in mishaps, a flat tyre becoming a lesson for Sam in how to change a tyre while Dad gives you shit and the other two giggle away like school children.

A smile attempts to creep out of me. A wave of anger follows shuddering through me, pushing it all away. I force myself back to him, back to my memories, deeply painful and comforting as they are. Some of our adventures didn't work out as anticipated and Dad never seemed to care. He loved the unexpected, experiencing the unknown. He would just stand back and smile like he didn't have a care in the world and time didn't matter, if only he knew. The car is silent. We are all in our own memories of Dad, a man robbed of his life too young. The lump is rising in my throat. I push it down, swallowing hard, clinching my fists and attempt to talk to Mum about the farm. She is not having any of it. We arrive to a little café that appears out of nowhere, finding a table. I go to place the order and thank the bejesus there were three eclairs left. Holy shit, that could have gone even more wayward. It makes me feel comforted that Dad is sort of here to soften the blow that is coming from these two, with the sugary goodness beholden in an eclair. My anger subsides. Fuck, I miss him. He'd know what to do about Evie. One beer, the shed, done. Why did he have to fucking die? Why did he do that to me? On my way back to the family intervention, I look away from the glaring eye of my mother and down the street. I see her, frozen to the pavement. She looks so good. I use all my might to not run towards her. I'm stopped on the steps, watching those hips. My god, she's gorgeous, what the fuck am I doing? Those curves coming towards me. My hands stretch out in the memory of her body, those hips I want to grab hold of. She is a woman, strong and yet so vulnerable. She's lost in her thoughts again, her golden tan, hair wild and curly, how I would love to hold it back and allow her wild to come out all over me. Those hips have me hypnotized. I'm rudely shaken back into reality by Ruby calling my name. I'm stopped dead in the middle of the outdoor seating area, spellbound. I walk to the table, failing to compose myself. I sit, unable to take my eyes from her. I want her to see me, internally begging, Evie, look up, feel me, look up. She catches my eye, she heard me. I almost stand, resisting and fighting with myself, fucking frozen, speechless. I want her. Why am I doing this? Why am I fighting myself, why am I lying to myself? No woman has ever done this to me before. My heart wants her, the thought shunting me into a silent mind. She's so polite, smiles, a nod hello, at Mum and Ruby, graceful, dignified. I'm the fucking idiot staring at her mouth open, dumb arse!

She's perfect, my perfect, and I've fucked it up. She's too much, I can't handle it, she needs a strong man, not this fucking weakness. I'm aching all over, yearning to feel her, fuck, I'm with Mum! My mind is racing with nothing and everything at once. I'm suddenly embarrassed, feeling the burning sensation of Ruby and Mum's eyes on me. Avoiding this is not going to work now, nowhere to hide. It begins politely enough. The first blow comes: "Who's that? She looks like a lovely lady."

Ruby jumps straight to "she seems different to your usual type?"

Without thinking, I snap at Ruby. "Type, I didn't know I had one! It doesn't matter, she wouldn't want a bar of me!" I'm so defensive and I don't want to be, I am so angry, why am I doing this?

The chocolate eclairs arrive, and I stare at it, feeling the pressure to share. I'm not ready, it's all too much, everything is too much. My thoughts sound so stupid now that I have to say them out loud. I attempt to piece together my reasons. She needs a strong man, not a weak one, thoughts rolling on a loop in my mind. In response to Ruby, I say quietly, "there is nothing usual about Evie."

Of course, instantly, both turn the heat up on me to share. I sit back in my chair trying to create space between us and the onslaught begins. It's like they are pecking at me and my life is the carcass. I'm angry, white knuckling it, answering some, swallowing the painful awkwardness of the situation, knowing that Evie is inside probably even seeing all of this and I wonder what she would be thinking. I'm a fucking volcano and an eruption feels imminent. I place my hands on the table, spreading my fingers, a big clue to them both to hear me. Through gritted teeth, I tell them to STOP, silence falling over the table. The waiter gives me a reprieve with the arrival of coffee followed by Evie walking past, no eye contact. I search for her and see her run at the crossroads, pained, the emotion of things spilling out. I want to go to her. I see her distress that I caused. The pit of my stomach churns. I don't want her to go, what is wrong with me? She is on another level, one I could never be on. Mum places her hands on mine, her soft touch instantly calming my panic. She gently asks Ruby to leave us. I say "No, Ruby, stay. It's okay, Mum. I'll tell you both, your son's a weak bastard."

Since we lost Dad, we are all a lot more honest with each other. I like it, less bullshit, although at times they both still take forever to get to the point. Mum looks at me and straight up says, "I don't need you anymore Sam, nor do I need you to be the strong one of the family anymore, you're not to take your fathers place."

While I am feeling stunned and in shock at Mum's assertion, Ruby pipes up with the same sentiment. "I want my brother back and not another father. I already had one and I think we all agree he was pretty great."

A well of emotion and relief bubbles to the surface. I feel sort of numb, like my brain has gone into shock, but in a good way. I feel lighter, in that I don't have to hold that full responsibility. It feels like I don't have to hold it all on my own anymore.

"Your father is still here, he lives on in us, and how we continue to love him. You have to forgive yourself and I've told you and will continue to tell you Sam. Now listen to your mother. You freed your father from pain, you did what Dad needed you to do. We all needed you. He and I are grateful for your kindness." Mum, holds my hand, looks at Ruby who nods and they both says, "it was a kindness."

Overwhelmed by the acknowledgement and emotions, a few tears come out under my sunglasses. Mum reiterates her beliefs. "Now you need to decide what you believe, because an accident killed your father and you, my son, eased his pain and showed such love to your dad in his final moments." When we lost Dad, I immediately took on the role of the strong one, being the man of the family. It's important to me that I protect my family and they come first, as that is who Dad was. Talking of Dad in past tense, hits me hard and I'm having flashes of my promises to him before he left us. Ruby and Mum both know my death bed promise to Dad. I would have promised anything to a dying man. I made many bargains with God or whoever would listen in the hope that he would survive. I made promises to give my Dad what he needed to pass, to alleviate his pain. When Dad realised it was too late, he couldn't survive, I agreed to take care of the family, to look after Mum, I would have agreed to anything to ease Dad's pain. I allow my tears to flow freely. Since losing Dad, Mum and Ruby know me so well.

I decide to tell them all about Evie. I take a large bite of my éclair to add in sweet courage, telling them everything, from our first meeting after we lost Dad, our date, to that walk on the boardwalk where I lost my shit. How it was too much, too soon, too intense, it was too, too, too. I fucking froze. I told them how I didn't tell her about Dad, how I sort of pretended he was still alive. Hesitant of their reaction, I look up. Mum is in tears, Ruby reaches out to hold my hand and I repeat I just can't, I can't... I can't feel anything... We had this intense moment and I almost became a blubbering mess, I felt her and this fucking emotion, just came from nowhere. I am not weak, with emotion attempting to climb out of me, I look to them both for help, feeling wounded and stupid.

Mum says through tears, "You had a lot of emotions going on with this young lady, and you are trying not to feel anything at all. You shut off everything after Dad died, and you can't turn off how you feel about Dad and her. Sam, you are battling yourself, feelings were developing. I know you are shut off to your grief, but you can't close yourself off, because it closes you off to everything. I know this, son, because I am still trying to not do this myself. I felt like my love for your father was leaving me and I couldn't feel the pain, I was numb to everything and I realised I wanted to feel the loss of your Dad and honour our love and life together, because I need to feel his love and even though he is gone, his love isn't, that is always within me and you and Ruby."

Mum makes sense. It's so hard to hear her pain. My throat is like sandpaper. Letting Mum know that it's too late with Evie, that door is closed, slammed shut. Mum reminds me of the connection we experienced and the feelings I already have for her. "Don't run away now, she's opened Pandora's box!" Ruby adds, "You can't close it."

Even when you know you're being a dickhead, you never like being told or admitting it, especially to your sister, who will proceed to give you shit for the rest of your life. I don't know about that, clearly, I'm still struggling with the emotion and thinking through my thoughts out loud with them both. When you are trying to be numb, and you feel something, I guess the floodgates or proverbial box open. I tell them about my stalking capabilities, embarrassed, my voice still hoarse with awkwardness. A level 10, I might as well go all in and tell them how I treated her. Ruby looks entertained at her big brother; she's chuckling at my stupidity. I announce, wounded, that it's over and there is nothing more to discuss. Mum smiles "Stalking must run in the family! Your father stalked me, you know. He used to stand at the gate to the farm. He would sit on the fence and whenever a car or my parents came near, he would stand to attention in the heat. Your grandfather thought he was short a few beers. He would always smile, politely and respectfully, at all going in and out of the farm. Sam, you know where she is," she says with that beaming smile that I have not seen in such a long time, "so go to her and start with a smile." Mum gives the best advice.

I stand, feeling hopeful, polish off my éclair, kiss my girls on their heads and go in search of Evie. On the way to the beach it's not long before my eagerness is replaced with confusion, not sure how, or what to do or say, tossing up whether to borrow my sister's words, even if I don't completely agree. Thoughts of Dad are beginning to rise in me again. I arrive at the beach. I can see a rug up in the dunes and I assume it belongs to her. I head up towards the blanket and the coffee confirms it for me. Hearing a scream, I look around and I think I spot her in the water. There is next to no-one here and she's in the white water, just letting the waves hit her. She's at their mercy. I want to help and yet I understand it not my place, so I stop myself. I can see she's in control, she's right where she wants to be in the midst of the chaos. Being thrown around by the waves, crashing into her body, fighting to get back to her knees before the next wave, taking each blow from the wave.

It's painful to watch, as she rises again and again, amongst muffled screams, braving her emotions. I am so ashamed. It feels terrible each time I hear her cries, knowing that I caused this. I can hear her crying and it is so hard to resist running into the water and holding her, kissing her hurts, the ones I caused, guilt rising in me. What have I done? Desperately trying to escape the rising emotion of shame from witnessing her pain. It feels excruciating and more tears fall down my face. She stands and walks further out, swimming beyond the breakers. Being near her belongings, feels wrong, watching her, waiting, while fear descends on me. She feels things so differently, so deeply and she's not afraid of anything. Look at her being with the pain, letting it out. Fuck, I shouldn't be here, I'm not the man she needs. Remember what she said in the garage, she told you to come and find her when you figure yourself out. My thoughts move to her body, how she experiences things, savour's moments of pain and joy. This is not how a man thinks or feels, well, fuck, it is, but well, I don't know. I do know, I want her in my life, and I want to learn to experience life how she does, I want to savour us, I want to be a better man for her, for us. I want to hold that body, while we both experience each other, my God. I can't ruin this!

A volcano is rising in me, of holding the last 6 months down, in the depths of me, of fighting with what I genuinely want. I'm struggling not to lose it, to explode. Trying to compose myself but watching her body roll gently with the rise and fall of the waves is completely distracting. I'm brought back to reality by her soft sobs rolling up the beach, this is torture. The lump in my throat has returned, hurting, my gut sinks. Having to sit in how I've hurt Evie is horrendous, reminding me of Dad and the day I found him. I couldn't breathe with the lump in my throat, until I had to pull my shit together and tell Mum the love of her life was gone, I just closed off, shutdown, I had to. The thoughts of Dad, the thoughts of Evie,

I can't hold the tears at bay anymore. I don't try stop them nor do I attempt to hide. Fuck, I held my Dad in my arms for his last breath... Dad's gone forever, I say to myself. A woman who could be the one, Evie, is out there feeling, being brave, expressing her pain. That's a woman that I want, shit, could I love her, do I? I'm so fucked up. I feel the urge to stay, not to run, not to fight my feelings away, to just stay and wait for Evie and to sit with what I am feeling, to feel with Evie. I can hear her voice getting softer and softer and its soothing me and my own tears begin to slow. Right, start with a smile, and the truth about Dad, as Mum said.

I'm caught in my own acknowledgment of my grief when, Evie's piercing eyes catch me off guard. She freezes on seeing me. I just sit in the one spot, like concrete that has set. I feel her on my skin before I've touched her, how do I do this? How do I actually say such horrors, such pain? How do I share with this woman, that I killed my dad? How do I tell anyone what I am trying to outrun, the pain of what I did, of further hurting people, the thoughts that live with me every day, haunting me! Fuck, am I considering telling her?

No, I can't. I can't even get the words out of my mouth, they reverberate around my thoughts, both in pleading that I did the right thing and that he could have made it and I killed him. Even the fact that Dad asked me to release him from the pain, that he was dying anyway, knowing the truth and reality of the situation doesn't stop my fears and thoughts doing a number on you, that 'if only' haunting my thoughts. A tug of war battles between my pains and fears of the way people would look at me. Evie looked at me as a man. I know it was the right thing to do for Dad and that even after what happened it wasn't another 30 minutes until anyone else showed up. It was an accident. I understand this and yet I still hear his screams at night, loud and in agony, my silent screams mixed with undertones of the smell of diesel. I knew then that he would die quickly if I freed him. I relive it every night. I knew the tractor was the only thing keeping him alive and he knew too. I fight myself every day about what I did, should have done, over, and over again, on replay. I am controlled by my pain, by that day. My pain is on pause, as am I. I know it, logically, I know Dad's screams remind me that I had the courage to carry out his wishes, to release him from pain, to love him, we both knew how bad it was.

In Evie's garage, in the moment when she looked at me, I felt her pain and it sent me right back to Dad. His anguish, pleading with me, the sheer helplessness. I felt being powerless to save him and instead helping him to die. I fight my emotions and acknowledge Evie's sitting behind me. I saw her expressing her emotions in the waves, open and honest. She isn't a coward, and even if this is the last time we speak, I need her to know, to understand, I need someone to know what happened to me, this is not the man I am, this mess of a man.

The day I lost Dad pours out of me, like the flood gates on a dam. I just stop holding back and I talk. It's strange. I know she is sitting behind me but it's like I am speaking aloud to myself and, I think, to Dad, really. It is like I am finally processing what happened to me, how I lost my Dad. I even share my thoughts when Dad asked me to move the tractor, the silence of knowing what that meant fell over me, when I realised how bad it was, even thought I was still trying to give him hope, he'd been there a while before I found him. How my freeze-frame memories are torment-ing me in the middle of the night, how I forced myself to be numb, to look after Mum and Ruby, to hold Mum's screams while covered in Dad's blood, how I became a zombie, closed off to the world, everyone and everything. How weak I am, how the responsibility of taking care of my family falls to me, there is no buffer, there's no more Dad, I am the man of the family. I could always rely on Dad, he was always there for me, a foundation and now I'm so alone and struggling to feel the gravity of shouldering that responsibility for my family.

The sense of shock that falls over me, also angers me because I am not this man, fuck, who is this emotional man? I have always thought people should just get on with it, until now, until knowing this pain, I'm a fucking mess. My idol, the one man I went to for everything, is gone.

H E R | Thirteen

Why am I smiling at him? Not a complete smile, but a knowing smile, hinting that our journey is not yet over. My emotional self is in complete opposition to what my rational self is saying. And yet I'm thanking the universe for dropping us in front of each other again and begging her to please help us work through whatever is going on. I know he's battling his own monsters. I saw it right before my eyes, and yet my little girl inside doesn't want to be hurt, she wants to protect us and run. I walk up to the rug and wrap myself in a towel. He looks at me differently, like he is looking beyond me. His focus remains out in front and he hasn't turned to talk to me. Maybe he won't? What is he doing here?

We are silent for what seems like forever, I'm screaming on the inside, playing it so cool on the outside, until I notice my hands are uncontrollably shaking, so I allow them to continue to shake. I don't hide them, in fact, I encourage them by shaking my hands more to help alleviate the anxiety that is rising and enable me to be present with him as it feels like a big one. I did tell him to come back when he has figured out what he wants, didn't I? Can I survive this emotion? Did he just watch me purge my heart out to my ocean? A wave of goosebumps adds to my trembling, turning my insides. I hug myself tighter to comfort myself and the emotional intensity.

Fuck it, I don't care, I can only be me and show up even as a screaming crazy woman being tossed around in the ocean, no matter what because this fucking hurt. He hurt me and he just witnessed the result of that pain. You don't need to hide, Evie, you don't, encouraging myself. I reach for the warmth of my coffee and wrap my hands around the cup to soothe myself, as I sit behind him sipping on it. He still doesn't turn. "Evie," is the first word spoken.

My name, full of emotion and angst, hitting me sharply in the heart. I immediately want to reach for him, the pain in his voice, in my name, it is with all my power that I stay seated without interruption. This is clearly not a moment that I need to fix.

'Let the man speak' rises from the woman inside me who recognises pain.

He clears his throat, an attempt to hide the emotion in his voice. I continue to hold myself and sip my coffee.

He begins, "Evie, I never told you about my dad," and I'm slightly perplexed as he talked a lot of his dad.

I listen without comment and somewhat holding my breath for what he is about to say, the energy, he looks emotional. Then a beautiful man tells the story of a father and son and I can feel the tragedy coming, air escaping my lungs at the understanding of unthinkable pain. I stopped breathing as my insides begin twisting in the recognition of pain that can't be healed, only lived with. Tears that I had thought all dried-up roll silently down my face as Sam tells me what happened to his dad. I'm tormented by not being able to reach or hold him. I want to feel it all away. As loudly as those feelings scream, I am also aware no one could or ever can do that for me, so I sit back, burying my feet into the sand, seeking grounding to prepare myself for the story I can't fix, as I am a guest in this moment, right now. I am listening and feeling what is being described, as this is Sam's grief, from all accounts the first time he's really shared what he feels, what he thinks, how this has affected him. I am the passenger, albeit a weeping one at the enormity of loss between father and son. One of the most challenging situations ever is to watch a loved one in pain and not being able to take it away, no matter how hard you want to. Sam's grief pours out of him, the responsibility he feels now for the family, the running the farm, together with the tremendous sadness that his dad will never meet his kids, too never being able to have a beer and talk about nothing and everything.

H I M | Fourteen

I feel ashamed of myself for falling apart in front of her. I try to reason with myself, I don't like what she is doing to me, fuck it's all coming out wrong. I know it's not her, I'm trying to show her there is a fucking man here. I loved Dad and I'm missing him terribly, he's gone, nothing, like he didn't even exist. My thoughts and emotions collide, and I let it out. I share with Evie the pain at finding Dad like that, thinking he was joking at first, then seeing those eyes, burning into me, pained, trying to be composed in his physical pain and the recognition for both of us that Dad wasn't going to make it. Dad was courageous to the end. He was my support even while I was freeing him from the tractor. I was a complete mess, crying, screaming, shouting, hopeful that I was wrong, hopeful that it was never that bad, hopeful that Dad would survive; he was awake and lucid. I was repeating 'Don't die Dad, don't die,' to the point that I was saying it aloud. Dad encouraged me to let him go, and telling me he was immensely proud of the man that I am. That he is incredibly lucky in life to have lived and loved so hard.

He was saying goodbye and I couldn't listen, I couldn't believe it, I still can't believe it, my life feels so surreal. I turn reaching for Evie, and she's not there. I can't bear to look at her, I call her name and she holds me, she wraps herself around me and my grief pours out of me. We stay like this for a long time and I don't want to move, to breathe. I want to close off to the world and stay here with her, feeling her kindness. I take a deep breath of her, to compose myself and feel more of her closeness, she moves and I help her to arrange herself next to me, feeling raw, exposed and not wanting her to see me so wounded. She's seen my worst. Why would she want anything to do with me? What do I even want? Fuck, I am a mess.

The story of a father tragically taken way too soon feels like a giant empty hole in the pit of my stomach. Then finally as my tears have slowed, Sam expresses that he's been trying to hold it all together, trying to be the head of the family and keep his shit together. He switches emotions and immediately is angry. I'm confused, he's like, 'I'm not this fucking guy and I'm not going to be weak.'

I desperately want to wrap myself around him, climb on top of him and hold him in my skin. An epic battle of grief is happening, grief and fear holding the floodgates at bay for Sam. I know it well, I literally bite my tongue, I can't try to fix it, I can't make him feel better. I force myself to stay put, mouth closed. Straight away he takes a sharp, clearly frustrated, breath, forcing himself to regain composure.

"This shit is new for me, Evie. We opened Pandora's box, bringing things out in me that I was trying to avoid, do you understand me? I have to live up to my responsibilities and what Dad wanted me to be and I need to keep my shit together, so I can take care of Mum and Ruby, even though they decided on a family fucking intervention today and unconsciously brought me right to you."

I'm getting desperate now in my need to nurture to take away his pain to shield him, even though knowing that I can't. I know loss, and this kind of loss is not one that can be overcome. The kind that is too big, the kind that you must learn to live with, not forget, live with, actually have a relationship with the love that exists, living on in the love you have. My God, I am falling in desperate messy love with this stunning man, his rawness and ability to remain masculine in his emotional pain, and share it with me. I feel honoured to have heard his love for his dad and sad that I won't be able to meet him. This is a man I would chase and hope to love, one day. I feel privileged to hear about his father and overwhelmed because all that I have ever wished for is in front of me. A little pang in the depths of my mind reminds me that monsters live inside me too. I'm quick to ignore my own pains and focus on Sam. A man who is attempting to be honest in his emotions permitting his pain to take its own course right in front of me! This is emotional truth and to bear witness is such a special moment of trust. I'm trying to just allow the space he needs, not making it about me.

I am also daydreaming about the father he will be, praying that I'm the one who gives him boys, because this man right now personifies beauty and sexy in one. I'm brought back to reality, and him, when he says my name. He's searching for me, trying to say something and it feels abruptly uncomfortable. I stand and move towards him, he turns and immediately we embrace. Him against my womb, my sacred womanly self, wanting to hold him. I want to embrace him now. I slide down his body onto my knees, so we are eye to eye, wrapping my arms and legs around him, half tumbling. Sam steadies me, sitting back, allowing my body to wrap around him tightly, taking him into my heart. Embraced. I'm not sure how long we hold each other like this, and I don't want it to stop. I lift my head from his shoulder and look at him, feeling quite exposed now at the realisation of our position and how it feels to both of us. I get off him, with his assistance, and sit next to him.

"Sam, I have no idea how to comprehend your loss, nor your relationship with your dad. You sound like you have a very loving family. I don't know a lot Sam, but I do understand pain a little and what I have learnt is when we lose people who matter they live on in the people who loved them. Our relationship with them doesn't stop, it changes, and we learn how to continue to love them differently. We discover ways to honour the love we had together, how they shape us, and continue to love us. The pain doesn't stop, we don't get over it, we just learn to love them differently. I've learnt to love my hurts because it is also a reflection of how hard I loved and love. Grief needs to find a way to live out of us, not internalised and controlling us. We need to be freed by the trauma of our loved one's final moments to live in the great times of why we loved them so. Why your dad was a great man and better yet, the best loving father he could be for you, Sam."

H I M | Sixteen

Evie's comments seem to make sense, in that I should stop fighting and trying to forget, I think. I feel lighter and I am not sure if that is because of the emotional release or Evie's words or all of the above. Right now, it doesn't matter, I've not held it all in. I don't have to get over it, he's my dad. This is how I love and honour him now. Her words are strangely comforting. She's right, I am incredibly lucky to have been born into my family.

Evie prompts me further to talk about my dad and so I tell her all about the first time we went camping and we managed to invite two snakes and some dingos into the camp site, while also managing to offend the local indigenous community by camping where we shouldn't have. It was a masterclass in what not to do and then how to make amends with respect. Truly an amazing experience for a young kid, to see outside of the farm, watch Dad befriend anyone and laugh about our mishaps with nature. Dad became friends with the local Elders, and we ended up staying for dinner. It was the first time I was considered a man by Dad and sat with the men. It is funny that I have no idea what we said but for me I felt important and equal to Dad. From that day on it was different between me and Dad, in a good way, and we became mates. I opted to not share how we all went traditional hunting the following day, which for a 12-year-old was the coolest thing I had ever done.

Evie listens like she sincerely cares, and asks questions, ponders what that would have been like. She asks about the small things, which is refreshing, like if I was scared sleeping under the stars. It's like she is trying to picture the memory. She asked about how Dad looks, after checking it was okay to do so, and prompts me, to describe him. It all feels strange but nice, as I've not thought of him in such detail. I've been scared to talk of him with the reality of losing him and yet now Evie has presented something different to me, to not forget, to bring him forth into my life, so that our relationship continues. I want to focus on how that evolves for me. After a while, silence falls over both of us, my thoughts racing, in a good way. Memories of when I graduated with my trade, Dad was so chuffed, and both Mum and Dad arrived at the worksite in their Sunday best and made a big deal. My boss at the time was in on it, we had a BBQ and a few beers, the boss gave everyone half a day, so the boys were pretty happy with me that day. Then we all went out for dinner to celebrate.

I cherish those times I was, NO, I AM so loved by Dad and Mum. As a man now, I can see that I have been so very lucky. I do want that in my life and to be able to love someone how I have been loved and my own family. What is this right now? This feels good, but what am I thinking, am I ready for this? God, the sensations of her feels good, confusion clearly still here. I look straight at Evie, asking what are we? She shrugs. I usher us to the rug as I don't want to stop holding her right now. Her in my arms feels like the most natural thing to do right now. I'm lost in my memories. Some I share, some I don't. We stay on the blanket for a few hours.

I want to ask Evie how she knows about losing someone and yet the pain in her eyes frighten me, holding me back from asking. It's enough now. I close my eyes and I actually fall asleep, startled awake and no idea how long I've been asleep for. Evie is still in my arms. I'm surrounded by her scent, the salty air of the ocean, and thoroughly enjoying the feel of our bodies together in embrace, sensing her relaxing into me, the sun tip toe-ing along our bared skin, the gentle breeze, it all feels like a dream. Evie sits up, folding her arms over my chest and formally asks me to dinner, ever so politely. Watching the words roll out of her mouth, slowly purpose-ful, tastes so good, while having half of her body pressed into me and her expressing her desire. I feel like a fraud, how can she still want me? What do I have to give to her? I hesitate and she knows. I tell her I'm not sure, fuck. She suggests we don't think too much. Who is this woman? It feels right but I don't trust myself right now, I'm all over the shop and not sure what is right thing to do. She feels so damn good under my hands and I nod in agreement. We part ways with a hug that holds time, one that makes my breath stop and then she's gone. Dread pours over me. I feel like I'm doing something wrong, that we are not in the same place, she wants someone that I can't be.

H E R | Seventeen

"Sam, your father sounds like someone I would have loved to have met. I would really like to learn more about him. From what I have learnt of you so far, the apple doesn't fall far from the tree."

We both pause while taking my comments and it's sometime before he says, "Evie, what are we?"

"I'm not sure, I don't know yet. Whatever we are we need to take it slowly, we both have histories that we are telling to learn to cope with and that takes time. I'm not sure, but I know I feel comfortable with you and want to spend more time with you and see what this is."

We move to my rug and without words naturally fall into a cuddle. A long time spent in our own thoughts and feelings while the sun nurturing each other's hurts without words, and we don't address the fucking giant elephant laying in the sun with us. Instead we talk of Sam's father and some family memories and it feels so nice learning about them, a supportive family, kind of like the family I wished I had. I love my Mum and Dad, but they both had families separate to me. They did their best and yet I was always on the outside no matter how hard they tried, and then bad things took the rest of what I could have had. I couldn't trust anyone.

The afternoon is lost. I just want to focus on feeling not thinking, I want to feel this moment, his warmth, his scent pouring out all over my body, sinking into to each other.

After what feels like not long enough, I turn to Sam, asking if he will join me for dinner tonight. I want to cook for him. He looks at me and says, "Evie, I'm still not sure..." Interrupting him, I suggest we just see how things feel, not thinking too much. I drop him at his house and head to the supermarket, where a complete meltdown ensues. "Let's not think too much?" You fucking nut job! My inner protector is screaming "what the fuck are you doing!"

He is grief stricken. Fear announces its arrival and sets up camp in my brain. It's like a TV series on rerun. He hurt you! "Let's not think?!" The dramatic finale he's still not sure about you and you're planning a romantic dinner with you for the dessert!

What am I doing?

I scream a little in the car and then scream some more, gripping the streeling wheel. It helps take the edge off. I'm trying to logically think this through, starting the peep talk with a little Buddhist-like chant: "you will NOT sleep with him" over and over, over again! I'm sweating profusely, my inner battle revealing itself clearly now as I attempt to contain the cascade of excitement. I burst into laughter as I know how much of a complete lie this is. I am contemplating buying protection.

Fucking pathetic girl, why can't I run with what I've said? I'm not sure either, why do I have to go with all or nothing? The anxiety monster is trying to bend my will. I want the complete package. My dream. I must acknowledge that my future picture of us is not necessarily his and how can it be fair to expect him to be on the same page, as me, with my needs and wants for a relationship? Why am I already trying to think for him? Sleeping with Sam now would also be the fastest way for me to destroy anything we could have, ruining any opportunity for real intimacy, my unconscious becoming conscious in the honest reflection, almost jarring. Overexposing myself to make me run.

I am already afraid, already fearing his response, playing his thoughts out in my mind. I am ready, trying to control the future, with panic in control. My inner coach rises through the panic. Evie, let the inner thoughts play out, remember they are being fuelled by excitement and the pressure of what might be. It is just dinner with someone who you want as a friend, so just try to be friends. It takes time to come together, grow and work out if this is the right skin for both of us. I need to check my expectations. I need some grounding. I've never felt this way before. I've never felt this alive in my skin, this connected to the woman that is inside me and I want her to be released in love, but need to remember that she's from within me not from an external source. I want to trust. I'm hoping that I am enough and to believe that I am for love. We are all different and I can't put a script on someone else as well as trying to protect myself. My heart joins the internal debate and fires back at me with 'uncomfortable and crazy often leads to extraordinary things.' I need to be vulnerable as well and be willing to fail, be willing to be hurt in order to have the possibility to love someone that I've wished for. I need to be not so vulnerable, not so invested to make sure I don't give all of myself away.

Love is a risk. It is being uncomfortable, vulnerable and accepting the other person in front of you, no matter their baggage or fears. We haven't even opened my fears yet! I have a tight lid on them, clearly. I am way too ahead of myself. I really like how he feels on me, next to me, his smell, sweaty, salty fresh.

No one has ever made me feel like this before, so if this is not meant to be then, I will enjoy these feelings while they last. I close my eyes, touch my hand over my heart and whisper to myself "I choose to spend as much time in these feelings as I can. Stay in the present."

I trust me and I trust that if this goes pear shaped, I have the capacity to work with my hurts and overcome. I loved, I received it and gave it to someone. He is all over the shop, as he should be with what has happened to him, and this I understand being at the whim of pain, of unthinkable sadness. He is moving through his pain and I don't ever want to pressure someone who is vulnerable. I feel such connection with him.

Perhaps I should explain myself, mind you, what would I even say? I remember people telling me all of their opinions on what I should or shouldn't do and that was not helpful. I'm scared to tell him that I think he needs to focus on family, shouldn't he? I know it has been some time now, but am I taking advantage of him? Confusion and shit are getting real in my head. Any amount of time with him is worth the potential pain of losing him. What do they say? To love for five minutes can be worth an eternity. Right? Sam showed up and that's what I want to honour, he risked rejection and was vulnerable, he showed me his pain. For me, that's a massive display of trust! I have enough hurts that he has yet to see, this theme on repeat in my mind. I realise that I might be hiding behind the all or nothing type cop-out, that by saying you need to be all in, I'm pushing him away, because what does that even look like? There feels like there is more than us at work here. What if I let my guard down like he did? The fear of the thought sends a shudder of cold fear through me. How can I even say that to him? Shit, I'm instantly reminded of my body sensation of him next to me today and how my body feels stretched out next to him and I know that my body will never lie to me, whereas these thoughts and over thinking they lie, lie, and lie…

My own story of survival breaks into my thoughts and convinces me that I want to show up. I wasn't triggered in his arms and all that touching today felt safe. He feels lovely. I was open, I didn't run and try to shut it off my feelings. I want to risk it, I want to be loved and hurt because that is how we love, to show up in my truth and allow him to show up in his. In other words, the opening and closing of our hearts. I've been so closed, my heart switched off to love. I've only ever dated men I could control and predict. I know that sounds bad, but for me it was about safety. It's not that I didn't have feelings for them, just that when it came to an intimacy level, I could control them to a degree. Although nothing's ever 100 percent, this created a level of control that provided the level of safety for me, allowing me to practice my triggers safely. It all gave me hope that I could love and I could receive care. It was a survival strategy too, in order to have moments of connection and intimacy, while feeling safe behind my caged heart. I have not been triggered with Sam. He feels so safe. I haven't wanted to run screaming in the other direction, only my mind is coming up with roadblocks attempting to protect me. I have to let go of control, as the focus has been him and not me, which has meant I could sort of hide.

Now I am fighting my own fears and trying to get out of my head. He has shown up and I need to as well, even if that means losing control and allowing someone else to help me to learn to love beyond this concrete caged heart. I have expectations of him to protect me and be there for me. He is telling me honestly that he is not sure. I need to respect his wishes and pull the handbrake on myself. How is it fair that I have expectations on this man? He has a right to his feelings, and they are just as valid as mine, just different, I think. I have run with the whole it is a 'forever' relationship and that is not fair! He has a right for it not to be that! It hurts to consider those feelings and try to risk it anyway. Opening yourself up to love increases your fears and my irrational thoughts are showing up to take over. There have only ever been two men before in my life of who I have let go of control. One I knew for an exceptionally long time and another was only a brief encounter, with an equally confident man who I just felt at ease with due to our level of vulnerability and intensity. Our connection was embedded in raw honesty and how we showed a mutual understanding of pain and how our confidence was a survival strategy. We shared moments of vulnerability taking risks in our connection and accepting each other. We both knew it was more about comfort and connection in a loving way, rather than sex…we had connected sex, where vulnerability was accepted and embraced with communication. Perhaps this occurred because we knew we were never going to see each other again. So, we were able to peel back our bullshit, talking of love, of hope, of what feels safe, of our dreams and fears in life. I have treasured these moments because they helped me to learn to trust myself again, in taking a risk to be accepted as me, not what I think I should be. It was two people who came together in their fears and accepted each other while also sharing hope for the possibility of those parts of us being loved in the future.

I have a world of anxiety thinking. This is the tip of the iceberg! I do need you to know that this is my fear showing up and that I'm gifting to you. This is the preparation I am doing because I know I want him, I want to feel his hands on me, I want to feel his love, choose to love. So, clearly, I don't have any control with Sam! And, well, control helps me to feel safe, so trust Evie, trust. Instantly, I revert to self-coach mode, which is a great opposition to my overthinking. Remind myself, remember to trust myself and to unleash the woman I am. Be raw, authentically you, it's the same as showing up. Evie, you need to show up emotionally, even if that is you shitting your fucking self.

I make a plan in the pasta aisle. Lasagne. I'll need to let him in on a little of my crazy, just a small amount. Please let me not be too much. I'm again begging God, the universe, the divine whoever will hear my call on the drive home, normal, please, let me be normal. He let me in on what is happening in his head and I'm not sure he truly knows what is happening for him. I think that this is okay and that it's okay for us to be in completely different places, emotionally and physically. That is how you come together with someone, the ebb and flow of opening and closing your heart, the peeling back of yourself, right? The hurting and the healing, right? I don't want to start with a closed heart, but I fear, that I am. I need to understand and accept that our doors could be closed but completely unlocked.

Opening your heart means opening it to everything, to all the parts you've closed the doors on, all the parts that are unresolved, you can't close yourself off to one feeling without dampening all feelings. I want to be open to the entire experience of falling in love. I guess I want to let him know that this is my experience as well, that I have been secretly freaking out the entire time we've spent together. Even though I know he knows this, I want to say it, aloud. I wonder if this is what happened to Sam? Opening his heart to me meant that the dam wall cracked, and shit began flooding out. He had closed himself off and when I came along cracks began to show. I want to be compassionate towards him and honour his relationship with his dad, honestly sharing what I can give and want. There will be a time when he needs to sit behind me and just wait, or whatever it looks like for me. This realisation brings a calm to me. I feel my shoulders relax and I'm beginning to check back into reality as I feel the cold milk on my arm, redness on my skin from the chill. Ingredients for lasagne balanced, very well I might add, in my arms. I laugh out loud as I wonder how many times. I've just been walking aimlessly around this supermarket deep in thought. Amazing things happen when you're in supermarkets. At the checkout, my thoughts softly murmur, 'our stories are different, and our internal battles are the same, both grappling with life, warts and all.' I know the best place to heal from relationship trauma is in healthy relationship however the practice of doing it is a different story.

H I M | Eighteen

Harold, my blue heeler, has been under my feet since I came home. He's been like this for a while and today appears even mores agitated. I ask him what I should do about Evie? Harold responds with a bark.

I'm not even sure I'm going tonight. I'm overthinking things. I know it, but I can't bear to hurt her. I can't have those eyes look at me, like that again, wounded. I can't be who she needs. I ask Harold and he just licks my face, and I laugh, somehow. I think why not, you're a good man aren't you? Am I? My God, it got serious quickly. Am I trying to ignore the pain of Dad? She just feels good, and being near her feels good. I just want to feel good, can't I just follow that? Just see what happens. I take a deep breath, giving myself some encouragement. Right. Put in an effort. She is so kind, I like the person she is. Remember about Mum and Dad and try to be a gentleman like he was. The word 'was' disrupts my thoughts and causes me pain.

Clean up, one foot in front of the other. I put a shirt on, and quietly ask Dad out loud to help me. Harold cuts sick at the door, barking, jumping through the doggie door and into the back of my truck before returning inside. Clearly, he's made his mind up. I'm stunned and comforted at the same time that it feels like Dad is helping me, and I need to trust it is him. I am choosing to believe it is him helping me. At Dad's farewell there were a few strange things that occurred, as if Dad were still with us. We all acknowledged it, not out loud of course, that would be too crazy for my family!

Ruby stopped me later, after I asked 'what the...' Her response stuck with me. 'You may not believe in it, but it believes in you,' in reference to the strange occurrences and her beliefs that Dad is still with us. It is sort of like what Mum and Evie said that Dad lives on within me and how I continue to love him. I did ask for help and I want to listen, Dad and Harold just gave me a pretty big clue. Particularly with Harold's weird behaviour. After a lot of coaxing Harold gets out of the ute, rewarded with a giant bone for his help. I drive forward towards Evie's, feeling more resolved and like things feel right. I guess I'm not arguing with how I am feeling, including just not knowing what is next... because I don't know, no one has any clue, we all just pretend we do.

Arriving at Evie's, I can hear old time music playing, the kind Mum and Dad used to listen to while Mum attempted to dance with a man who had two left feet. She used to stand behind him, swinging his hips in an attempt to get him to dance. He would always give her a clumsy jig and her smile would light up the room. Small moments were what made them both light up. I knock and there no answer, but the door's open, so I invite myself in. I see Evie. She's dancing and I'm transfixed immediately. She moves her body in a way that mesmerises me, and I feel hypnotised. I'm watching her body, picturing her riding me, moving to the music, slowly. I think I have my hands stretched out towards her when she turns after noticing me, but I can't be sure.

"I knocked," stumbles out of my mouth.

She says it's okay, giving me another swing of her sex in my direction. Well, I am done in. I'm struggling trying to contain myself and keep up with the conversation while watching her. The way she looks at me feels amazing. I notice I am puffing my chest out, its comical really and yet feels primal. This part of me is showing strength to her. It feels electrifying between us. I can smell her, taste her in the air. She's sweet and musky. I'm leaning into the space. I can see her flicker, from the excitement. I'm getting so hard, pushing my own manhood out towards her to feel for her. She moves, and I want more, so I feel her, taking that body and letting her experience my manhood, while tasting her lips slowly. Showing her that I'd take her passionately, tenderly, and fiercely over and over again. I feel her body change under my hands. Rigid. Too much. I pull back, steadying her hips to feel me. She takes the control of the moment with a passion-filled kiss, pressing her breasts into me. Fuck, she feels so good. We both try to slow down in recognition of how that felt. She tastes like beer, without thinking I say the beer tastes good, breaking the ice a little, releasing the tension from engulfing us both.

The local radio station is smashing out some classics. I feel good, show-ered, restored and determined to be authentically me. I have a beer in hand to relieve my nervous angst and some dancing to take the edge off the anticipation of his arrival, while the smell of basil and tomatoes fill the air from the lasagne.

Etta James, 'Sometimes I Get a Good Feeling' comes on. I am owned by the soul of an epic song, from a time when every song lit you up from the inside, speaking to your soul. The purest form of creativity and expression that I have is dancing, where I can spend my emotions. I spin myself around my kitchen dancing with an invisible partner, dreaming of his hands on me, to find Sam standing in my kitchen in a trance watching my body. I'm embarrassed and giggle like a schoolgirl. "I knocked," he declares.

The cheeky woman inside me flashes him a swing of my hips, telling him you're welcome! I walk around the bench to greet him and he smells so good, a spicy woody tone, showered and clean. Blue jeans and he's chosen a nice shirt to wear for me, towel dried hair, very sexy. The shirt shows off his body, making me wonder if he knows how sexy he looks, or if he pulled the first thing out of his wardrobe. From what I know of this man, I think it would have been the latter. He is particularly good looking, and as I take him all in, suddenly, I feel inadequate. I let that thought pass on by as my sassy self internally laughs with, 'I'm the fucking prize!' My very own internal rebuttal. I'm in front of him, looking into those eyes. His hands immediately reach for my hips as I reach for him, standing there taking this man in, feeling the moment, him and our energy rising. We are not moving and yet a dance is occurring, our souls are caressing each other, finding their tune, our flow, reconnecting. We are about to move apart, the energy swirling around us increases, my breathing quickens. I'm having a hot flush, sweating, my hands on his chest, exposed, fighting the urge to kiss him, fighting my excitement, attempting to tame myself and to contain the moment. The part of me that is fearful, is the part of me that doesn't want to be hurt again, the thought causes me to flicker, to move. He responds completely as if tuned into my body and moves me closer to him. Ever so gently he runs his lips over mine, hands reaching for my face, tasting my lips, holding me in him. Turning the volume to right up to max in our energy, the room is spinning, my heart is thumping hard against my chest, dread rises, my heart panics, racing hard against the cage she is in. Fear is coming in this moment, and I'm triggered completely, I feel the rigidity arrive in my body, so I push my feet heavy into the ground and press my chest against his and take some control of our kiss, setting the tone for myself, so I can accept the bodily experiences and recognise this as pure connection and it's new and I need practice.

I practice that change in me, feeling both wonderful and terrified to work with it, allow it to live here until it doesn't anymore. I soften into the space. Sam now takes back the rhythm of our embrace, penetrating my every sense. My heart thumps to find flow, lips quivering, searching for our own beat, feeling the warmth of him, his sweetness, all of me held, synced to our rhythm pulling me closer to his body, his soul, I slow us. I need to breath, I step back taking a deep slow breath, while taking all of him in, I push my feet into the ground, my legs feel like jelly, fear attempting to crawl out of the darkness and yet a smile comes out of me, in the knowing that we have begun, I have faced it in the presences of someone and our rhythm and our tone is creating safety for me. We move further apart, I feel completely surrendered to the mercy of this man, he feels incredible, he knows only the way a man does how to hold your centre of gravity while you are lost in the feel of him wholly. And you trust that this ever-present source of man's strength holds you right there, right where you need to be held to explore the man before you. I'm overwhelmed by his natural instinct to protect, without even knowing he is doing it, I think. He's got me like an anchor. Sam's voice breaks me out of my thoughts, "the beer tastes good!" I smile at his cheek and grab him a beer.

While we talk about nothing, politely avoiding what just happened and it all feels so surreal. I serve dinner and somewhat regret the formal nature of the dining table, wishing I had of opted for the kitchen bench. The formality of it increases my anxiety. I'm already on edge after my supermarket attack of the looping mind and it all appears blank after tasting him. I'm committed now so over the first bite, I start to slowly tell him how I feel.

"Sam, you scare the shit out of me!" Internally, I'm screaming at myself for my epic fail at slow and slightly yelling at him. "I want to run towards you and away from you at the same time and this is not just about what's already happened between us. The reason why I want to run away from you is because of the baggage I come with and how I desperately don't want to ever be hurt again. I am battling those old wounds that used to keep me scared and now they show up in big moments like this, with you because I like you. I know that's a stupid way to live, hence why I'm also trying to share with my experience and trying not fuck this up, yet I know we will hurt each other, I understand you will hurt me, and I will hurt you too. What I believe a relationship is the practicing accepting each other while hurting and repairing, rinse and repeat." Sam instantly reacts, and I interrupt. "Sam, please bear with me, I know I am stumbling though, when you say you're not sure, I feel hurt and like I'm not enough, sort of like you are rejecting me and that's ok because you're being honest with what is happening for you and my feelings are also okay too. I guess I am trying to let both of us be okay in being different places while dealing with massive emotions. I'm trying to respect your wishes and allow space for my feelings to evolve as well. I am scared to open myself up to love with someone and to learn to experience the love of another. I am responsible for my choices and us being in different places is fine and tomorrow I might be in a very different place too and I guess I just want you to know where I am coming from and I understand where you are at, I think. I know this is probably way too full on for you right now, but I want you to know I respect your wishes and also want you to understand my feelings and that I get that we both are 'not sure,' just in different ways. I know we will hurt! That's part of learning to love and I'm figuring out what that looks like and what my expectations also look like. Sam, I come with damage and it will show up, sort of like now! I hope it's something that we can work through together and I can overcome for myself. I learnt this a long time ago but today in the supermarket, all my fears showed up about you and I wanted to run, then I realised I don't want to be hurt! My fears are real, and I will still show up in them, I just need to feel them through. I am open to feeling what we look like without expectation knowing that being hurt while working out if there is any possibility of feeling what I feel for you now, is worth it. I am confused, I am struggling with my desire for you and the reality of us, while wanting to get to know the man you are. Trying to keep my feet on the ground, which is what I mean we are at different places and are different people and I guess, I am trying to work with my expectations and overwhelming feelings while acknowledging and giving time for that to be ok within you. I am trying to be open without judgement and expecting you to fit my ideal."

Throughout this anxious rambling, my internal fears are oscillating between negative thoughts of myself and attempting to look half rational in what I am trying to convey here. "I understand how my fears work. I get that we have no idea where this will go. It is complete bullshit to say I am ready for you and what this could be, because when you're near me, I feel like I don't have any control and when you touch me..."

I take a slow depth breath to compose myself. I am trying to ride the wave of my feelings while having a cascade of emotion, desire and fear-based thinking overcome me.

I look up at Sam, and I am not sure of what he is thinking. I am rambling so much, fuck.

"Well, shit, that doesn't sound right. A relationship has good and bad, and I know that's not us too, we are just seeing what happens, what we feel like for each other and I am happy. After hearing your love for your dad and your family today, your honesty and understanding why you didn't want to see me, why it was too much for you, I want you to understand, I am also struggling with the intensity around us and I want you to honour your father and your feelings for him without me in the way. I wanted you to know a little about me too and I want to be true to myself and true to you, I might get hurt and it might not be what I want and I may be a little crazy, yet I inherently know that I will survive and love that I showed up gave us a chance, without holding back. Sam, I like how I feel when I'm with you, and I'll chase any amount of time with you even if that consists of going on mad tangents over lasagne."

Sam's attempting to be cool, calm and collected, I think. A wave of emotion is rising in me, awaiting his response to the first flood of anxiety spilling out of me. "Evie, thanks for letting me know, I get it and appreciate you seeing where I am at, when we shared our first kiss I felt all of that and your vulnerability and it felt too much. It showed me what I was trying to outrun my own emotions." He squeezes my hand and adds, "now eat."

I'm dumbfounded and falling in so much crazy love with Sam that all I can muster is a smile as we both return to our lasagne.

After a few moments of silence, I say, "I was attempting to show you how much I wanted you with your hand on my chest," while giggling.

"My God, we are intense, hey?" Sam smiles and squeezes my hand. I add "I will try to stay out of my head so much. This is just new territory." I'm trembling while I'm saying this to him. Thankfully, he simply responds, "I know."

We enjoy the rest of dinner in comfortable silence. It has been a massive day, with a smile here, a gently reassuring touch on the arm, on the hand there. We do the washing up together, enjoying the moment of dancing in each other spaces softly. He laughs at the fact that I like the doing the dishes rather than using the dishwasher and attempts to educate me on water saving. When I explain why I actually like it, he smiles. This used to be a time that families would spend together. I potter around, and he retreats to the couch, it feels so unbelievably normal and this is the first time he's really spent any time in my house. My space suits him, and I smile at the thought of him naked in my kitchen. Sam calls me over and we both stare at the box, I lie down and rest my head on his lap. The last thing I remember was him playing with my hair.

I wake suddenly. I'm awake, alone and cold. I call out "Sam!" He's gone and there's a note, a simple 'goodnight.' I smile and am grateful for the note as for a second. I thought he had deserted me again. I take myself and the note to bed, waking again to the buzzing of my phone. Its' 6 am, wow, I must tell Sam that I'm more of a sunset than a sunrise lady and roll over to sleep some more.

H I M | Twenty

Evie initiates small talk. The desire of our kiss lingers, driving my want for her harder. It's difficult to focus beyond her body. She is rambling and her nervousness feels amazing. She's confident and yet so delicate and it's the fragility that I hope to protect. The thought shocks me.

Fuck, I really do like her.

There's fucking bucket loads of chemistry and she's utterly captivating. Am I embarking on this with her? Is this love? Fuck.

My thoughts are interrupted by Evie announcing I scare the shit out of her. Fuck, well, that is left of field! She feels so certain all the time. Her announcement makes me nervous. I'm caught like a deer in her headlights, while the smell of lasagne below my nose makes my taste buds dance and my stomach growl. I strain so hard to focus on Evie. Fuck, this feels too much. She wants to run away. I get that completely. It's too instant, and it feels out of control. Wow, she's honest. I think what she's is telling me that it is okay for us to be in different places and have different ideas about where we are at.

Fuck, she is just as messed up as me! I want to help her, make her feel safe. I get it, she's right. It is overwhelming and I do get what she is saying but I'm not sure what to say to help. Evie starts to stumble over her words, and "I know" falls out of me. These emotions are full on and yes, it is what it is. I try to show her comfort and help us to relax. We both end up with a nervous laugh at our honesty and I see she is trembling. I want her to know that I hear her, and I don't want her to think that I didn't, so I attempt to convey that understanding.

After dinner, we do the washing up old school and it feels nice. She's still seems a little fragile, as am I, if I'm honest with myself. I want us to relax so I ask her to join me on the couch, encouraging her to lie down where she places her head in my lap. I watch her face as her eyes close slowly and she struggles to stay awake. Her hair falls over me, her hand on my knee. I play gently with her hair. Both she and the room smell of garlic, basil and tomatoes, her skin soft and smooth like silk. I've been playing with her hair and watching her for a while now and I wonder when is the point that it becomes uncomfortable? I've already stalked her, now I'm watching her sleep.

When would a gentleman leave? Sliding myself away, I place a pillow under her head, managing to leave without waking her. Standing over her, I wonder what happened to her, what's her pain? We clearly both have a story. Her comments on having a relationship with our losses, makes me wonder what that actually looks like.

Driving home, I find myself telling Dad about Evie. Dad would say that for sure, she's a keeper, I think. The conversation with him feels painful and the tears flow because I can't be sure that is what he would say. There is a gaping hole in never being truly able to hear his voice. It has been a massive day, highs and lows and all throughout, the pain of Dad. I get home and Harold is waiting, looking up at me. I tell him and he barks in all the right places, then I tell him about Dad and that I'm going to talk to him. He turns and plants his arse on my foot which, I think, is him telling me this is a good idea. It's enough for my thinking to diminish and feel like sleep is a possibility.

HER | Twenty-one

Unable to truly return to sleep, I get up and potter around the house, reliving all that has happened and the crazy lady who showed up at dinner last night. Did I even make sense? Dread forms a weight in the pit of my stomach while I'm dissecting everything. I need to shake it off, welcoming all the crazy that I am purging into my diary, so I can be a normal person. I recognise that my emotional hangover is here. Everything that I said to myself that I wouldn't do, I've done at least twice today in my daydreams. I've married us, pictured him playing with our son and then found myself sobbing at the fears that repeat over in my head. Deep down, I know I am also washing off the emotions and stress off the last few days, so I stop resisting, jump into the shower and unleash all that I have down the drain. My thoughts loop on my decisions I've made and conversations with him that haven't even happened. My head is doing a number on me and I'm panicked and feeling exposed, feeling like I'm too invested already and completely pissed at myself for feeling this way. Classic psycho! Part of me is loving it because I've never had this before. Feeling in full appreciation of having these thoughts and wondering, holy shit, how do I stop these thought patterns?

The shower helps and the thoughts of actually appreciating these experiences with Sam, washes psycho down the drain. While in the shower, it came to me, that I should, write my experiences as I know it, even if it's just a place for an anxiety dump or my fatal attraction to show up far, far, away from Sam.

I don't think I'm entirely crazy, otherwise I'd be telling my story to a head shrink within a facility with white or greenwash walls. Don't ask me how I know the colour of the walls. You know how when you bring the inside thoughts out into the open, the value of them changes? Putting them into a voice or pen and they lose their power over you, as the importance of them becomes different, like saying them aloud. Well, for me it's writing.

I hold my lips together, close my eyes and dream of his mouth, his touch, those lips. Just to breathe him in, soaking myself amongst his strength. Imagining his hands on my hips, as my body surrenders to the thoughts of him capturing my womanly centre. That moment in the garage where he seized my hips, with my body instantly responding, my back arching, and I was against him. It was our bodies in control, the recognition of our souls reaching for each other and responding in kind. The sensation of him leaves a residual effect on me. Shudders pass through me at thought of him. As I stand, I take a moment to feel my body draped over him, the sense of soaking myself in his skin. I reach for my heart and engage the emotion allowing it to engulf me, encouraging the sensations to rise within me like a wave. Closing my eyes allows me to feel further into the pulsing energy moving around my body, as I feel him, I desire him so. I want that soul connection and a stirring occurs in the depths of me, I'm not even sure what I am asking for. My womanly self-rises, screaming for a lover, a man, a partner, an anchor. She's raring to be unleashed, to be stroked and played with while terror plays its own song in the background.

H I M | Twenty-two

I've decided that the oldies of my life, Dad's era, knew a little something so I have a plan. I can't stay away! I tried that and it didn't work, so I'm going to get to know Evie, slowly. I'm dealing with all these other feelings and it is overwhelming. The only thing I can think of is to help us both, is trying to be friends. My plan is that I'm not really sure about anything at the moment and jumping into a relationship feels too much. I want to listen to what Evie said: she is scared.

Well, fuck, I am too. I can't have her look at me like she did that day in her garage with those wounded eyes. I'm bringing out the big guns, going old school, in honour of a man who knew a thing or two, unhurried. We can see what develops with this amazing chemistry. It is so good for her to understand and, I think, be okay with us being in different places. She's one of few that has helped me make sense of what is happening to me, along with Mum and Ruby. It feels like I'm closer to Dad now. Even though I lost my shit in front of Evie, I didn't crack up, I didn't lose control and she supported me. I feel like I finally accepted what has happened and let someone else see my pain. I let someone help me.

Getting it all out has surprisingly helped me. I feel more in control and comfortable with my feelings being expressed. Dad was my first big loss, my first tragedy, I guess. How do you even know what the fuck to do?

Evie didn't try to fix it, she didn't tell me to let go or even get over it. She kind of just witnessed me while I took the brakes off and hugged me when I needed it. In my weakest moment, I didn't feel weak.

With Evie, it felt good to just be. Beyond my genuine appreciation for what she has done for me, it worries me to think about what has happened to her, how she has suffered? How else could she know what was happening for me? It was foreign for me. I can't see her look at me with pain, I don't want to hurt her, and I want to explore a friendship.

So, I've decided we are going to date, with all the trimmings of dating! Old school-like. We need to cool our jets and I want to respect her. To take things slowly, handholding at most. Five dates with the aim to get to know each other and have fun. We both need to slow things down. I want to be a good man and I have a fair idea on what that looks like and hope that I can live up to it. As I consider my plan, excitement and sheer terror builds in me, getting the shakes and all.

I kind of laugh as it reminds me of Evie last night telling me she's shit scared. Well, fairly sure we both are. Evie is utterly captivating and clearly has no idea how desirable she is. She's a natural woman who feels comfortable with herself, which is sexy as fuck. I am really going to need to restrain myself from wanting to touch her and yet completely excited by developing desire with her.

I ring her and formally invite her to dinner on Wednesday. She agrees, and it feels like we have a plan. Part of me wonders if I should tell her about my plan?

I call the next woman I want to make it up to, my sister, Ruby, and demand she meets me for a beer and countie meal. I will not accept no for an answer. It's something we haven't done since Dad left us. She giggles and her response to my instruction is "Hi bro, nice to have you back!"

Fuck, I love my sister. I want to apologise and tell her about what I have learnt and about loss and pain, and, of course, some of what has happened with Evie. I think it's time to get my sister back, not that she's gone anywhere, but I got lost in my grief and I want to change my course. Ruby has never steered me wrong. She will always tell me the truth even if it hurts and I am grateful that we have that level of honesty. Ruby and I go to our family pub, it's basically Dads' local. As we walk in, there are a few head nods and couple of handshakes and thoughts of Dad which feels nice, I think for both of us. As we head to the back for a quieter spot, two beers are delivered on the house. There is a silence between us first as we are both in our memories of Dad. I toast, "To Dad" as we drink.

Ruby's face is stunned. She says, "Sam, that's the first time you've acknowledged Dad."

I ask if she feels okay if we talk about him. I see her swallow hard, clearly a family trait, followed by a gulp of her beer, as she nods in agreement. We both fall silent again into our memories. After some time, I look at Ruby and say, "Good talk!" We both laugh. I tell Ruby about what Evie had said and how it makes sense to me and that I wanted to tell her to continue to make sense of it and also to spend time together. To start trying to find a new us, without the big fella. The sound of big fella coming out is enough to choke us both up, the name lodging in my throat. We both have a few tears fall out, as another round is silently delivered to the table. I just love our local community out here.

I tell Ruby how I've started talking to Dad and Harold. She tells me, I am bat shit crazy and she's been doing the same, so we both are then. "There's no rules to this Ruby, I've been struggling with what I am supposed to do, how this works and what I needed to be for everyone else. I also had no idea I could be in shock for this long. Fuck me, who would have thought this shit would even be coming out of my mouth? Rubes I want to share with you what's been happening, and I am trying to not hide what I have been feeling. I was doing one day at a time, trying to get on with life, hiding everything. I'm forgiving myself and letting myself have a bat shit crazy relationship with my dead father and I finally don't give a shit what that looks like. It is what I need, I want him to live on in us, Ruby, and how we keep loving Dad."

Ruby tells me that she thinks Dad is still around us. I encourage her to have whatever relationship she needs with him and let her know that I am here to listen. Ruby says she needs some time to chew on my new-found revelations and acknowledges it feels good to talk about him and how things have been for both of us. Rather than the pain of everything being endured separately. We also talk about Mum and I wait for Ruby to ask about Evie. It doesn't take long, and she thinks that my idea is a great one and likes that it is something Dad would have done too. It feels good just to hang out and we have a few more beers, some food and we agree next time that Mum is coming whether she likes it or not. It's strange. I feel like I have a way forward. Not that everything is squared away, but I have an idea on a way forward and I'm okay with not knowing the future.

Evie and I have three very polite dates. I'm basically having cold showers before and after in order to not be a crazed horny teenager. I really don't know what slow means when it is either too much, or not enough. She is so hard to read and ever so kind. She always askes about Mum and Ruby and really looks at me when she does. She is kind to everyone. I really like her. It is true in that there is a real friendship here. I love our banter, a sharp wit that feels playful, both of us testing the waters. She has a remarkable smile that she freely gives to everyone, from smiling to the old man walking his dog, to random people in a restaurant. The way her hair falls around her neck, the giggle that puts you at ease and her sharp mind. Wow, she is smart and difficult to keep up with.

She's people smart, and she's got me sussed quickly. She tries to break her thinking down for me. I can see this will frustrate me, like she is giving an enormous amount of useless information. She only does it when she's nervous. I notice her vulnerability, scaring me slightly. I'm desperate to connect with her and make it all go away and frightened that she needs more than I am. Sometimes in conversations she goes somewhere, like she checks out for a second or two before coming back. It's hard to know if she is being considered or if there is something else happening. We have talked about Dad a lot, and it's difficult and nice.

She's so easy to talk to, although it's like she is thinking too much at times. I can't put my finger on it, but sometimes I want her to relax. It's like she is careful with me. Perhaps it's because of Dad, I don't know or maybe I'm still sensitive? I want to show her more of me, and I need to go to the farm, so I plan to invite her. Then she can see me, and me is the farm, that's really where my heart is. The world can fall away there, and we can just be us. I also think it would be so good for her to relax, separate rooms and the whole nine yards. I am kind of worried that it might be too soon, too much and the aloneness of the farm will be wonderfully too much.

I want to build her the outdoor bath she told me about. I want to appreciate her. I want to give thanks for how she has helped me, and whatever it is we are growing into.

There is an old bath left from renos we did a while back, so it won't be too difficult to do. I call Evie to invite her to the farm for the weekend. I have this entire reasoning behind why she should come and that there are plenty of rooms and no pressure whatsoever. I've practiced my speech about three times and before I can get any of it out. she's like 'please.' My God, that is the sexiest word from her mouth and the tone in her voice lingers around me for hours.

H E R | Twenty-three

We have a few more dates, a couple of coffees and getting to know you type dates, very safe and public. They are fun and so very normal. I've loved it! We've laughed so much.

He is very structured and planned or maybe he's trying to impress me? He seems so cool, calm and collected all the time, but I don't know how. I meet Sam for breakfast. It's one of our safe dates. I am super early, so I sit near my car before heading into the café. There was some commotion in the car park where an older gentleman is struggling with his car and trailer. Out comes Sam from the café, clearly a lot earlier than me. He offers to guide the man and I can hear them talking to each other. Sam is so supportive and encouraging. Sam ends up jumping in and moving his car to make it easier for him. All I am doing is beaming a giant smile that I am dating a man who is this kind. Sam does this often, not like he goes out of his way, but if an opportunity presents, he assists, offering kindness when no one is watching without expectation of anything in return. It is simply what you do according to Sam, who is a man of integrity. It is daunting to hope to live up to and at the same time inspiring. Don't get me wrong, he is not saving the world, but he wouldn't turn a blind eye and that is such an important value of mine.

During breakfast we have our first debate about politics, about the land and climate change. Thank God he is not a climate denier! At least we are on the same page there. However, what makes a difference and offers a way forward is that we are on differing ends of the spectrum and it felt good to have a heated discussion, watching our passions play out and feeling comfortable with disagreement. Our dates bring out a friendship and a playful banter that is igniting our fiery passions, feeling more like foreplay for the mind. Our playfulness continues for most of the date and it feels nice to explore the boundaries of us and also getting to see our true selves rather than presenting the best careful versions of ourselves because we want to be liked. In between normal banter there has been magical moments of long stares, where I'm caught in his eyes, holding space for our feelings. There is a lovely gentleness to us that I can't find words to describe.

I think we both struggle with our flashes of magic, of no words of chemistry and closeness. My God, I am so frustrated that it's not funny! We have pulled the handbrake on our touch, and the intensity and anticipation feel too much. We feel like we are both trying to manage our emotions better.

It's like the pendulum swung too far in open emotional communication and now has swung completely back to a friendly, safe, not too emotional, not too physical space. Strangely in the backdrop of this friendly space, our intimacy grows, safety grows, and nothing eases me, nothing! This unwavering need of this man, it's punishing. Evie, I scream at myself, slow, you want to take things slowly. We have taken slowly to the next level. Internally, my head, heart and desire battle.

Yet, to feel held internally by this beautiful man is a dream I never thought could be real, so relax. I have spent time connecting with my heart, spending my emotions, not caging my feelings and attempting not to become them, as I fight completely with desire and not wanting to fuck this up. I'm petrified that my desire is blurring my ability to see if I'm falling in love, or not. Is my desire making me focus on sex rather than connection? It is the connected moments that my terror shows up. Or am I focused on the idea of love? And what it should look like? Am I absorbed by the idea of the Sam in my head and not the Sam in front of me?

How do you know if you've never known love?

I also feel rejected, by us slowing things down, with the handbrake I asked for now torturing me. Are we afraid to touch each other? Perhaps we've built it up too much? Perhaps we've missed the giant fucking boat! Today was a kiss on the cheek! FUCK, I feel rejected and crazy. I know it's not stupid, and I know it's slow and I asked for slow, with that stupid speech that made little fucking sense anyway!!! HELP! We are building trust and he's respecting me and, and, and…

I'm unable to think and beginning to feel manic. I fall on the floor, on the cool tiles in my kitchen, and sob my crazy little heart out with the kiss on the cheek reverberating around my head. Followed by fits of laughter at the stupidity of two grown adults; my need for him is driving me crazy. I want to be ravished. To be held tightly and toyed with, like I know he wants to. I want to curl myself inside in those arms, be gazed upon with those eyes, touched with those hands, feeling his energy inside me.

These are new feelings for me, and I question, have we missed it, are we stuck in limbo? My desire to explore myself in him, to feel every inch of him against me, how our flow will evolve, freeing myself of control while welcoming trust and tenderness. Could I be so focused on my need, my desire, as a way of hiding from the feelings that are naturally developing? Like our bond, our flow is finding its own rhythm. To trust and release control, to allow love to evolve is hard. Pace yourself and learn. Be the tortoise not the hare.

I don't want to be triggered, I reassure myself, I want to love. Reminding myself of my tender heart, in thought and touch. I don't want to control this either, but control is what has made me feel safe, control has protected me and sitting in the unknown is extremely uncomfortable and triggering. Control really is one of the ways I've survived so I am fighting battles of my past and future at once. I try to just allow these emotions to emerge letting them wash over me, cry more tears and soothe myself, as I go, I am triggered. We are taking it slow, snails move faster than us! How do I not be that person who pulls the handbrake while hitting the accelerator at the same time? 'You'll wreck the engine!' A rebuttal to my own thoughts hisses up, complete with smart arse tone! Even my thoughts have attitude. It's lucky as it is enough to bring me back to the reality with a grateful smile. Evie, just be in the present moment. I'm nervously excited and overwhelmed by my cravings, all rolled up in a huge ball of emotion inside my body. I've never been loved properly, and it feels terrifying to work through this while learning to love at the same time. I'm a feeler, can you tell? I understand my emotional expression and still, I fight with myself all the way. I have had to in order to survive and thrive in life and yet this is a whole new level. I am a nervous wreck. Sam physically reached for me the other day and I jumped. I wanted him to touch me, I'm just so on edge and so is he, I feel it in both of us, or at least I think I do. My mind flashes a visual sensation of him on top of me. I tell myself, slowly, Evie. Breathe. I coach myself and hold my body tightly, focus, find your focus. I push my feet into the ground and decide to go for a fast walk to move some of this angst in me.

My phone rings. It's the man himself! He is going to the farm for the weekend, wants me to come. I think "yes, please" was already out of my mouth before he's even finished asking. He chuckles, and I acknowledge that clearly I'm keen! If I wasn't so caught up in the weekend and the direction's he's giving me. I would have been embarrassed by my eagerness. He is heading up tomorrow to get work done and I'm following in a few days.

I manage to focus on work and have a few productive days. As there is limited phone reception at the farm some space from Sam and our intensity has been good. Time, to breathe, to attempt to wash off some of my stress and hormones with purpose. I triple my normal exercise and some self-care options to help me use up this pent-up energy, to take the edge off my manic self.

That is, until the morning when I'm packing and allowing myself to get excited and to ponder what might be. To take time to think of his body, his hands, working hands, rough, yet tender, a life of hard work. The strength in those hands as I imagine them steadying my hips, steadying me.

I manage to get stuck into my day and before I know it is lunch time and I'm rushing out the door for the 3-hour drive. I'm so feeling good, blasting my music to help with my daydreaming of him on the drive. I eventually switch off the radio about halfway into the drive to catch my breath, shutting off the busyness and trying to ground myself. I do some of my breathing techniques and talk with my heart for a little while to ease into my feelings for Sam and our weekend.

H I M | Twenty-four

The farm has provided some space for me and I've managed to get loads done, but with the anticipation of her arrival getting closer I'm becoming more nervous. The outdoor bath is all set up and waiting for her. I really hope she likes it, as it is a hack job, not a fancy bath at all. This house represents me, and, I guess, what I can offer and I'm terrified it's not her style. I've cleaned up and Harold's here with me too, all washed and looking his best. I walk around aimlessly for a good hour before I hear her car, waiting till the thud of crossing the cattle grid before I walk out from the house, to not look too keen.

She's just sitting in the car, so I walk down to greet her, hoping she's okay. She jumps out and I embrace her, showing more emotion that I would have wanted.

Fuck it, why am I holding back?

I really show her all the things I want to do with her, slowly, taking my time, she holds her hands on my skin and it feels like fire on my stomach, our eyes burning with longing, a long pause in the feeling of each other, before I say 'Hello.' I don't feel like this is real. She tells me how good I feel and I'm embarrassed and she completely loves it, shooting me that smile with the cheekiness of her enjoyment in teasing me. I collect her bags and show her the house, suggesting sunset and beers on the deck. She smiles a lot and is taking a lot of deep breaths. It's difficult to tell if that is a good sign or not. We dance around each other with giggles and stunned mullet moments.

I feel like a fucking teenager again, trying to kiss Carmen Bone behind the sheds at school. Desperately trying to hide my hard on. Thankfully, I have a little more control than my 12-year-old self, poor Carmen.

I glance across at Evie sitting in my chair, watching her take a swig on her Cooper's beer and lean back in the chair with a great sigh. Fuck me, that right there is sexy as, and I need to calm the fuck down. I take that as a cue to exit and allow her to enjoy relaxing. Heading to the kitchen to finish cooking dinner, leaving Evie with her thoughts and to make herself at home. It's not long before she's under my feet in the kitchen, helping me to get my shit together. Fuck, I didn't know I was going to be so fucking nervous. The normalcy of this woman in my house is equally terrifying and exciting. I feel exposed and yet I'm enjoying her and desperately trying not to feel inadequate and be charming. Clearly, dinner is not on either of our minds as we both push our food around the plates, apprehensively. Desire runs rampant here. Dreaming of that kiss and wanting each other badly. I don't want to fuck this up, with the memory of Carmen Bones freaking me out.

H E R | Twenty-five

The landscape around me changes from urban to country, from grey to green as I'm chasing the mid-afternoon sun. Golden hour, my favourite, is not far away. I'm happy, smiling at the world around me. It feels so nice to be in flow with my world. I find the farm easily enough and there he is, standing on the deck of an old-style white Queenslander, my favourite style of home. I realise he never described the house.

I sit in the car staring at him, taking it all in, kind of blank with disbelief. All that I've dreamed about is in front of me and I'm not sure any of it is real, if he's real? I choke down a wave of emotion, calling to myself, Evie, air in and air out. Trying to force myself to breathe. He is walking over. Get your shit together girl, dreams do come true, even for people like me. Okay, here we go. I'm out of the car and it's just us, space and us, well besides Harold, the dog. We walk towards each other, he looks different. He feels, well, he feels like home. It's an embrace that takes us both by surprise followed by a kiss... A kiss that brings us right back to that first one. Slow at first, tempered, with his hands on me, unleashing my desire, intensifying the kiss by pulling me even closer to his body. I feel all of him at once and I just want to collapse myself into him, his taste, wrapping myself in the energy of him and this farm. I put my hands on his skin under his shirt, his stomach and I'm lost in the moment feeling the pulse of our energy flow. He slows us as our flow had rapidly intensified, reading my body, the feel of me, of us, my hands still on his stomach. He looks at me and smiles.

"Hello."

"You feel so good," I respond. He blushes and I love it. He holds me until I'm steady, until I stop trembling. Ever the gentlemen, Sam retrieves my bag and provides a guided tour of the house. He grew up here and then it became his when his parents built on the other side of the farm.

"I'll show you the rest of the farm tomorrow."

We watch the sunset with a beer from the steps of the deck, enjoying small talk, long glances and schoolyard giggles that feel, absolutely amazing, and yet terrifying with tones of normalcy. I feel so at home on the deck, with the colours of the land, and the sounds of animals in the distance. I'm far from a farm girl, yet I can appreciate the life and respect the beauty in this land. It is breathtaking. Sam's getting dinner ready and while I enjoy the colours of the sky. Nerves and excitement are rising in me, and I'm grateful for the Dutch courage in my hand.

I head into the kitchen to help. While carrying out the official table setting duties, I can feel his eyes watching me move around his kitchen. I love the feel of it, the way his eyes follow me. I know he is thinking about us, about the things he wants to do to me. Our energy is soft and playful, and it feels like we are feeling into our space, like our senses are heightened and setting the tone for our flow. We play physically with each other as well, a brush here, a touch there, testing each other. We eat, both grazing over our meals, before returning to the deck, silent in anticipation.

I move over on the steps to seek out his warmth, finding myself on the lower step between his legs. He instantly feels uncomfortable. I turn to him and he grabs my hands and begins to say something. I stand without letting him finish, or even begin really, telling him to come with me.

I walk to his room and open the door. Without words, in the soft light of his lamp, I usher him to sit on the bed before slowly I begin undressing. Watching him watching me, enjoying the moment of his eyes discovering my raw self, feeling him burning into me with those eyes while he sits back and takes me all in. I've never really celebrated my body nor allowed her rawness to fill a space like this, with a man desiring all my curves. I've never loved my body before, like I do in this moment, acknowledging her beauty, with all my parts bare in front of Sam. Standing before him my body is on fire. His eyes burn into me and I wait, holding this space for him to take me all in. I enjoy him exploring me as our friction continues to build. Finally, his eyes meet mine, his want penetrating as my confidence rises with his need. He stands, so I move towards him, grabbing his shirt and say, "I'll do it."

I begin undoing his shirt, reaching my hands along his chest and running them over his shoulders and down the inside of his shirt. His eyes scorch into me. I brush my nipples against him, and he pulls me closer, his tongue searching for me, hands on my breasts. In one fluid move he turns me around, gently laying me on his bed. He stands, removing the rest of his clothes. I'm given a brief moment to take in his manhood before his body lands on top of me. My confidence is immediately out the window, as I see he's big. Sam looks at me with intent, pausing and seeking my permission. I appreciate his gesture and acknowledge him, saying "please."

I'm caught in my own energy of what is happening and then he's inside me. "Sam," I gasp a little too loudly. He feels the slight pain in my voice, searching my eyes. I reassure him, "I just need to get used to you, slowly." I take a breath and get lost in the sensation of him, the heat, the burning of him as we find our flow. Sam comes, and my body is still caught in the moment. He knows it and reaches for my womanliness, discovering my body, feeling those hands everywhere, as they search out my pleasure parts, following my moans. My body plots the course for him, and he can hear my soul crying out. I shudder underneath him, our bodies entangled, and he owns me again and again. I'm lost in the pleasure of him, the feel of his energy inside me, I want him deeper. He knows I'm ready for our bodies to take over, and they do. Hours roll by in touch, in unleashed pleasure and purity of connected sex, again and again. Both of us trying to alleviate our pent-up energy, that grows in desire, despite our releases. I collapse into sleep, surrounded by him, arms holding me close, held in his presence. My body still shuddering and aching from him, as he sleeps quietly while holding my hips.

I wake, still in his arms. Peeling myself away from him, I reach for the blanket on the ground and head into the bathroom. I hold myself and check my womanly parts. Holding my warrior woman, I connect to my vulnerable parts, taking note of my heart's feelings and asking her how she is. She swells in a wave of emotion, embracing the feeling and the sensation of him. I head outside and find myself on the stairs, wrapped in his smell, his taste, him, under the last of the night stars. I again feel my womanly body. She feels different, the fire that's in my belly, basking in the hours of that man's tongue all over my body, a giggle at my own bold-ness and feeling of my sensual self, the slight rocking, reconnecting to his flow, the dance of my body beneath him establishing our connection.

H I M | Twenty-six

The tension rises as we eat, I urge us to retreat to the deck after dinner. The space of the outdoors eases our anticipation. Evie moves to sit between my legs. Her proximity challenges my ability to be slow. Her closeness feels brilliant, and yet anytime she's close to me, I feel like I have to be very careful. I'm desperately trying to restrain myself as I want her to lead when she is ready, not to feel pressured. I need to be careful, her aroma is intoxicating.

She suddenly stands, grabbing my hand, and says come with me, dragging me off the step. I'm desperately wracking my brain, trying to come up with something that doesn't sound stupid, that "I really care about her" and "slow." I give up, relinquishing control to her.

I sit on the bed as she starts taking her clothes off, seductively, uncovering more of her beauty. She's strong, and the curve of her hips call to me. She's not sure and incredibly sexy at the same time, as the space electrifies around us. She has scars on her stomach and legs. I notice but don't linger, as her heavy breasts are released for me, nipples soft pink, waiting for my tongue to tug on them hard.

Struggling to contain myself, I need to lay her down on the bed, desperate to feel her softness embracing my cock before I explode. Her nipples are hard now against my chest. I draw her in, tasting her with my tongue. I lay her down, standing back. Watching her eyes, I let her see me all of me, watching those eyes erotically trace my body. I need to know her. She opens herself to me and with my body against her she says "please." I tilt her hips slightly, entering her deeply. Watching her face, with her eyes lighting up as she calls out my name. The oily scent of sex hangs in the air. I hesitate but she encourages me to slowly move, rocking against her hips, gently for as long as I can. She feels amazing and it's not long before her warmth and softness caressing me takes me to my limit. I watch as her body trembles, looking into her eyes. I reach for her, I need to know her, feel all of her. She leans into my touch, adjusting her hips and opening herself to me, meeting my thrusts.

Shit, I came quickly.

I can feel her arching and immediately I begin exploring. Watching her, seeing how she responses to my touch. My tongue feels all of her parts, listening to her sex, tasting her, letting our naked selves get to know each other. I can't believe this sexy woman is letting me explore all of her.

She falls asleep in my arms, spent, with my scent all over her. My mind is blown. Holding her body against me feels so surreal. Even my cock is nuzzling into her. The thought makes me hard again. Fuck, this feels fucking amazing and terrifying. The fucking intensity, wow. When a woman looks at you as a man, you feel superhuman, and that's how she looks at me.

I wake to an empty bed, and an aching cock, yearning for her. I find her naked on my front porch, thank the Lord. She stands upon realising I'm behind her, opening the blanket out to her nakedness and calling me to join her, arms open, revealing all of her to me. She attempts to wrap me in a blanket I don't need. I'm entertained by her efforts and playfulness.

She responds to my cock calling to her, and out comes this woman, who takes control, feeling the tip of me first, all the while keeping my focus. She comes down hard and deeply, arching her body to take as much of me as she can. A growl crawls out of me, she feels epic, holding my eye contact, boldly commanding our flow. I'm feeling all of her, my hands wrapped around those hips steadying her, encouraging her while feeling complete ecstasy at each hip thrust as she expresses herself.

HER | Twenty-seven

My thoughts are full of flashbacks of our bodies, our experiences, the nature in which we came, the surrender of my body, to him, the feel of his hands, of him. My thighs throb as the memory of our dance beats through my mind, followed by the hormonal cascade of those emotions attached to our night.

I turn as I hear the screen door open behind me in all his glory. In the breaking of the day, my man stands before me in all his glory. I immediately open the blanket, revealing my naked body. He smiles and joins me. "How'd you sleep?" I smile, attempting to fit him in the blanket with me. I stand and wrap myself around him, my thighs still throbbing from last night. He immediately he shows me that he has other ideas and my thighs find a new strength. I surrender to the feeling of him and hold my wild woman gently against him, easing myself on to my man, embracing my man with my most intimate parts. A deep growl rises up and out of him and it's like a call to my wild heart inside me. Encouraging her, she takes over. Sam steadies my hips and I set her free. Holding his gaze, his eyes alive and wild looking back at me, he surrenders to me, to my flow, to us, the tug of war emerging in between pleasure and surrender. I feel the warmth of the rising sun on my bare back and wonder in awe of my womanly self, taking her man on the stairs, unleashing and allowing my body to lead, submitting to the purity of us.

Exhausted, I curl up on him and after we catch our breath, he lifts me up. My legs are tingling and weak. Sam half carries me, and I half walk to the bathroom, where we shower together in silence. Sam washes my body with kisses and hot water, towel drying me, finally dressing me in one of his t-shirts despite my clothes being right there and putting me straight back into his bed. I think he kisses me on the forehead, although my sleepiness can't confirm this. After a few hours I wake and find a note next to the bed. "Evie, working, text me."

I get up, grab a coffee, and check into my body, physically and mentally. Holding myself, holding my newly emerged, womanly strength. I'm proud of myself. I'm proud that I expressed myself lovingly and genuinely. How she feels and, holy wow, my legs, my thighs are so sore. I smile at the thought of him leaving his mark on me and I like it. A few yoga moves will stretch them out.

The feel of the place without Sam is nice. I don't feel uncomfortable in his space, in fact it feels comforting, and, well, it gives me time to process, to think about all the things I want to do to him.

I eat some fruit, stretch out, and make like a cat on the makeshift daybed in the sun. Allowing Mother Nature to warm my body, I resist the urge to bask naked in the sun, opting to stay in his t-shirt. I feel the sexiness of my body, with his shirt not really covering very much, and I feel empowered in my body and my sex. Our flow came so easily! I smile at our slight tug of war and hope that it continues. I text him a picture of me lying in his shirt in the sun. He responds with a cheeky shirtless shot of himself, all sweaty. That right there, my friends, well!

Within an hour, he returns and I'm still laying in the sun sort of snoozing. I tell him to put a shirt on, that he's shameless walking around half naked! He pounces on me straight away, attempting to take his shirt back to put away his nakedness. After some playful wrestling, he settles on the daybed with me and tells me what he's been up to while I've been in the lap of luxury. The conversation moves from new fences to how my body feels, while he checks me over with his hands. I blush at the unusual topic of conversation while my man is holding my lady parts. Sam smiles at how my body responds to him. I tell him she is well rested. At that, Sam eyes light up, "I'll go clean up." I grab his hand, "please don't! I like you like this. I want to feel you like this, sweaty and manly." Before I can finish my words, we are skin to skin, his mouth searching my body, completely lost in his touch.

"Take me like this Sam." Lying naked on the sunbed the heat of him pouring over me, he's lying on his side, his manhood resting on my thigh, me holding his hand, stroking his fingers with mine. We talk about his dreams for the farm. His ideas freely roll out of him, his excitement clear. He talks about wanting to create what the farm was like when he was little. I move on to my side to directly face him. He immediately adjusts the pillow and himself to make sure I am comfortable, with a soft kiss on my shoulder. I reach to hold him in that space, to feel him close, to lean into him and the feel of him being attentive.

Sam feels different here, his eyes sparkle differently, he lets me hold the space of his nearness, he feels softer than I anticipated. I try to articulate to Sam how incredible he feels here, like home. He smiles at me and traces the outline of my nipple with his fingertips and then his lips. Even though he didn't respond with words, his tenderness showed me his acknowledgement.

The afternoon is a blur of kisses, pleasure, laughter and exploring our each other. Our playful desire continues while experiencing one another, gentle wrestles, testing and feeling each other out through touch and intimacy. I have found he is strong in connection. In his search of my soul in my eyes, our souls dance. He seeks out and holds my gaze, like my eyes are windows for him. He is even more protective than I could have imagined, his passion equal to his care for me. His eyes are full in protection and nurturance. His wanting to care for me only builds my trust. He follows the teachings of my body, to points I have not known.

I have my first trauma trigger. I knew I would eventually. I tried to prepare, I've had little ones and kept the monsters from Sam. Not this one though. I froze. I expected it, never ready for it, momentary panic. I think Sam knew something was up, but then again, I can't be sure. We are embracing, him on top. The sensation of being trapped, caught, and the world stopped briefly, as does my breathing. Frozen. Squeezed my eyes shut, I instigate a position change, slowing our tempo to aid in my panic subsiding while fixing on his eyes, seeking to take control, to create safety, focusing on the physical in front of me, the present, feeling into what is happening right now. Sam. Taming my monsters, my thoughts repeating: he's mine, you can't have him. That bear hug type, I can't be freed, feeling trapped, depths of my body immediately rigid, beginning to turn to ice. Pained, I breathe, slowly, purposefully. Right to the deepest pit of me. Reach out, I grab my anchor, hold my heart, and return to my body. Coaching myself through the terror, allowing the trigger to be there, but focusing on rewriting the experience. It was a moment. I knew would come, so I was able to work with my sensations as I've learnt so much about how they act out. Firstly, stuck in concrete, paralysed cold sweat, mind completely slow, then run, feelings of move now, followed by dread, trapped, a flood of images and sensations of what happened to me, voiceless dreams, all at once. I go through the checklist, encourage and accept new feelings. I am not allowing my trauma to taint my Sam, or this moment.

Practice, Evie. Practice the uncomfortable, practice the pain, the new, you will feel triggered while you reclaim this you. It rolls through my mind like a kindness mantra. Stay with Sam. Telling myself to feel in him, he's safe, you're safe, trust yourself, spinning around my head. Without realising, Sam's gentle hands are nurturing me. My god, he makes me feel safe. Control helps me, it helps me to be intimate, when his connection terrifies me.

Does he know?

The tenderness of his care pushes me back into the light, and my panic doesn't turn into my demons taking control. I am called forward by my heart into love, the love that is within me, that I am born to give. Again, he steadies me while my warrior self, fights demons, wins and returns to his arms.

Does he know my story?

Late in the afternoon, Sam sits straight up in bed and announces, "I have something for you!" And he's up and away! As I put on his t-shirt, he looks me up and down and says, "you won't need that."

He takes me to the back deck. Right in the middle with pipes running from the laundry is an old clawfoot bath. I'm speechless, frozen. I previously mentioned that in my dream home I'd love an outdoor bath. I look at him, overwhelmed, fighting back tears and the giant fucking lump in my throat. Dumbfounded. He listened to me and created this for me. I'm barely able to contain myself, when he looks up like a man who is going to be endlessly thanked for his thoughtfulness and says, "hot bath?" I just stand there staring at him. He walks over, kissing my forehead before leaves me. I'm desperately trying not to cry, failing of course. He has no idea what this means to me, how this makes me feel, what it means, that if I didn't love him I do now. A massive gesture like this, although small to some, is enormous to me because it signifies being heard, accepted and honoured. No one has ever taken the time to show up for me like this. I have never felt special. The bath is ready to go after the smallest amount of time, steam rising, afternoon sun saying her goodbyes. It's dreamlike.

I'm not sure if I'm in shock or not. My thoughts are telling me to wake up, that it's all not real. I walk over towards him where he is crouched down checking the water temperature. Holding my arms up in the air, he follows my lead, running his hands up my legs and removing his t-shirt. As I am slowly easing my body into the bath with the aid of Sam's tender touch, it's beyond bliss.

The sun is almost behind the hills in the distance, it's golden hour. The water is scalding hot and I'm in heaven. I don't care if Sam sees my tears of emotion; I am unable to speak. How does this happen for someone like me? I try to wrangle my hair, failing at the mess and rolling back into the water, setting myself free to soak. Sam leaves me for a while, so I submerge myself in the disbelief of this magical moment, of being worshipped, of the woman that is shining through and being held in who she is, who I am. Giving myself full permission to feel all of my emotional self. I really like her, this me. I love that she's honestly real in what she feels, good and vulnerable. I'm not trying to be someone I am not. This is a massive gesture of kindness that I will never ever forget. One moment of appreciation, of thoughtfulness, can enable a lifetime of love. I stretch my body, bending her and feeling her. She feels different, she feels alive and loved. My body is tired, raw and tender, and yet alive in the same vein, in ways I've not known. The moment of solitude allows time for my body and heart and mind to come back to the ground, for me to check in with all my parts, showing her love and kindness for the gifts she has given me. I glide my hands over myself, nurturing, celebrating her femininity, thanking her feel. I feel powerful. I feel my body is stronger than I ever knew, that wild warrior who has so many parts, including her resolve, her strength, all being loved, nurtured and brought to life, all being awed by a beautiful man and by me. The little girl who is scared to be hurt, has been kissed and held; the confident woman stands tall in her beauty; the unsure, overwhelmed, emotional woman has had her fear subsided, shocked, embraced and allowed, fears expressed and felt. The wild warrior who stepped out of the shadows, perhaps only in a glimpse, tasted her man. All the parts of my body are expressed and freed in front of him, now all of which are slowly coming together inside me, the evolution of my emotional selves, good or bad. Those horrors that ruled over me in the darkness, that I'd thought shameful, I'd thought unlovable, damaged, that lived because of what happened to me, old hurts, are now coming together to receive a tender hand in trust.

I smile with a tear rolling down my face, holding my inner self and thanking my body, my heart and my mind. The trust within me to experience emotion freely allowed myself to unhook from the need to control and allow love to be set free from the cage within me. The realisation that love is not external, it's a response that ignites within you from what you already have within, hence why people always go on about self-love first. I learnt to trust myself as me, who I am and it's the love I have for me that helps me to feel this now. Gazing at the sun dropping behind the hill as the colours change the skyline, a bright tangerine with soft pink fairy floss clouds against the dark green hills, entirely dreamlike. I would do almost anything Sam wanted, trusting in his heart's desires. I dream about what that might involve. I feel like I am in slow motion and the rest of the world is in fast forward. I continue to dream a little of love. Every ounce of me feels in awe. I think this is what happiness would feel like. I realise Sam is behind me, not sure for how long, he must have realised my moment.

Hopefully he's not too spooked by my emotion. I'm puzzled as he has my bathroom bag in hand and a cup. "I thought you might like to wash your hair" Sam manages to stumble out. He truly must have known I was deeply immersed in my feelings and completely unable to contain them. I smile at his kindness and let him know that I don't have the energy to do it. My body is happy and I'm giving permission to submerge myself in these sensations and love it.

He smiles, dragging a chair over. "Sit forward." He speaks in a tone I don't recognise. I immediately comply. His voice is tender and firm, as he looks at me with care and I follow every instruction. He is intense, and the most natural and sexy thing of my life occurs. Sam, with those amazing hands, manly, rough and lived, those hands that pushed my body, that search out my dark corners, show new depth to tenderness and intimacy. I think it unexpectedly overwhelms both of us. While he washes my hair, rubbing my shoulders, affectionately rinsing my hair, I am searching for the feel of it now. The warm water, the pink sky, my feminine self, the focus he has. Each touch sends waves of love and care throughout me. Goosebumps begin covering my body and my fears of falling completely in love with him rise from my dark parts. I know I can't go back now, but nor can I stop the avalanche of my love building for him. A shiver creeps out across my body. He assumes I'm cold, but actually I'm experiencing a wave of fear, that if I lost him now, I don't know if I could recover, I don't know if...

I stop, forcing the thoughts away as he tops my bath up with warm water then thankfully sinks into the bath behind me. His arms rest on my tummy. I curl up, embracing his arms and resting my head on his chest. My happiness just pours out of me, the emotions of the last month, the feel of him in this very moment, feeling safe and nurtured. I don't need control, Sam has me.

I announce "Sam, you were right, I would only need one bath in my dream home."

For the first time in my life, I trust someone and receive pure love. I allow this man to love me and accepting his protection and tenderness. The tears briefly flow. He knows. I feel him get uncomfortable and he sits with it.

I eventually tell him, "It's been a big few months. You make me feel safe and protected. I'm choosing to enjoy it and not shield you from my emotions."

We watch the stars become bright in the sky and leave the bath. It's cold and I've begun shivering, although I'm not sure how much of the shiver is the cold and how much it is the years of emotional baggage and perhaps the beginning of an emotional hangover.

It doesn't matter.

I just let go of a little and allowed my true self to shine.

I firmly announce, to break the emotional energy, that I'm cooking and with limited options, shared omelettes and frozen chips it is. While I go about figuring out his kitchen, Sam starts preparing a fire in the lounge. I can hear him moving things around and making a lot of noise, and then building a fire. I'm in a trance already from the crackle of the flames. I can't even see it, but the sound, the smell, transports me there anyway. My body sensations are so amplified, everything feels like the volumes been turned up loud, like I can feel the fire on the inside of me and all my senses are heightened. Every cell in my body is awakened - love does that. My internal voice shakes as the thought of leaving passes through my mind, sensations of terror and joy, followed by "No." Begging myself to let that thought train continue to roll on by.

The weekend has been perfect. I have been myself, whole heartedly and felt accepted. I get a flicker of the weight of tomorrow, with reality bearing down on us. I don't want to leave and I'm not even sure this weekend happened. Pushing back the creeping darkness, I refocus on dinner and reconnect myself to the moment in front of me, him. I couldn't tolerate hearing "I'm still not sure" to come out of his mouth now, after all, that we've shared, all that he's done for me this weekend. It couldn't be possible, he wouldn't...

I'm startled, turning to see Sam dragging his mattress into the lounge room where the fireplace is. I smile at his sheer brilliance.

We eat with soft music and the roaring fire in the background from the lounge. The fireplace easily heats the house, and I no longer feel cold, despite still shivering. After dinner Sam strokes my hand and says, "come to bed with me." His voice is tired, but purposeful. I stand with a smile and we walk into the lounge. He's laid out candles, the mattress is in front of the fire and soulful tones are playing. It's simple but elegant. The fire is well alight now and the pungent wood burning smell fills the room.

Sam undresses me, starting by untying my hair. He brags about his excellent efforts as he softly pulls my hair out, before bending forward to run his fingers slowly up my body to remove his t-shirt that I am still wearing followed by my underwear. I stay standing while he undresses, walking me over to the mattress laying me down in front of the fire. The warmth tingling on my skin. Sam kneels and takes me all in. His gaze is soft and exploring, while his fingertips continue to dance up and down my legs, my thighs. He bends, scattering kisses all over my stomach. It feels lovely and yet the creeping fear in the darkness, his level of intimacy and connection frightening me, take the lead Evie. I'm already aware of Sam's needs, so I focus on him, it feels safer for me. Our bodies blur in our touch, our scent circles the air, oily. His want, impatiently showing now, draws me into our nakedness, our stripped bare, self-exposed and wanting, needing release. I stretch my body over him, as agony and bliss surround us, battling each other, inside me. Sam is full and heavy, gasping for air, pained by the closeness of my key to his release. The heat between us, the sweetness of him, allow our pleasure centres to climb their way out toward each other. His manhood takes me, pushing deep into my soul. A wild cry flows out of me, followed by moans pleading for him to NOT stop. He takes me hard. I'm squirming underneath him, body shaking from the inside out. His own groan is loud and earthy, holding my hands down above my head, my hips tilting to feel his final throbs inside me. We exchange sweet kisses until Sam pulls me on top of him, falling asleep with him tenderly holding all of my body.

H I M | Twenty-eight

Lying in bed, half snoozing while thoroughly enjoying this very sexy and very naked woman in my arms softly running her fingertips over me, I feel happy. It's been so long since I've felt content with my lot in life, till right now in this bed with Evie. I don't know if I have ever felt this happy and, well, ever this connected to anyone before. I have this overwhelming need to take care of her, to protect her, shower her with kindness, while carving to be inside her, pleasuring her. In such a short time this woman has made a massive difference in my life, and I am grateful for that. It is sort of strange, like in the shower this morning I wanted to wash her, touch her, savour all of her and she let me. Looking at the curves of her body, tucked under my arm on her side, she feels so vulnerable and intoxicating. I want to prevent the world from coming in. I feel a pang of guilt. How am I able to be so happy during one of the hardest times in my life? How can I have this amazing thing happen to me, right when the most terrible loss of my life has happened?

I'm starting to figure out that when I have vulnerable times, I bring Dad up because life is moving forward without him. I take a deep breath and swallow this painful realisation. I want my thoughts to stop. Focusing on Evie, like this and we can both just stay here in bed. As much as I try, my thoughts begin to cascade, of losing Dad and then the thought of losing Evie, now, of what if. Fuck! I get it. I move and watch her body move in tune with me.

Then it hits me, the bath, the fucking bath! Evie's face is priceless when I drag her out to the back deck to show her what I had made for her. Then she just stands there and it is instantly awkward, fuck. I just focus on getting the bath set up for her, well, moving around her while she is, I think, a little shocked at the gesture. Perhaps feeling like it's too much? It's just a fucking bath, I am confused. I busy myself with getting it ready and testing the heat. Its ready, although perhaps on the boiling side. I kneel down to check the water and it is as I suspected, near boiling. I glance up and Evie has finally moved from her shock and is standing in front of me with her arms up in the air, looking bewildered, prompting me to remove the shirt, eyes red with silent tears. I have never experienced such raw beauty. I'm stunned by her purity, this natural emotional beauty floors me.

I remove her shirt and hold her hand while she slips into the bath, not completely knowing what to do with myself, nor what is truly happening with her, it feels like I have walked in on a private moment, like I shouldn't be here. I step away when I see Evie, fighting with her hair, thankfully giving me an out. I'll go grab her bathroom bag for her hair. Fuck, I didn't mean to upset her, noticing her silent tears have now turned to sobs. I go inside searching for her bathroom bag, completely terrified I've broken her. It was meant to be special a way of thanks, I thought she would have loved it. I take a few deep breaths and return to Evie. She is caught in something big; she has her hand over her heart and is sobbing. I'm beginning to feel overwhelmed by her outwardly expressed pain and not wanting to interrupt her nor having any idea what to do. Feeling helpless, while mesmerised by her beauty in vulnerability, her expression of pain. I see her sink further into the bath, as she slows herself and submerges herself briefly. The tempo of her breathing slows, she sighs loudly and suddenly, she is aware of me creeping behind her. I raise her bag and suggest washing her hair. She's exhausted and I need to do something.

I want to help in some way, I feel useless. Evie sits forward and I attempt to wash her hair. It feels unexpectedly intimate. I try my best to be gentle and nurture her. Our closeness; the warm water, running down her body, the way she puts her head back for me; the silkiness of her hair, the aromas of sweet fruits against the bush smells of my land; it's all intoxicating. I rub her neck, shoulders, comforting her how I know to, to show her kindness. I may not understand but I can do this, reassuring myself. I strangely love washing her hair, the feel of her hair, her body, her surrender to my touch. It helps to relieve the feelings of inadequacy. There is not a lot of words spoken, our bodies are doing the talking. Evie obviously has a deeper story, one that I know is going to be hard for me to deal with. I already care so much about her and there is so much I don't know. She's is kind and very affectionate, she's vulnerable and freely shares her emotions and has a burning fire inside of her. A resolve, that I think has helped her to overcome what ever happened to her. I know she knows pain. It scares me to think of the pain she's known. What she has endured. I lean back and admire my clumsy effort on Evie's hair. She moves forward, and I take that as an invitation. I want to hold her and I feel relieved at being able to comfort her. Even in the bath together I feel her tears on my arm, and I just hold her. She tells me it's been a big emotional rollercoaster and I make her feel safe, safe to feel whatever she needs to. Relief pours into me at her words.

Reality dawns on me, with my body quickly following suit. Fear attempts to set up residence as my adrenaline comes down, more of a crash landing from the weekend. I'm awake. It's early morning. I have reached for him and he's not there, the bed is empty. I try to adjust - the fire is stoked, and then I hear the shower going. Empty, it all feels empty… Reality and I'm scared. It's normal, Evie, needing reassurance. The morning is trying to be stock standard, I'm uneasy, perhaps a little confused. Sam is all business, talking about his workday and all that he needs to do. I'm still hooked into my emotions, so I panic, scull my coffee and announce its time for me to leave. I want to abandon this pretend normalcy, both politely imitating Mr and Mrs fucking Brady bunch.

The bath. I should have been more composed, less emotional, what was I thinking? I couldn't stop the tears. He carries my bag and is all gentlemen like. A kiss, passionless from us both, and he is in my rear vision mirror. I'm a fucking mess. My fears screaming at me 'it's over' and a little soft voice of 'what was that?'

Hang on, I was just as weird as he was, after releasing some of the pent-up emotion and knowing that I felt it from him too. Did we quietly panic into operation be normal again? He felt far away from me, and I wanted connection. I had a weekend of pure connection.

I'm arguing with myself while crying out my little heart, finally acknowledging that I loved hard this weekend, that I felt so much, this freak out and feelings deserve to be felt and kindly ask myself to sit in my emotion and not fight or deny myself. They are emotionally accurate, aren't they? When I've run out of tears, for now, and wash off all the emotions from the weekend, my mind begins its tsunami of questions. My brain attempts to problem solve them all and, from somewhere, my reasoned self appears, taking command and forcing the crazy to sulk in the back seat, thankfully.

I have the time on the drive to go through all of the emotions and assess everything logically. This is my emotional process, it just feels awful, and I think it should feel different, thinking my feelings again. I know it was strange. The weekend was like a love bubble and I think we both shed emotions and skin in coming together in the way we did, exposed. I think it was full on for both of us. I need to ebb and flow with our moments, trying not to read into things. The pit of my stomach is heavy, churning with emotion and hormones. Crazy takes the wheel for the second coming and it is flowing out of me. I allow it and stop arguing with myself, stop blaming myself, stop judging myself and just let my crazy run freely out of me. Thankfully, I pull the car before it became too much and I was able to scream a few times, a release. The cascade of fear, of emotions and judgement run through my mind like a show as negative thoughts torment me, but I know they are lying to me. The ones that dig deep and twist in the knife have half-truths, these old fears on rerun: 'you were too emotional.'

Then sadness grips me, I'm in the middle of nowhere and I walk straight into a paddock, falling to my knees screaming to the world, a healthy side of ugly crying pouring out, and out of me. I comfort myself, tucking my hand under my armpit searching for my heart, I feel it pounding in pain, crossing my other arm over myself in a sort of hug. Cuddling my pained heart, reminding her that this is beautiful, a beautiful mess of feeling to be encouraged and accepted, fear expressed. I'm aware nothing really is going to calm me down, and I need to listen to my emotions and feel, allow them out, break free of the cage and the ability to do this with grace does not fucking exist. However, I will ride this wave and allow it to pass with a healthy side of release rather than holding my breath. Attempting to fucking mindfully breathe in the depths of my darkness is a tactic that has never fucking ever worked for me. In the darkness of my emotional meltdown, I know the path of least resistance is the way to go, so I don't fight my own emotional expression. I try to attune to my feelings understand my wave, I embrace, allow and scream the fucking house down as I need to meet the intensity of my darkness. Not attempt to pacify it or shut off, but embrace my monsters and love them, set them free, and then I am free, since my demons are real. This is how I tame them. This is how I have learnt to control them and not have them control me. I'm aware that I've been triggered a few times with Sam and that's okay. I know that I trusted, and that when he felt my body go rigid, he focused on me and somehow knew that, well, I don't know what he thinks, but I know he responded, and I felt safe. I breathe, and my inner warrior comes through the darkness.

"Evie, you don't need to define it."

I feel the wave subsiding and it comes to me, like that, that this is a lot of shedding. This is not just him, this is years of pain, of hurt, of all those unlovable beliefs, of my demons controlling me, it's all washing out of me. I'm no longer bound to my hurts, to those who hurt me. I'm free, I let love in. They didn't fucking win. I'm not damaged, I am loveable. The battle scaring me. No matter what happens between Sam and I, I am so very grateful, to have felt the love of a true man, of a man who's far from perfect, a man who I see feels so much and is not scared to feel with meaning. My God, we opened so much this weekend, and we both need time to process it.

Sam is comfortable in his skin and knows how to read the skin of a woman, can take his time to learn her body and understand her heart. A

man who is not afraid to nurture and care for. A man who seeks out connected intimacy, a man who showed me passionate love this weekend,
in heart, mind and body. At times, his sexual intensity was too much
for me, but he didn't battle with me. I lead, and he let me push away the
connection if I needed to. Sam didn't try to fix me when I was emotional nor did he ignore me, he was there, in the background, letting me
do what I needed too. Whether he was completely aware of supporting
me doesn't matter, it is that he did it anyway. This last wave of emotion
reverberates around my body, tingling and thumping into the corners
of myself as it dissipates, tears silently expressing the sadness and joy of
my revelations.

I stay in the dirt for a while, feeling the earth underneath me, as the sun on
my face dries my tears and my mind quietens. I just allow the space to be,
without judgement, before returning to the car to head home. My hands
are shaking with aftershocks of my emotions and I know I need to get out
of the car again. I stop in a small town to find something to eat. While
I'm waiting, I walk around and shake off my hormones, with a purposeful
walk and some jazz hands to take the edge off.

It works and I'm back on the road feeling strong albeit not sure about the
reality of us and grappling with it being okay not knowing the future. He
did feel so very different this morning - disconnected. I must remember
to keep my feet on the ground and stand in my warrior self. We are just
seeing what we feel like, to follow the flow. Basically, begging myself to
stop picturing us married on that back deck. To remember that we both
have stories and if I am feeling this amount of emotion, he will be to a
degree also. Equally understanding that the last time he felt different, he
disappeared, so I am coaching myself through that fear, believing it is different. We are different. Reaching down in the depths of me and dragging
hope out, while holding my heart and breathing into her softness. I start
the car, smashing out some music with a healthy side of back up singing
and some shoulder dancing. My mind is slowly accepting reality, exhausted
with an emotional hangover. I don't care either way really, it's just silent,

from accepting the uncomfortably uncertainty. I focus on being grounded and not thinking, playing it cool with a side of wanting him to know that I want this, him, whatever we are, I am all in.

As he's at the farm for a few more days, I can throw myself into my work and the energy that pours out of me is amazing. I manage my thoughts well - they are crazy - so I'm reverting to thinking about them like TV commercials. They're on in the background and I'm not paying any attention to them. I'm also upping the ante on my physical efforts to burn the stress and emotion hormones while fighting with the unknown of us.

I am choosing to not allow those fears to set up house in my head. Every day, I'm having moments where my body trembles at a sensory memory of him, or the prospect of what I want him to do to me. I feel him whispering into my ear, as my body yearns for him. I find my hips are dancing, seeking out the memory of his touch, the rhythm I have inside me is bursting to get out, to be expressed.

It feels fantastic, I feel fantastic.

I've surrendered to the fears and they are on in the background, but not running my show, which feels a new sense of good, but shaky. I'm trying to enjoy the sensations of him. Each day I have felt the need to stretch out my body, to expose her to the sun, to feel the slightest breeze on my skin. Savouring my energy, the pleasure, the moans that creep out of me, my senses are alive and wanting and I am not trying to stop them, nor judge my bodily expression of felt love. Every bend, every tingle, completely aroused and at his mercy, despite the distance. We've talked and texted a few times, which reassured me. He got back last night and is coming over after work today. Will our energy be electric, will he want me still? Have the flames fizzled, or is this love? Did our weekend together freak us both out? Overexpose both of us? It feels like careful small talk now. I'm not sure if that is based on how exposed we both have been and now we are a little unsure of what to do with ourselves. Wondering how to peel back or move forward, like our intensity our emotionality has made us retreat in hesitation. We fucking thought too much and fear took hold. I know it, Evie, fear... like now...

Self-talk rises to attempt to calm my thinking and return hope. Those feelings are okay, just don't let them control you. It could be the sharing of fears that has us locked in this strange space, we both have histories, Evie. Well, fuck, everyone does. Remember that you both fought demons and both are so awkward at times. You know it is about coming together in that space and showing up, in the emotion of us, in our hesitation too. Remember hesitation is the way your brain says 'hey, this is important! Pay attention!' In fear, it's a green light for 'this is significant.' The hesitation makes you feel the magnitude of it and allows you to chase it. The warrior self concludes my pep talk and I feel somewhat relaxed. I don't need to fix it or him, I just need to feel it for me and let it evolve, don't force it. Breath into the uncomfortable space and be you in your want for this man, be your truth. We will only know when we are standing in front of each other, and that is tonight.

He's running late.

I'm going all out with a roast lamb and I'm so nervous. God knows he probably feels the same, attempting to reassure myself, and scared that he might not even turn up. My hands have been trembling most of the day. I'm relishing the anticipation and embracing the anxiety to a degree, but now trying to compose myself, I'm not succeeding as much, as I hoped. I try to shake it off, and my entire body feels like its shaking on the inside. I attempt to encourage my body to shake more, and it helps take the edge off, thank god. Right now, I am so grateful for that little anxiety hack. I'm so scared of rejection or not being loved and in, that morning we had on the farm, I felt rejected. Even though I know, deep in my heart, that was not his intention at all, the rejection still set up camp in my heart. My thoughts begin the rerun of my personal horrors and reminding me why I'm so damaged. We are coming at this with different timing. Remember

Evie, balance. The right timing for waves to hit the shoreline means that a flow has to be established and wrestled with, you're in that part, before the breakers, breathe and keep your strokes steady.

I bring out the big guns, some old school Otis Redding and dance around the kitchen. It helps me get out of my head and back into my body. I allow my hips and body to get lost in the swing of the music that plays around the house, eager to be caught by Sam, and physically being caught by him at the same time, as he has found his way right into the kitchen. He is staring at my body, eyes alive with desire. I feel hunted, wanted. He just keeps staring at my body, my hips, so I keep moving them to the music and he encourages me with a quick glance at my face before returning his eyes to my body, lingering on my hips. They are calling him over, as I allow him to watch and savour my body. My God, he is sexy. I walk towards him and our eyes lock instantly. I can see he's emotional. I show him how I missed him, so he feels it, deeply. He's so responsive and hard. His hands explore his favourite parts of me, as he pulls my head back, his wanting written all over his face. He seeks permission and finds it in my eyes, taking control immediately and showing me how he missed me as I savour all of him.

H I M | Thirty

I lie in bed next to her nakedness, watching her and struggling to make sense of what is happening to me. The weekend has felt amazing and primal. We've connected and I don't want to let her go, nor do I feel worthy of her, afraid that she will get to know me more and I won't be able to fulfil her idea of a man. Arguments run wild in my head.

Yet she has accepted me and been herself. She is fierce in her connection, her will to love, to be open, while trembling in my arms, tears falling from her. That sheer beauty floors me. I really believe that we both have been wholly ourselves this weekend, I think. Is this what I want? Am I all in? How can I ask myself this now! I've got to get out, I need space, shut it off. I peel myself away from Evie, moving through the morning routine while hating myself for being distant.

Fuck, panic is starting to set in. I've spent the entire day in denial, avoiding feeling what happened this morning. Worried that I'm too invested, I've smashed out three day's work in one, needing to burn my frustration. She's in my head, full force, that smile, the way she lights up. I feel sensations of her throughout the day, as if she is here, beaming at me with that twinkle in her eye. It feels great and entirely bonkers. She's so very fragile and strong at the same time, sort of like me now. Feeling so fucking great and then so fucking horrible to have found her, to feel happy, and like its wrong. I know I shouldn't but sometimes the guilt is too much. How do I stop it? The knowledge that Dad died less than 2ks from the farm. It's like my reason keeps failing me and I'm reminded of that day when my body shakes, sadness engulfing me. Dad wanted me to be happy, he'd wanted me to settle down for years.

Why am I tormenting myself? I fucking like her. It feels like Dad is here with me when I'm working on the land, our farm. Harold walks over to sit by my leg, clearly seeing my distress. I tell him about my thoughts and what's happening with Evie. I know Evie is who I want and that I am ready to give this a go. I plan to ask Evie out, smiling at the thought that Dad would have done a formal request with Mum. I will not be so formal and yet I am still honouring the family tradition. It is funny that even after all we have shared, what I have experienced of her, the thought of asking her to commit to a relationship with me turns my stomach, petrified with sweaty hands, heart racing, the whole nine yards. I want to love this woman and feel like I am sure now, so let's give this a go. I crack a beer for me and one for Dad, and let his beer sit next to me. Harold gets some water. I tell Dad now all about Evie. I tell him about his emotionally vacant son, one minute, and then how emotionally needy I am, and it feels like a conversation we would have had. I tell him what I am struggling with. I think, between over thinking about her and over thinking feelings. Feeling out of control with my emotions and yet after being emotional with someone, I feel more in control. It's fucked up. I didn't want to lose control and yet that is what gave me my control back. I am trying to figure out so much with my life and the feel of her in my life is overwhelmingly wonderful. I know for sure Dad's head would be spinning too with this newfound epiphany, so we agree that it's a good idea for me to have another beer. Dad's sitting on his. Then we talk like he is truly here. We talk of the wave of guilt I have been feeling and I swear to God he asks me to let it go. That was a tough pill to swallow. I know it's me talking, but it feels like him and definitely his style, so I take a deep breath. The words tumble out.

"Dad, did I kill you?"

They are closely followed by tears that I can't hold back a volcano of emotion explodes from me. The true depth of my fear is what would have happened if I had waited for help instead? I logically understand it was the right thing to do, to relieve his pain, but my thoughts play tricks and it feels different staying it out loud. I am choosing to believe that my dad came and gave me some sound advice, that moving the tractor off him meant he was released from his pain. I rationally understand that, but it is still my dad, it happened, and I know I will go over it many times and that's okay. I love my dad. I'm instantly reminded of what Ruby said the other day, thinking something and feeling it are two different things. Stop trying to think feelings and fucking feel them. Rubes has an astounding handle on the English language for a lawyer. I smile as I polish off my beer and feel like I have accomplished something. I can't control things, but I did have the courage to ease my father's suffering and I am proud I could do that for both of us. The thought actually brings a level of relief and I feel like I ease a little. I know I will grapple with this for the rest of my life, I loved my dad and would do anything to have him back, hence why I am fighting with myself and the reality of what happened. Pondering my thoughts, the landscape, the sense of freedom I feel here, along with the images of what I shared with Evie this weekend has me smiling at how life has changed for me. I'm standing with Harold and a refreshed beer, talking to the ghost of my father, watching the sunset, thinking of her. How she giggles, the way her smile moves across her face, how good it feels to be listened to, how she just is herself. At times she feels like she is being careful with me, and I guess I am too. The 'getting to know you,' and we are trying to 'take it slow,' even if that was thrown out the window this weekend. My god, she is kind. I desperately don't want to hurt her. I'm in, with her, completely.

Fuck, life is different.

After dinner, we are washing up together when Sam looks at me and says, "I missed you."

"Me too, it was hard to leave you. I'm not sure what we are, I feel you in my skin, I feel you in my body when you're not here." As he turns me to face him, my trembling voice continues, "I want your eyes on me all the time, I want to be with you all the time."

He stands back, leaning against the bench, looks at me, and watches my body for a moment, enjoying the space he is creating between us, electrified again, heat and passion filling us both. I breathe it all in deeply. I allow him to take his time. He says he's not sure what we are either and he 'is in.' He pauses, looking into my eyes. "With you. I'm in this."

I'm a crumbling ball of emotion on the inside and can't stop my smiling. With as much cheek as I can muster, I ask if he is asking me out.

He clears his throat and I can see this is important to him.

"Evie, exclusively?"

"Sam, yes. I would like that very much."

Sam responds with good and declares he's sleeping over, playfully whipping me on the arse with the tea towel. I put my arms around his shoulders, drawing him into me.

"I am grateful you asked me out and let me know that you are sure you want to try to see what we can build together."

Our banter turns quickly into a shower, exploring each other in our newfound commitment. I feel more grounded, accepted, safe in the recognition of emotional vulnerability being held and nurtured. He didn't run for the hills. In fact, he chose me, so I show him how grateful I am. The energy is swirling around us, his touch like a dancing fire tracing my skin, lightening me up.

My body feels tense, strained, yearning. I need to harness what is out of control. I feel this pent-up energy rising in me. He's sleeping now and it's been a remarkable night and yet I'm restless, somewhat like a speed freak, Evie… Plugged in. My thoughts are racing, lying next to him, when like that, suddenly, click, I understand why my body is reeling.

I need to learn to love, to learn what the practice of what loving for someone like me looks like, for all of me. Exploring the parts of my body, my heart and my traumas, as those fears show up and swarm around me. The focus is on me now, I can't focus on Sam, he's in. I'm holding back, scared to completely release me, to truly trust, hence why I am wired and full of this energy. Instantly, my body relaxes. The best source of confirmation is my glorious body and she was screaming at me. I now begin the next level of letting Sam into my skin and letting go of my demons, without running away or self-sabotaging, I beg myself quietly in the dark, please let me out of the cage.

A few weeks have passed since my midnight realisation. Fear has become a continuous creeping shadow in the dark. I'm experiencing the torment of my monsters. I know I'm triggered, wondering what happens if he discovers how broken I am? I am attempting to roll with it and to try to see the punches coming.

I know unhooking myself has been hell. I'm seeing the depths of what healing looks like in a relationship, while also discovering our normal. In between learning about him, my monsters play games. They show up constantly when I'm vulnerable, attempting to play games with my mind, telling me how bad I am, damaged, the negative reruns, becoming louder and so full of hate. When I see Sam feeling down or struggling about his dad, I automatically focus on him and supporting him, and my fears lessen. Then when he is good and seems okay, I sink. Why can't I support myself like that? The ordinary exists in the way he tries not to be in a bad mood after a tough day, when he chokes back emotions when he is reminded of his dad, when he reaches for me to feel his pain, when he laughs. I close my eyes and feel his smile, his joy, savouring those lucky moments, like music to my heart and body. When he tries to impress me with gifts, little things, small moments of acknowledgement. The way the man says hello, good morning, goodbye and good night all send tones of joy and appreciation throughout my life.

Keeping myself normal-ish with Sam and keeping my demons at bay has been difficult. I feel so exhausted all the time and sensitive, like everything is amplified, sensory overload. Which equals more triggers, sleepless nights, flashbacks, body tremors and my brain in survival mode. I understand I'm trying to make sense of the new, trying to unhook from old, working to create a new story written by us not by my past. I up the ante on those things that are good for me, including more touch with Sam. He loves it although has no idea how much he helps me. Skin to skin time reduces my anxiety, I know this, and even though it feels physically painful at times, I practice. I am rewriting my story of touch, of love, of feeling safe with a man. I have gotten myself to a point of being able to love. The doing of love and working with my fears is simultaneously revealing new layers of my trauma.

However, it's a whole fucking other level to go through it and hard work because I am fighting my own demons while learning to trust and love. I've made attempts to avoid Sam a few times. Our connection is so strong and overpowering, I feel my body disobeying me or is it that I'm disobeying my body? My soul calls to him. How do I practice trust? Confusion fills me, I churn and churn, not about Sam, I'm sure of him. But of, my demons wanting to take me from him and the fear battle occurring in my brain. I know in a roundabout way they are attempting to protect me from feeling that kind of pain, again.

My stomach feels stretched tight like I'm going to vomit all the time, and it is like a lump has permanently set up in my throat.

I'm trying to think my feelings. Fuck, I don't know. I've had panic attacks, my body's way of screaming at me to listen after I try to ignore my emotions. My heart is the loudest, she aches and beats out of my chest cavity, all over shaking, out of control and covered completely in sweat. I'm so cold, so very cold, bone cold, hold me. Once, I vomited when I was in such a spin of fear, hiding in the bathroom, how it tried to control me. Some nights I repeatedly beg 'let me love,' in the dark. Wishing for release, to break free of these bonds. I feel like a dam wall is breaking and I'm doing my best to plug every fucking hole before Sam sees the crazy tumbling up and out of me. My all shakes constantly, battling my demons and working with them is taking a toll on me.

I'm stuck between the possibility of two different worlds, even now I'm shaking, my inside shivering. Knowing how one can be loved but not allowing myself to receive it, feel worthy of it and love beyond the demons in the darkness is my torment. To let light, grow from within, while a hurricane of connection, affection, laughter, tenderness, protection, looks down upon me, as our intimacy grows. I'm trying to accept my feelings. Knowing that I'm not even sure but he feels so safe. How does he even exist? Some days I feel like the luckiest human in the world and then I feel so deeply sorry for him. Having felt the darkness of pain, loss, hurt, betrayal, means as much as I want to love, I'm battling my own exposed monsters by experiencing a love that is safe, how someone should be loved, should give love, I'm losing my struggle. My own history of all the fucked-up shit that I knew was there and hoped I had worked hard enough to never let it own me again, then feeling like I'm under complete control... followed by the thought 'sure, dickhead.'

How much personal development is enough? Fuck, I know myself too well sometimes. I am my own monster, not just what was done to me, but my coping strategies keeping me from living. How much convincing do I need? I'm damaged goods. How do you stop thinking?

Now, I do understand this is the next level of taking my life back, of no longer allowing anyone else to dictate my life, including my past hurts, but to live my authentic life, as a loving woman, giving the love I have to Sam, reclaiming my power in love, I need him more than ever, am I drowning in darkness? I want all levels of love in my life. I am attempting to break my brains habit of being a victim, of being too broken, too damaged for love. I am none of these things, believe me. I will no longer allow fear to trick me into believing I am, fear can't convince me anymore. I will thrive, with or without Sam. Fear cannot live here, I have choice. No matter what I'll be okay. I want to chase love even more now as I'm feeling all of me. My darkness and light, it all feels unstuck, like I'm learning and expressing and being dragged back into the thick mud of it, all at once. Then hope rises through and it feels like my darkness is allowing the light to grow, an internal tug of war. Love helps me to find more of my own trust and releases me from those pains, my two sides, fear-based, and love based. Both win as doing the very thing that scares the shit out of me is how I found self-love and being able to open to Sam. I love how it's the feeling of love that pushes me, and the possibilities I have with Sam. I'm fighting an epic war on my own that I will fucking win. The more I talk aloud the more I gain perspective, the more it is out of my head. The more I am free to experience him, to experience us. Trying to stay in my body while she screams, she argues and I shake uncontrollably. The deeper we go, the harder I find it to shield him from those monsters; he never needs to know, no-one ever does. I am the monster now. I'm lying next to him, betraying him by not telling him, after all we have been through, after what, he has shared with me, after what, I have asked of him. Fuck, I'm a hypocrite. You see, the fear, these thoughts that I feel, I need to share with him, and I will.

Time, I need time.

I want to take my power back. The power out of my fears, out of the ability for me to self-sabotage us and that I choose to tell him, and am not forced to, not out of fear. Oh, Sam, please be patient with me, please hear my silent pleading in the dark. I need to jump off the edge of the cliff into the abyss of me, to unhook myself from these fear patterns and to feel alive, practice new, chase my happy and fight for us. I need to not think, stop worrying. Let me just make this clear, I have a beautiful, strong man and our forever is amazing. I feel him in my skin like I have never before experienced. I continue to nurture my own story and our love story so that my heart opens. The more we become us, the more I'm feeling the possibility of loss, of hurt, so I'm chasing my natural instincts to love and connect while equally wanting to run like the wind in the other direction, in fear, which leads to a life of more of the same. The fear of being broken, unwanted, never seen. My brain wants to protect me, attempting to convince me to protect myself from him. I'd be happy alone, but would it be an extraordinary life: NO. I want, and can have, extraordinary. I know my past hurts are trying to save me from future hurts. I've felt loss, the horrors of fear, it is the part of me that survived that cuddles me in the middle of the night while I am frozen in terror. It's my brain that protected me and took me away. It's my heart and brain that knows the sadness of loss, I felt, but it's my survival mode that protected me. You see, I'm in a battle with the very thing that I need to survive, that has both consciously and unconsciously protected me. My brain and heart are my own internal knight and shinning fucking warrior, because no one came! I showed up for myself! I fought! I still need those parts of me to live as I might need my survival warrior woman again.

I know I will hurt again. I know that I will feel loss. I will have hard times. I'm equipped to deal with whatever comes my way, to process the feelings and stay in my body, not my head. Knowing this and the practice of living it are two very different things. This is the first big challenge to that resilience in me, because it's not that I want it to stop, because I need it to protect me and to trust myself that if I fall, I can catch myself. I'm truly not sure I could survive hitting rock bottom again. I'm trying to expand myself to allow love in, both self-love and to receive Sam's love, while loving Sam, to unlock that magic within me and allow light into my dark parts. To overcome is to make friends with my survival self to bring forth the abilities I have within: my self-trust, allowing me to have a different relationship with my past, and my fears, so I can be adaptable and have the life of my choosing.

Even if it is not forever, I am willing to lose and love. I choose to feel the protected strength of a man, not for Sam to do life for me or fix me but, for me to feel the safety of a man and turn down my survival mode. I first and foremost can protect the hell out of myself. I would love to feel protected and feel into my softer feminine self so as I don't have to fight as much, for someone to show up for me in that way. This does not change the fact I am strong, and fully capable of protecting myself. I know Sam loves that about me, however I want to choose to feel the protection and safety of a man, as that is my desire. There is freedom in my femininity, in my want for protection from a man who also is seeking meaningful true connection. I wonder the woman I can be not shaped by the terrors of my nights. My need to feel safe and allow another to provide for me, in that way, reflects the human being standing before me. I want desperately to feel the strength of this man to feel my basic human need of protection met for that cup being filled by a man. I've spent so long fulfilling that for myself that I just want to feel safe. Just as a strong woman allows space for another strength to evolve, equally for a man to show both power and vulnerability, there is nothing sexier and more of a turn on when those traits exist side by side within a man and are freely shared. It is a sign of a good man with depth and integrity. No one is ever comfortable sharing emotions but a willingness to do it anyway, to face the unknown, to hesitate and do it anyway, that's strength.

From that day on the beach with Sam, he has continued to be that guy, that man, showing up in all of him and in a willingness to be okay with all of 'this', with me. Every person out there in the world no matter their sex, whatever their sexual orientation, whatever, we all want to feel loved, safe, protected, trusted. Finding meaning within ourselves and with connected others, the rest is just life. These are at times slightly different, but when it comes to connection and love, there is no difference in soul love. We are truly the same. We all have hearts that open and close based on life experiences, challenging fears, seeking out the same connections, same loves, same moments, arriving at same destination, sometimes at different times with all sorts of baggage. I guess I am also changing, I feel like I am softening, like I am not so hardened. I had to become hard and cold to a degree, to protect myself and now, I am seeing little moments of softness and I wonder, could that have always been me? Or is it because of the way he looks at me, that means I don't have to fight so hard anymore? The key is the battle of un-pretzeling yourself and allowing authentic love to grow within.

H I M | Thirty-two

Tonight, Evie is meeting my boys, the men who mean the world to me. I know they will like her. We have an epic banter and bounce off each other so well. It's just easy. Evie has been a little odd of late. I know she is feeling things in the dark, and I don't know what to do. I try to just let her know I am there without pushing her. I have no idea what else to do except wait for her to ask me for help or to say something.

I don't want to wait, I want to help, and I'm completely useless. So, I wait, reaching out in the dark to let her know I am always here waiting. I can't force her. I know she is fighting something, so just as she didn't force me, I need to be patient.

Arriving at her front door, I take a deep breath in of her scent at the door before walking in. She feels so good, beaming one of those smiles at the me. The way she checks me out in my shirt, I know she likes it and am slightly excited by her reaction to me.

I can sense the under tones of her struggling. Her face is serious as she sits me down. The weight of the moment and fear make my heart pound into my rib cage. I'm not completely sure what's happening.

Evie tells me she's falling in love with me, which makes all of my panic dissolve into relief, but I know there's more to this. I know it is about the other thing, not feeling ready, not sure what to do. My panic rises again, as Evie attempts to tell me her story. I try to do what she did for me, waiting, letting her have time. She loses it, trembling, with pain pouring out of her. I'm helpless, again someone I love is hurting. Fuck, I hate this feeling, it reminds me of Dad. I need her to be okay, I desperately want her to be okay. Evie curls herself on to me and I do my best to hold her tightly with the most love I can muster. My mind is blank on how to help, what I should say. I feel frozen in this hug, hoping that it's enough, that I'm enough for her. I shake myself. Focus on Evie. Encouraging myself to connect with her. I think we should cancel tonight, trying to protect her. Internally I'm screaming - what the fuck happened to her?

Randomly I try to breathe with her, gently rocking and it feels like the right thing to do. I hope it is, as Evie's breath slows, coming to a steady rhythm. Dread rolls into my stomach, sinking with the possibilities running through my head of what may have happened to her. Reminiscent of being helpless again settling into the churning of my stomach. It doesn't fucking matter what happened to her at all. Nothing she tells me will change anything. I want to tell her that! It is important, but it doesn't matter. Fuck I don't know, if that is the right thing to say? I wouldn't want her to think I don't care, fuck. I convince myself to follow her lead. She sat back for me, so I need to for her, and my opinion here truly doesn't matter. I just need to be there. Literally, that. It is helpful and made a massive difference for me.

Evie refuses to cancel tonight. She's all over the shop though, eyes panicked and darting around. The pressure of expressing herself and meeting everyone might be too much. I want her to trust me, so I stay with her, to show her that I am here, but also, I'm not really sure where to go. I want her to know that I can be that for her. I tell her I know how she struggles in the dark and that I'm here when she needs me to be, in whatever way she needs. She begins getting ready and again I follow her, not wanting to leave her alone, worried that it's becoming too much. I try to encourage her to ride our wave and the waves of what she is feeling.

She tells me she needs me close, as she initiates sex. I'm unsure as she so fragile, but oddly it actually feels like I'm helping. I release all control to her and with her first thrust, I feel connected again. I can see the change and feel of her body, less rigid, softening into me, flow, the feel of how she holds herself on me. Suddenly, she pulls me out of her and tells me that's enough for now.

"What the...?"

I'm confused and my cock is pained. While I hold myself, I look at her, noticing there is a sparkle back in those eyes, my sassy woman has returned. It's like I have my Evie back and now she's playful. I'm not sure I completely understand. I think she needed a way to stop her feelings from running amuck. I think that is what she is saying. I'm not sure I understand, but I trust her and know that this is not over, so right now I take one for the team, attempting to pull myself together. I feel like a volcano that's going to erupt anytime now. The energy between us is sensational and all kinds of fucked up. I think, well, fuck, I don't know. I'm watching her and her body like never before. I feel fucking focused, and sensitive to the world, alert, I guess. We leave for dinner and I'm acutely aware of Evie all night. I am engaged and focused, I feel good, like I have more strength.

After dinner Levi starts giving me shit about Evie. "Could you be any more into her?" He encourages me to play it cool and finishing his intervention with 'my son', imparting his attempt at wisdom. Some kind of Yoda, commentary. Little is he aware that during our current exchange, I have to take a breath as the words 'my son' linger in the air. I know that Levi is completely unaware of how this feels like a punch in the guts. He clears his throat and all of sudden everyone at the table is quiet.

Evie thankfully is in the bathroom.

Levi announces "Seriously, be careful not to look the fool!"

"Levi, I'm happily the fool, have you met her? She's amazing and I will do anything to love her. She's thoughtful, kind and fiercely independent, all of what I find sexy in a woman. I found her. I am going to chase her and I intend to make this work, I intend on loving her how she should be loved, and I don't give two shits what it looks like!"

Levi is clearly taken aback by my declaration, as am I. We have the entire table's attention. Levi adds "I have a lot to learn, Yoda." and we all laugh. I take a swig on my beer and say, "no time like the present" and head off in search of Evie.

I manage to steal a few moments with her that only increase the erotic energy between us. She feels into our moments. Wanting to feel her moan vibrate within my body is like an ache within me. I like the trust between us. My desire feels frightening and fucking epic all at once, pushing the boundaries of what I know, pushing the limits of me and us. Our private moments are displayed a little too publicly and I need to get out of here. We leave and my house is closer so I flag down a cab to take us there.

I feel out of control and yet completely in control. It's strange, like I'm watching myself. We push the boundaries of our bodies and the fire between us, entering her time and time again. Our bodies lose control in our sex, this raw and primal connection, tears at me for release. Evie's groans, guiding my cock deeper into her. Breathless and worried that I've pushed us too far, I reach for her. Cradling her in my arms as firmly as I think is good for her, I tenderly hold her shaking thighs. I half carry her to the shower before kissing all of her parts, showing her how grateful I am for the experience. I want to nurture her body after our emotional roller-coaster tonight, and I know showers and water are her thing. I'm freaked out we went too far. She's quiet, yet I'm reassured by her touch, her gentle kisses and soft eyes, both looking a little bewildered. I lay her down on my bed, kissing her forehead, and she grabs my hand. Opening her legs to me, saying "I want to feel you inside me, slowly."

I want to hold this space for her, I want her to let go, to feel completely safe with me. I feel into her slowly, with delicate movements at first, rocking along the curve of her hips. Finding a motion in tenderness, engaged with those blue eyes, as they sparkle up at me, encouraging me. I feel energized and in control of my own orgasm, feeling more able to be there for her in this connection. I feel myself growing harder and harder within her. I feel her trying to resist the urge to move faster, moving more deeply and slowly, staying with our momentum. Evie trembling beneath me, her moan different, uncontrolled, craving her release, sharing her vulnerabilities with me, wanting her to trust me to hold her here. I'm watching her every move. She's begging me now, using her hips to attempt to quicken my pace. I pull her back, slowing her body. I'm willing her to let go, to go beyond her limits and to trust me. When she does, we float between these spaces of pleasure and release she eventually surrendering wholly to our experience. Flooded by emotion, her pained sobs, loud and uncontrolled, frightening me. I hold her gently yet firmly, partly for her and partly for my own emotional release. Even though there are a lot of tears, from us both, it feels right, it feels good. I lean into holding us.

H E R | Thirty-three

Sam, the hurricane, comes over. I know he feels something in the air, as the pressure has been building for days. I feel it too, a hesitation. I know it's coming from me, as I decided two days ago to tell him what happened to me. Tonight, he is introducing me to his friends. I'm really looking forward to it- meeting the people who love him. He has that white shirt on again, the one with the long sleeves. He knows I love that shirt, cheeky shit. I can make out all of his torso and he is aware I'm watching. Beautiful, it's enough, he's enough. He won't run away from the crazy person to the hills. I can tell him how damaged I am.

Can I?

Oh my, Evie, breathe, deep breath, reassuring myself. My negative thoughts are racing in circles. Allowing space, I grab his hand, I need us to sit, walking him over to the couch. He searches my face, recognising I want to talk. Okay, ready, crazy is going to show up briefly, then Evie will be back to normal.

"Sam, I am really enjoying us, and completely falling in love with you more and more each day," He kisses both of my hands and looks back into my eyes. My God, he has restraint, he's clearly been waiting for me to say something. He knows without a word. Fuck, I'm losing it. My monsters scream 'he knows how fucked up you are!'

I swallow hard, dragging all of my willpower out of me as we both seem to take a deep breath at the same time. I'm struggling to contain myself. I feel overwhelmed and fear is shaking my body. It is reassuring that I am less willing to hide my bodily responses from Sam. As my feelings are growing stronger, I'm becoming more scared that my history is too much, and I'll lose him. The crazy tears begin to flow. "I want to tell you my story, I just can't find the words."

He holds me, curling me underneath his strength to find my spot on him and smiling at the safety of having a spot. I feel completely encompassed by him and surrender to receive his comfort. My freak out is pathetic, I can't even get past my fears of love. Fuck, Evie I can't find the words, how do you even start a conversation like that? I'm triggered. I immerse myself in Sam's presence and just allow myself to soak him in, words have failed me. Reverberating around my head is 'some horrors don't have words, Evie.' Part of me hates that I must contaminate us, and fears that he will look at me differently.

After a few moments, I sit up, look at him and feel his love pouring out all over me, in one look. He asks, "shall I order in and cancel the boys tonight?"

"No, Sam, No. Give me a minute to clean up and we can go, I've been looking forward to this, shittest timing ever!"

Sam joins me in the bathroom. He's so comfortable in here with me, I find it funny that he can watch me do the most mundane of things and be aroused by me. He stands behind me, holding my hips. "I'm fighting fears too, but we need to be honest with each other, we are okay. We don't need to struggle separately in the dark." Sam finishes by acknowledging my nightly struggles and his awareness of it.

Fear shudders my heart into a pause as the man has reached inside my body and held my heart in the dark, knowing I'm there. He has been there in my darkness, the whole time, calling to me. The knowledge of this brings such joy and comfort to my heart. I feel pained that he must feel shut out.

"Sam, I'm trying to overcome and tame my monsters and attempt to be normal."

He interrupts. "We are not normal Evie! Let's just ride the wave, together." Adding a pause before 'together.' I feel my fears rising, he knows so much about me, he probably can guess what's happened to me. He probably also knows how fucked up I am. Crazy is coming out and I'm unsure I can stop it. Brain screaming 'I'm too broken. Beginning my internal coaching... Go with the sensations of what is happening in your inside, trust your body, bring him close' Wisdom coming from a small voice within me, as I'm completely triggered. My safe place of control is blown, and I feel the fear rising in me. I'm frozen by the darkness creeping up my legs, attempting to drag me into the black abyss. I look at him and hold my hands on his face, on his chest, the touch of him, is shifting me, moving my impending panic. "Sam, I need to feel you inside me."

Sam looks at me, happily bewildered.

I tell him, "you make me feel safe and connected. Right now, I feel exposed and am struggling to contain my overwhelm. Your touch is so grounding for me, our raw touch tames me so. I need to feel you in the depths of me, close, inside me, please." I genuinely need to feel secure in my insecurities of being too damaged.

Sam's eyes are sparkling. Hastily, I push him backwards into the chair in the corner of the room. He's still hesitant, unsure of what I mean, perhaps we both are beginning to see that sex is something I use to feel safe in being in control. I wrap myself around him, taking just the tip of him until his manhood is ready for all of me, thrusting deep within my vulnerable self. We both moan instantly at our emotional energy. It is like I can feel myself pushing the pain out of my body, fighting back while Sam holds me. His eyes lock on to mine he holds on to my shoulders, guiding my movement, drawing me into him and I see he feels this is different. I exhale loudly, he sees my body relax, naturally wraps me in his embrace. This feels like home, like I've put the cage back around my heart and locked down the horror story. I don't know if my emotional pain has an expression. I collapse further into his arms, warped in the shell of my man. I feel, accepted, with him inside me while embracing my fragile self. He holds me tightly, arching himself within me. We instantly feel the change in my body, as I retreat from him. The confusion on his face is almost comical. I feel a pang of guilt, and dread, that I'm using control in this way to achieve safety. I don't want to do that with Sam. I fix my clothes and return to getting ready, frozen in my thoughts and fear of what I am doing, disconnected from my emotional turmoil. It also gives rise for me to focus on Sam and not me.

I explain I'm not trying to torture him, we are late and maybe we could be beyond our orgasms, until later? I bullshit reasons why, as I think it was control that actually helped me here and I feel ashamed of doing this to Sam and don't want to admit that control had a hand in this. I instead tell him that I needed to feel him in my soul and our connection is beyond pleasure, the need to feel control back in my body. That with him holding me, I can fight anything. Which is true. I look down, filled with embarrassment and admit it. "Sam, I think I also need to feel in control of the situation?"

He smiles, telling me to stop thinking so much and just roll with it. Immediately I feel accepted and relieved. 'Just roll with it, Evie,' pumps through my thoughts.

I do want him to know about me. I am worried what he thinks of me or what has happened to me. I am desperate for him to not see how broken I am, and I don't want him to look at me differently. I guess, I want to prove

I'm not broken. I'm disappointed in myself that I'm dressing this up as a distraction rather than using the safety I feel when he is inside me. "I just needed to feel you protect me. Sam, we are just beginning! It's just a pause until later tonight." Stupidly I respond to Sam as if it were about sex, even though we both know it is not. I begin telling myself that I want us to go to this place together. A new level of us, and it scares me. I'm listening to my body's needs and wants. I feel like I'm disrespecting Sam, so I try to describe what is happening for me. "This feels right, I am not trying to hurt you and we can finish now if you like, although it also feels right to wait, did you feel the energy? Did you feel the release in me?" He looks at me puzzled. "I think so…" comes out of him. He says he does feel good, frustrated, but good.

Let's see what happens, roll with it, Evie.

"I want us to be solid so that our monsters run from us, that way we love so loudly in body, mind and heart that our fears dissolve."

I think he can also see I'm battling bigger things, things he's not sure of, maybe? Pushing us beyond our limits and our relationship is important to me. I don't want normal, that's not us. I want magic, we fucking deserve magic! There are monsters in the wardrobe, and they don't get to define me or us. The man stands, holding my hand. He trusts me implicitly. I'm not overly sure what I am doing but, it feels good and I feel strong, my monsters tamed for now. I attempt to explain what I am feeling while internally wishing I would shut up.

"We inhaled each other's skin and for me you are safe. You ground me." My voice is clearly shaking.

He pulls me forward and holds me saying, "okay, okay, I'm just feeling the moment as well." He smiles, promising "we will finish this later" as he pulls me even closer. Running his hands through my hair, he draws in a giant breath of me, pressing into me so I can feel his manhood, feeling his lips linger against my ear, traversing the nape of my neck. He does the one thing he perceives I find irresistible and I do. Grabs my hand and walks me to out the door to the car, my legs entirely jelly, and he knows it. We arrive at the pub, I am meeting his nearest and dearest, filled with nervous energy as I want them to like me and his taste lingers all over my body.

Why did I do this tonight?

I'm dressed smart but casually. It took me ages to figure out what to wear, I want them to like me. A light, black button-up shirt and jeans, comfortable, yet stylish. I'm trying to distract myself from thinking about something other than his touch. My demons are finally quiet now, consumed by his promise. I'm trying to focus, to remember their names, to navigate what my nerves are and the anticipation hanging around from our earlier encounter, all the while, feeling him looking at me like I'm in trouble, his prey. I feel strange, a mix of disconnected emotions, fill me.

I offer to buy a round for the boys, half because that's the kind of woman I am and half to compose myself from Sam's eyes. Standing and heading to the bar, he's next to me, not touching me, but close enough to feel the intensifying fire between us. He can see I'm having a hot flush, with the excitement pouring out of us both. He stops me, pauses, looking at me, before slowly and carefully saying "My tongue is going to saviour every corner of you, so slowly you'll beg for my cock to release you." His eyes are burning, with drive, with passion. My body trembles and waves of shock tingle through me at his promise. I reach for him, as he grabs my hands and moves us to a discreet corner, luckily, it's a busy pub so we can steal a minute. I move for him again, but he seizes my hand and says "Don't."

I look at him, with words escaping me.

He holds me away from him, leans over to my ear and whispers, in slight desperation. "Everything feels incredible, every part of my body is on. I can't have you touch me yet!" I stand back and look at him. He smiles uncomfortably and says, "My senses have come alive, you're mine and I will share this torment with you. Now get your arse to the bar and buy me a beer!" He finishes with a cheeky slap on my arse, and all I can do is laugh at the beauty of my man, battling his desire while loving the space, at the same time. 'What have I created?' crosses my mind, with a wave of emotion firing through my body. I can't stop the smile from beaming across my face. We have dinner and I can feel his intensity. I think everyone can, and I'm slightly embarrassed. I manage to concentrate on his friends. They are a great bunch of men. Dinner has lots of laughter and a few stolen moments with Sam. As I walk out of the bathroom after dinner, Sam's suddenly there, swinging me into his arms. I crumble into those shoulders, as he holds me against the wall, embracing every part of me. Hands on my hips, thighs, mouth, arse, everywhere! I can feel his body fully against me, feeling his need, wanting every inch of him. My body responds to his and for a second, we forget, and he kisses me so passionately, showing me what is waiting for me. I respond to his need by sharing mine, sucking his tongue. He moans, and I am immediately brought back to the pub. I push him away, "Sam!"

He firmly tells me "We're leaving."

Just before we are back at the table, he mutters. "Drink fast. The boys love you."

I naughtily take my time with the beer, half preparing for what is coming and half to play with Sam, prolonging and allowing him to see, to watch me. It becomes clear to his mates that he's checked out, his eyes on me, not moving. It's time. I finish the rest of my beer, stand and say see you soon to the boys. We leave the car at the pub. Standing next to each other without words, without touching, waiting for a ride, is epically intense. In the taxi, he reaches for my hand, holding it gently. I'm reassured, immediately surrendering as my nervous energy disperses, trust.

I can see his eyes on my body, lit by the dim streetlights. His eyes move down to my breasts, following the rise and fall of my breathing, as I am attempting to control my craving for him. I undo the first button on my shirt, and he follows my hand, rubbing my neck. His eyes take over, searching all over my body, calling my parts to him. He places his hand on my thigh, and my body reacts to curl under his touch. Sam grins clearly aware of his touch and how my body yearns and responds to him. His eyes move to my chest again, seeing the goose bumps before gliding back to my mouth, breast, lips as he squeezes my thigh. Oh. My., God. I am nervously ready. We arrive, and I realise we are at his house, when normally we are at mine. I look at him; he beams a mischievous smile back at me. A new wave of nerves rises in me. He's behind me as we walk up the stairs. I can feel the movement of the air. My senses are on full alert, blood pumping my awareness into overdrive. Sam's gaze is unflinching, penetrating, as he presses me against the door. His hands find my breasts, he pants heavily into my ear, with his manhood hard, pushed into me. My back arches to feel more of him.

"Sam, babe," I'm begging him. "Please, Sam, open the door!"

Totally entangled in desire, he unlocks the door somehow, still pulling at my jeans. "Sam. Open. The. Door!"

The door flies open, and we fall inside. Disentangling myself from him, he closes the door while holding me against the inside His desperation is clear now.

I turn and kiss him with all that I have, as he pushes down my jeans and directs us to the kitchen, taking me hard against the bench, wildly and powerfully. As we catch our breath, he gently places his hand on my lady parts, turning me around. My whole body feels like jelly, my thighs weak, pulsating inside out. Sam gently removes the rest of my clothes, with soothing kisses on my rawness before guiding me to the bathroom. I feel like a deer in the headlights. We move in silence, overwhelmed by our wildness and tender from our efforts. He sits me on the bathtub and turns the shower on. I think we both know we pushed some boundaries tonight, in a healthy trusting way. Entering the shower, I allow the water to stream over my face. The heat is tingling on my skin, his arms are around me, holding us. I submerge myself into his chest, into him. I feel pained and a little panicked, but my lover is cherishing me, kind hands holding me, showering me with compassion.

I feel worshipped by him. I turn to him and smile as he wraps me in a towel and dries off my body. My legs feel weak or perhaps I have more unspent energy? He walks me to the bed, removing the towel and lying me down. I feel so safe.

I invite him into me, opening my legs to him and asking him to enter me. I want him, to move inside me very slowly, to explore the slightest of move-ment, to build our connection. I want to feel the strength of Sam grow inside me. Sam leans down and places a kiss on the crevasse where my hips meet my thighs, his signature move. As we begin, I whisper "slowly, very slowly," and use my hips to guide him. He recognises my vulnerability, interlacing our hands above my head, as time falls away from us. I'm pained and overcome, with him, with our efforts this evening and it's not long before I'm begging Sam. Pleading him to move faster, feeling his souls' touch, needing him to love my pains, my panicked self. I'm lost in us, as my hips call him, driving his timing. He knows how to pace me, to steady me beyond my limits, and slows me. My hips are pushing him to liberate me, my begging beyond any comprehension. Soon I turn to pleading, not to stop, lost in the feel of him. It's excruciatingly pleasurable. He is holding this space, slowly, for me, and it's all pouring out of me. I'm feeling his love. My body quivers, exploding as we release, and I lose it entirely. My emotions unleashed, as uncontrolled sobs reach out of my heart, engulf-ing my climax, body trembles, pain releasing, rawness pours out of me. My body, my heart, my tears, all pained outwardly. Sam holds me tightly, still inside me, as I cry a thousand tears of unleashed love, of complete trust and setting myself free from my demons. My body convulses in emotion, in a freed heart released from its' cage. I reach for my chest, my hands over my heart, feeling the pounding of my heart, physically holding my hurts.

My silent cries, never before felt in the presence of another, are expressed and held. Finally, my warrior self and womanly self are coming together, trusting me to move beyond my boundaries, for pushing and fighting for my love.

Sam. A man who could show up in my hurt, hold my pain, steady me with strength and knew to follow his instincts to gently help me to trust myself in love and him. To bring forth my love, to bring forth my warrior woman he so loves to play with. A man who understands that I need to save myself. He can hold my hips, caress my shuddering lady parts, hold me while I cry, and laugh with me at our exposed selves, and we will feel the strength and boundaries of our love evolve. That's a fucking warrior man. Don't save me, hold my hips while I save my fucking self! Tonight, that was Sam. I am not sure how long I have cried for, nor how long we lie in silence. A smile creeps across my face, it's over in the dark, a smile of holy wow! I'm proud of my emotional expression. He feels the change in me and releases his hold on me, planting a kiss on my forehead before rolling over. He reaches back for the touch of my hip and, when, just like that, he's asleep. I contemplate and relive the night at least three times in my head, before I fall asleep. After all, I am the crazy one in this bed.

H I M | Thirty-four

Holding Evie tightly in my arms, in my bed, in my house, feels incredible. Breathing her in, walls have crumbled down for both of us. I'm happy, right now, I'm so happy. Simply holding the woman, I love in my bed, both of us carrying pain and learning how to love each other anyway.

I have a sense that I helped, that I was able to be there for Evie, hold her, take care of her, free her. I know we are not perfect, and I don't ever want us to be. I want us to be real, extraordinarily imperfect in our own right. I truly feel closer to Evie than ever before right now. I want to understand her experience, I want to hear her experience of us. And mostly I want the reassurance that I'm helping, I think. I decide I'm not going to hold back. I want us to be involved in understanding what is happening for each of us.

"Evie. Tell me how your body feels, how you feel?" I wait.

Initially she's like a deer caught in the headlights. I know it's a risk and I said I would wait for her to be ready, but I also want her to know it's okay to trust me and I want to learn how to love her. I feel like we have hit a new level of trust and I want to keep it going, so I wait and she opens. I listen and learn. It's hard to hear about her bodily experience as she describes it and how our desires aided her panic to subside and then to feel comfortable to release and to receive love, to be loved. I ask her about our intimacy levels and I really don't want it to become an emotional crutch for us. Even though I'm petrified of her response, I have to put it out there, about control and us both having healthy control. She immediately agrees and it feels like we reach another level in our trust and communication. We talk about our intimate needs and how our desires are playing out. We even talk about pushing our boundaries; how it felt and what we both need. I tell her how I am trying to be open to new, even if I don't truly understand.

"I feel this rawness under the surface, with my emotions bubbling away and I'm trying to contain them as I don't want to hurt you or expose you to my weakness." I know I am navigating a delicate cliff and I've no idea what's at the bottom, I want Evie to know and feel like I'm standing with her, even if I don't fully understand.

Evie queries, what do I mean by weakness? And I am actually lost for words. I add stupidly, even though I know it is not a truth, that emotional weakness is not a sign of strength.

Evie asks if I think she is weak, or, better yet my dad? I'm choked up instantly, aware of the heat rising in me. Sweating in my own pain's arrival during our conversation, followed by anger at thinking for a moment that Dad or Evie are weak. My thoughts race to make sense of what I'm discovering. I'm now the deer in the headlights, attempting to clear away my emotions. Pulling Evie closer, feeling the rawness of my realisation while Evie allowing me the time to ponder her reflections. I'm wounded but so appreciative of her insights. Not knowing what do to do or say. Evie holds my face closely, looking me dead in the eye. "The sexiest thing on a man is when he can share his emotional experience authentically and still be manly, there's a strength in both - the lion and the deer." Fuck there is a weird synchronicity in completing each other's thoughts.

She goes on to say that she wants us to continue like this, in opening up and trusting, and honestly sharing, even when it's hard to hear. That she needs me to express my emotional self, as does she. We both need to find our own way in expressing it. I tell Evie how exposed I feel, after dealing with years of bottling things up it will take some time for me to figure out what this looks like for me and to try it out, I guess. We both shed some tears from the pure overwhelm and acceptance. I ask Evie if it was okay that I stayed inside her last night, that I wanted to feel that connection for me and to be there for her while she was expressing her emotions. She again holds my face to emphasise her point.

"It was perfect. I felt the strength and beauty of my man so I could fall apart." She traces kisses down to my heart and we both lose ourselves in touch.

H E R | Thirty-five

I feel him stirring in his sleep. The sun warms my naked legs as it streams through the open window. I'm wrapped in his sheets, with his hand placed steady on my hip. Absently, my mind wonders how he always manages to find and hold one of my hips all night.

He pulls my body in close, burrowing in behind me, without words, holding my left breast over my heart, my body engulfed by his. I arch into him. I can't help it! He moans softly in my ear, knowing full well I love the sound of his manly rumblings, as his sounds reverberating inside my body, lighting me up. He feels my body smile at him and chuckles. We cuddle while our bodies play with each other, without words and yet so much is spoken in a touch, a brush of the skin, an almost touch, his breath on my neck, soft and soothing, his smell. I draw all of us into me. I'm almost asleep again, hidden in my man shell when he speaks.

"Tell me how your body feels? Tell me how you feel?"

I'm stunned awake, with questions being asked of my exposed soul. I thought we were brushing that one under the carpet. I turn to look away from him, take a deep breath before sharing my experience of last night.

I expose him to what was happening in my body, all my sensations. I tell him about my body panicking and pained. My emotional nakedness shedding to the bones of myself. My voice shakes but I express my emotions and how safe I felt and how grateful I am of him holding me in that space. I share how much this means to me and how I feel about him in complete trust. He reciprocates, sharing his feelings and what he felt last night, too. We talk about the nature of our lovemaking. It is freeing to hear his side, his thoughts, his feelings, his vulnerabilities. We both reveal that our level of intimacy is new ground for both of us. He is listening to me and running with what his body wants to do, adding that he feels so energetic. He briefly alludes to letting go of some pain that he wasn't ready to acknowledge last night, both of us emotionally shedding. He expresses feeling unsure about his own emotional release, he felt equally held in his own feelings by me and reassured that we could be in the moment together. I never considered that my freak out could help him, that he was also expressing emotions. I turn back to face him. My quivering voice tells him that he embodies the strength of ten men and the heart of a true lover, my lion and deer. He looks stunned at my words and my directness, but I cannot let him believe he is weak, when he is the complete opposite. Our feelings that had locked us away are unleashed. We hold, we hug, we touch, and we soothe for most of the morning. Cherishing each other's emotional hangover.

He is laying on my stomach, hands still holding my hips. Looking at his naked self, his beautiful back, I'm lost in the feel of him on top of me. I am pure happiness and my smile is permanently etched on to my face. I feel like the luckiest girl in the world and am appreciating it too, with this remarkable man in between my legs.

I am so wired, that I feel like I can do anything. In the last 24 hours I feel like we have pushed ourselves to beyond our limits, sensing a quiver as the thought crosses my mind. I now recognise with Sam we are always going to push each other, in love and life, because that is what our relationship has started on. He has entered my heart so deeply; with the love I have felt for and from him. I never thought anyone could show up for me like this. I'm learning to receive his love and be present with just him in the tender moments, to outlive my history. I'm brought back to this moment and to my body by my man kissing my tummy, saying "mine, mine!" I acknowledge him with a smile, as he declares: "Food."

H I M | Thirty-six

Things were going so well! My brain runs this on repeat. I've been blind-sided by Evie, fuck it. The morning was ideal, what happened in the café, the day had felt so right. She's helped me to open up and now I feel shut out, confused and trapped. Fuck. I hate these feelings. What happened? I don't understand, and I'm terrified I've done something horribly wrong and have no idea what.

Perhaps we did push things too much last night and today?

My thoughts are crazily panicked, and I am blowing everything out of proportion. I can fix this. My brain thinks up a thousand ways to ask her what happened? All of them provoke more anxiety. Wait, just wait for her. I had a freak out, this is hers. Yes, wait, slow it down and let her speak.

In the car, we are both overwhelmed by the tension in the air. She begins to speak, and her panic overwhelms me too. I'm somewhat relieved she's panicking as well because I am freaking the fuck out over here.

She's confused? Not about me? It wasn't what she was meant to say?

She is becoming more and more agitated and having a panic attack, maybe. I reach for her, trying to help. She pushes me away. I feel rejected and hurt, desperately trying to listen to her and push my own feelings down, so I can just be here. I want to be here for her. I'm frustrated that she won't let me speak but know I must be careful with her.

Fuck, just say it! Stop trying to be careful with me!

Evie is again telling me what my feelings are about what is happening, being careful with me. I get it, it's her way of protecting me, but I don't need protecting from her. My thoughts are running high. I'm trying to listen to her and also ridiculously gripping the steering wheel like it will break off any minute now. After what we had talked about and being so vulnerable in sharing ourselves, I'm not sure what the fuck happened or how we even got here! I feel so fucking inadequate right now. Dread churns up my stomach, reminding me of being helpless again. Someone I love is hurting and I'm fucking useless. Steadying myself and forcing myself to focus on Evie. Steady, be here, just wait. I am coaching myself to prevent rage from coming out, and to stay focused on her, not my emotional responses right now. I reach over, placing my hand on her thigh. I just focus on feeling her skin, on loving this part of her as best as I can. Letting her know I am here but not taking over, just witnessing her in pain. I focus on what she did for me and to be solid next to her. The sensations of her shaking under my hand, heat rising through my fingers and I'm helpless to do anything. The palm of my hand fills with sweat, sickness fills the pit of my stomach, desperate to stop the situation. I can't control this, no matter how much I need to fix it for her. I know I can't but knowing this is not fucking helping at all. I listen, feeling defeated by my inadequacies. I listen and try to be gentle with her, holding my sweaty hand on her leg. Slowly, Evie begins to shift out of panic, and slowly she also begins to make some sense. She feels overwhelmed and I think it is strange for her to love me or receive love, so she needs time with it!

'Fuck,' I think. This is so hard. It hurts my brain trying to make sense of what is happening. I'm doing my best, I think. I want us to work so I have to learn what she needs not what I need for her, to learn how to love her, just as she is learning how to love me. Fuck, it is accepting our fucking freak outs, best guess. I want her to need me. It's so hard, she has a right to her feelings, and I think they are coming out wrong because of how I'm reacting. I want to fix us, not even sure we are even broken, although it sure feels pretty dreadful. Knowing this and not knowing what the fuck to do is driving me bonkers. I do feel rejected although not comfortable to tell Evie, ever. She moves my hand to her heart and I'm so relieved to feel close to her. Her touch eases the tension, it's not me. My god I think I love this woman, even now in this moment, she is striking beautiful and her resolve indescribable.

Evie starts trying to be gentle in explaining things to me. It's agonisingly frustrating and like I'm this fragile little boy. I need her to stop, just stop filling the air with words!

"It's okay, I don't understand, but it's okay!" I snap at her. Fuck, I should have done that differently, but fuck, someone needed to stop the out of control train. I tell her I'm in, like truly in with us, and what we are, even in this. Whatever this is right now. I'm in, Evie. I'm not fucking going anywhere. I tell her to tell me or not tell me what is happening. I trust her. It won't change anything for me. Please stop being careful with me. We are different and that's what I want! I know we have to figure things out for ourselves and together. Our histories are different and that is okay. I flash her a smile and begin driving towards her house, not sure this is the right path, but it feels okay. I walk her to the door and hold her tightly, kissing her hands, face and lips so she knows how I feel and that I am in, even in whatever this is. I trust her. I tell Evie, perhaps a little too firmly, that one day she will do this with me, and she will let me hold all of her while she does what she needs to.

H E R | Thirty-seven

Sitting across the table from Sam, who is now looking at his food in the same way as he looks at me, fills my soul with joy. Watching him eat, I'm overwhelmed by happiness. He catches my eye, which are glassy with happy tears. I beam a smile at him as he chews. He says, "eat, you will need it!" That cheeky smile is plastered all over his face. I look at him in delight as a lump lodges in my throat. Naturally my hips defy me, responding to his call, his lust caressing them under the table. I take a deep breath and the shithead loves it, pulling my body back to myself.

"Sam, I need to go home. I need to check in with myself, I need to spend a little time trying on this unleashed woman, time with these unfolding emotions. I want to soak me, in my tub, nourish my body, cleanse and soothe my aching thighs, soak my tender lady parts, try out this skin that has awakened from within me. I need to consolidate, I need time. I feel ever so deeply, please let me feel this and allow the time for me to grow into this woman." Well, that is what I was trying to say, what I wanted to express. What came out of my mouth was not that. It was stupid and fear based.

Why did I fucking do that? Where did it even come from?

I'm happy, what am I doing?

Sam's wounded eyes burn into me. He closed off to me immediately, and the energy that was freely dancing around us is now closed, shut off like a slammed door. The life force feels like it is draining from me now, and I'm panicked?

I just sabotaged us.

Or do I feel uncomfortable with feeling happy and had to ruin it?

I don't even understand myself. I want to scream, tear at myself, as the energy shifts into a gaping hole developing between us. I just... I need some time, make it stop, make it stop! Help! Now we are being polite and withdrawn with each other and it feels terrible. This is not us, not after all we have been through. Sam's driving me home after silently retrieving his car from the pub and we are hurt. Quiet in our own hurt feelings. He's confused, I'm confused, and I don't know why I'm not expressing myself well.

I say. "Sam, I'm not coming across well." I nervously start giggling. He looks at me with so much intensity. I say, "Sam, this is not what I meant! Panic set in. I know crazy, like I just wanted to tell you what's happening for me and this crazy 'I need some space' comes out, from nowhere. I am sorry I hurt you."

The solid wedge in my throat is now the size of a fucking tennis ball! It's making my voice scratchy. I swallow hard and put my hands under my legs, feeling cold sweat pouring over me. Sam realizes I am not okay and pulls the car over. The heat is rising in my body, and my heart has gone from racing to thumping in my throat. No more thinking is occurring, my body is seized in fear, screaming loudly in a full-scale panic attack. I allow the waves to rise, trying to match my breathing with the intensity of my heart, desperately trying to focus on my bodily sensations while my hurricane watches on, attempting to help me. The panic passes in sweat, heart thumping tremors, heat, muscle strain, and coolness. I feel into the space that is my body in fear, my body screaming at me. I squeeze my legs together tightly and finally say out loud: "Please don't fuck this up."

Sam reaches for me. The panic is clear in my voice. He wants to nurture me, to help me.

"Wait," I say. "Please let me get this out." He sits back and waits. He's frustrated with me. I can see that clearly, maybe he's scared of what ridiculous crap will fall out of my mouth next? I'm scared of what is going to fall out of my mouth next! He places his hand on my leg and looks out the front window. I search for the words, busy breathing and arguing with my thoughts before fear launches another full-scale attack on me. I allow the waves to pour over me, accepting the fears and panic while it all floods out of me: how I want to nurture my body; how I want to spend time with the parts of me that I never knew existed; how the unleashing of me, with waves of mental and physical exhaustion, allows my panic to subside; how I want to love him, saviour him, this moment, our growth together, my body changes; how I feel; how he is mine as he's claimed me. I have him, in the depths of my heart, the corners of my body and the mysteries of my mind. I'm badly trying to convey my feelings in words to take back how I wounded him.

"It's all trying to consolidate, within my heart, body and mind while you love me ever so loudly and I want to feel it. All of us, not get lost in you. So, I need to surrender to it and rise as me. I need time to step into that woman, to feel this new vulnerable skin that surrounds me and continue to prepare for us and how we will evolve, whatever that may be. It's been massive. I'm not sure, but I also think at the restaurant I felt happy and content and I freaked out. I need to bring all of this together in my head and heart. I need some time to scream in a paddock, fuck... and for you to not see the batshit crazy hormonal lady that you had lunch with today."

Sam finally speaks. "Evie, I'm relieved but I don't understand… I appreciate you telling me, I trust you, you need to trust me, if this is going to work." He looks away. I breathe loudly.

My fear speaks. "I can feel this," hand gesturing to space between us, "this haemorrhaging hole, building here. Right here." He looks at me again.

I rush to plug the hole. "I do. Completely! I do trust you, like I've never trusted anyone before!" I'm frantic. Moving his hand from my thigh to my heart, I continue. "I want to be honest with you and I'm trying! We both have histories we are fighting and a world of emotions. Fear is completely operating the show that is me right now. I'm anxiously searching for reassurance that this man will not run from my fear show. I don't want you to feel rejected by me, or wounded, I don't ever want you to look at me like that again, I can't help how I feel and the ways in which I work through them, I know what works for me!" Breathe.

"I know I showed up in fear. I'm not really operating on all cylinders right now, clearly. I understand that we are both feeling a lot of emotions and I will continue to be honest and try to share what I'm feeling, like last night, I was so overcome and I'm not completely sure I'm finished, I feel so raw. I am sorry, that hurt you and I will try to just tell you minus the freak out about what is happening for me. It feels like my brain is being operated by someone else with all this rambling to justify bullshit that hurt came out of my mouth, I freaked, and fuck I'm sorry. Please, stop speaking. I know ridiculous is pouring out of me right now without a filter or ability to stop. I want you to do the same, even if you know it will hurt me, we need to be honest."

He nods in agreement.

"Sam, you are all that I have ever wished for, when I never really knew what I wished for until you showed up! Literally, you are more than I could ever have hoped for."

He reaches for me, and I let him hold me. I want to push him away, but I don't. "Sam, please. I need to finish, to get this out of my head, for us to be healthy. I need me to be truthful. You know I need to share some things with you and I'm trying to be ready. It means that sometimes fear controls me without a lot of reason and then I have to work backwards to figure out what I am battling. I am trying as hard as I can. I just never want you to see me do it. I hope that's okay, I don't want us to change. I want us to grow together, to evolve on a solid foundation!"

My thoughts keep falling out of my mouth, as if trying to clean up the road train that has already crashed...

"Stop, fucking stop!" Sam shouts from behind gritted teeth, both hands now on the steering wheel, knuckles white, like he will break it off. Thank God he is stopping me. He's angry. Oh God he's going to leave! I'm too much, fuck, fuck, I'm frozen in fear, waiting for his next words, although grateful someone stopped my crazy train.

"Evie." There are tears in his eyes. "I'm in this. I understand, I'm having some crazy shit happening over here too. My emotions are fucking bonkers. Stop waiting for me to fucking leave! I would have left already! I feel us also. We do need to listen to ourselves and our needs, and I hear you need time! Stop thinking you have to be careful of me! Be you! I won't let you down, let the chips fall where they fucking fall. I know you have some important things you want to tell me, and I want you to, whatever it is, but only when you are ready to tell me. I trust you."

Tears are streaming down my face. Sam continues. "Nothing about us has been normal, Evie. That's why I'm here!" He turns and looks at me. "That's why you feel so different, that's why I want you, even with your crazy ramblings, but don't work me."

He smiles with the cheekiest of smiles while kissing the back of my hand and squeezing my thigh, he tells me to nurture myself, prepare my body for him because we will together explore her limits, bringing the same intensity. The tennis ball lump in my throat is instantly back.

I muster a quiet. "Please."

Sam slides the car into gear, and we are off again. The gentleman opens my door, aids my hips in getting out of the car, walks me inside, kisses me so I will remember the taste of him for days before leaving. As soon as he's gone, I feel the emptiness of my home without him.

I stand naked in front of the mirror, reacquainting myself with my body, feeling my body and the momentary loss I feel from him walking out the door. I smile at the anticipation of his promise. As I'm tracing the newness of my body, feeling his hands on me, I realise he is embedded in my soul. My everything is raw, so very achy and in dire need of Sam. I can't have him be my emotional crutch, I need to do this for myself first. Tears begin to fall. I think thoughts about how much I trust him, how he brings lightness to my soul. Feeling happiness at my emotional nakedness, laughter at my boldness, comfort in his protection, while creating space for me to unleash, to feel the full power of his love and the love that exists within me.

I think, I felt content, like I was experiencing happiness at the restaurant and I went a bit cuckoo bananas. Warmth creeps over me, from the inside out, like never before. I can only describe it as my soul's smile, the recognition in my own capacity to love, shared, the trust I have in my own love, vulnerability expressed and held. The enormity of what has grown within me and between us dawns on me in a wave of emotion encompassing my body in the experience of love. I step myself in to my version of solace: a hot bath, candles, and music. Soft waves of emotion pass over me and I feel the excitement and gratitude of felt love, of receiving and in letting go.

I focus on me, gently feeling each part of my body. I feel into my legs, starting with my calves. Massaging, asking my body to soften, to feel rejuvenated, then my arms, neck and shoulders. Welcoming this new connection to myself. Nurturing and holding all of me. I leave my thighs, hips and lady parts till last, the most sensitive, encouraging and thanking those parts of my body, to be soothed, to embrace the aching of my sex, my warrior woman, soothing all of my parts that showed up in love, with love, accepted and self-appreciation for the gift that stood forward and is now awakened with me. I really like her, this Evie. I want to step my life forward with her. I've found within me such courage, self-trust, and a self-love like no other. It is like I am standing tall for the first time. I'm overcome with gratitude and a grateful heart that is healing from love, I am free, I am free. I reach for my phone, take a picture of my legs and send it to Sam. I caption it: *Dinner tomorrow, legs or thighs?*

He responds immediately. It's a picture of his legs and a toothbrush emoji: Two can play at this game.

I soak in the warmth of my bath, the feel of my man's response. Closing my eyes. I feel him everywhere, hear his voice, that laugh he has, a strange chuckle alongside an epic smile, that feels like home. His firm heart beating against mine, heart to heart, finding their connected flow. Strong arms holding me in place, a genuine heartfelt embrace. His face, rugged, that shows a story, a lived life and a softness for me. I now understand his hesitation at the beginning of us, when he's in, he is all in. I ponder the thoughts that float by in my head. Some are completely ridiculous, some in anticipation of him, some in dread of the day I tell him my story, some of our wedding, our children, my crazy. It's all, welcomed, allowing all of this to roll on by, like a TV commercial, paying little attention. I put myself to bed, quivering at the thought of my man putting me to bed like he did last night. Nourishing myself in tenderness and lovingly feeling the skin of this warrior woman. I feel like I am visualizing my little girl inside all grown up, standing alongside my warrior self, all coming together within me as one and standing tall.

I've finished preparing for dinner. Why am I feeling so anxious? How lovely does it feel at the same time? I literally sink back into myself and the space of nervous anticipation reminding myself how grateful I am. Giving myself permission to savour the feeling as good, to enjoy the mood. My skin feels tingly, I feel the excitement in the air. I hear the door as he walks in. I have to stop myself from running to him. I can hear his sexy swagger, the man strut, as you know, I love when a man swings his hips for me, it is more of a flaunt than a swing.

I say aloud "Fuck it!" before running to Sam. He laughs and opens those arms for me to be swallowed in, home. My God, he feels good, so good. As I think it, he says it out loud. I reach under his shirt for his skin, stretching my hands all over, to his back. It's not enough. I want more of his skin, more of him against my skin.

"Sam, take your shirt off," I request, as I'm already taking off mine, "I would like to cuddle."

Smiling, he follows my lead and I feel like I'm endeavouring to wrap myself in him and it's not enough, I want more of him, I need more. I stop thinking and just go with my body, removing the rest of my clothes before dropping his pants to the floor. He's excited and gives me a look as his eyes change, expressing his want. It's a look that sets me on fire. Standing apart at first pausing, taking each other in. Suddenly, a wave of vulnerability spreads throughout me, maybe both of us? He reaches for my hand and I give it to him, he then places over his heart. It's beating a million miles a minute. He reaches out and holds my heart in his hand. It's beautiful. A silent tear rolls down my face in joy and knowing we can get back here. He looks exposed and unsure, feeling the gravity of our connection and love in the air. He pulls my body to him and we embrace. My mind owns me at first, internal fear saying, 'you're crazy, you're stupid, what the hell are you doing?' Just fear attempting to sabotage our moment. I allow these thoughts to roll on by, not engaging with them and they run out of energy. The thoughts quieten and emotion shows up in waves pulsing from my heart, from Sam's hand still holding my heart, connection embraced, and it feels like it is coming from both of us.

I'm present in love and the fear is gone.

I tilt my head up to him. His eyes are closed at first, but then he opens, gazing deep into me. I feel our love as a thing, as an expression. Right now, I'm wholeheartedly content. This is our love being expressed.

I kiss his chest, his skin, and I can see just how much this has also meant to him. Intrinsically, he knew this was different and he is slowly getting used to my unusual requests, as am I. Naked, in the hallway of my home, I stand cuddled with the love of my life. I feel his love, I feel close to him. Our connection swirls around us. I'm able to share my love with him, hold him and our flow, while we hold our love in our hearts. His trust of me and willingness to explore a deeper level of intimacy has me beyond words to describe how I feel about this man. He is more than enough. We held each other's hearts without the need for sex. We just experienced a moment of pure connection, safety, and love. It was not about me or him, it was about 'our' us, our love. While dressing, he looks at me and says, "I'd be okay if we did that again."

My response is simple: "Please."

We finish dinner and there is a softer feel to us, a comfortable flow to our interactions. Sam grabs my hand, sliding his fingers down the inside of my arm, another trademark move. It's one I adore, after learning it began from his nervousness and missing when he tried to grab my hand. "Come to bed."

We walk to my bedroom. Sam stands back watching me, turning the lamp on, light off, pulling the covers off the bed. He mirrors my movements in undressing, he kneels in the middle of the bed, with his hand outstretched to help me kneel in front of him. He's serious and yet feels quite playful. I feel him calling forth the lover that exists within me. Naked in front of him, face to face without words. The space building the fire that exists between us, he is fixed on connection, I feel the scared flicker within me as he is holding this space, holding my hand, feeling him sharing his tenderness. Sam touches my hips, drawing me closer, adjusting himself to align our bodies, wrapping his amazing arms around me. A gentle hug encased in him and my heart is beaming. My hands naturally wrap around his back, my head resting into his neck. I could stay in his man cocoon forever. It's quite some time before Sam releases a reluctant me from those arms, that chest. I'm unable to hide my bliss, he kisses me softly and lies me down.

Still not a word uttered, he traces my stomach with his fingers, kissing my body, my nipples ever so lightly, watching my reaction to every touch. He moves my legs apart, kissing my thighs, slowly applying pressure to my inner things, playing with pressure and my reactions to him. Sam drapes his body over me, and my body opens to him.

Sam speaks, "slowly, let's take our time."

I'm not sure I can, the tenderness is wonderful and yet the flicker is now anxiety, the vulnerability is becoming too much. My thoughts start pleading with me to stay with Sam, to follow him, to feel comfortable with him. This level of emotional nakedness is confronting, and fear is growing in my belly. Sam clearly can feel the change in my body, in me and he rolls off me. I use this as an opportunity to take control to shift the focus to him. I traverse his body as he did me, listening to his quiet moans, allowing them to guide me, to push him, what I know he likes, what I know will end this quickly. And he lets me.

I turned something beautiful into a fuck. I wonder if he is disappointed, full well knowing that he is frustrated with me and my anxiety. I can't have him show me too much care, he can't be so good to me. This is ridiculous. I know, I avoid affection from Sam, the exposure of my emotions, of letting go in trust, terrifying. Fuck what am I doing? I can't have him care about me. My thoughts don't help. I've made our love making all about him, controlling the level of intimacy. I'm doing my best and a different kind of sadness engulfs me, shuddering my insides, as I'm wrapped in him holding me while sleeping. Shame.

Early on Sunday morning, Sam suggests we head to the local beach, to our spot, where he found me. It has become a little ritual for us to stretch out in the sun, on our rug, soaking in the rays and swimming in the ocean. It has become a healing spot for both of us. It's lovely to connect here after the last six months of intensity and emotion.

On the beach, Sam sits up suddenly. Looking at me, he says, "Evie, I want to tell you a few things. I would like you to please listen and let me finish and then I would love to hear your thoughts."

His formal type request places the fear of God into me and after last night. I take a deep breath, sit up and attempt to prepare myself. My body has just frozen, completely rigid, in panic, I am a deer frozen in headlights.

He begins. "Remember the discussion we had in the car after the restaurant, it felt like you were trying to work me or soften the blow or something. When you were trying to tell me you needed time to nourish yourself? Well sometimes it's like half of the conversation we have has already happened in your head before I even become aware of it. It's like you have already discussed it with me, and you've decided how I am going to respond. I guess it's like you have already made my mind up that I will take it badly and begin talking to me from that point. I hear you clearly that there is something big you want to share with me. I need you to understand there is no pressure to tell me, ever. Tell me, or don't tell me, tell me in 50 years. It has no right here with us. My relationship is with you and is not determined on what you have to tell me. Yes, as you said the other day things will upset me, and that is actually a reflection of how I feel about you, so be raw, argue with me, stop trying to protect me from your past. It is in the past for a reason and I am your future. I want you to know I will hold you."

His voice shakes with emotion.

"I will hold your hand, naked cuddle you, all of you, heart, body and soul as you say, in my way, the way my feelings develop. You need to let my affection grow for you how it needs to evolve, not the version you are creating in your head. Fuck, I am now doing what you do, rambling! Seeking some reassurance from you after asking you to listen to me!"

He reaches to hold my hand as tears are stream down my face, and I'm smiling internally at my beautiful vulnerable Sam. Wondering how lucky I am, because he is right. I nod at him, encouraging him to continue.

Fuck, in this moment I realise that all that I have been doing in the way of healing and practicing how to love, has actually just kept me in the thinking of things rather than in the feeling of the present and feeling with Sam.

Sam says it is now time for our trust and bond to develop another layer. We talk together about what that actually looks like, in complete honesty. Unguarded communication takes hold of us both. Freely expressing our internal thoughts, good, bad, indifferent. My God, I learn so much of my man, and him of me. We were both trying to be ever so careful of each other, that we failed to talk.

We soak in the sun, with a side of naked cuddling in the dunes. It feels like this man has climbed into my skin and understood me, accepted me, and kissed all my hurts, slain my monsters and freed my caged heart.

We leave the beach renewed and head to Sam's house. As we arrive, I am reminded instantly by my body that she remembers how he touched me the last time I was in this room. How his touch owned me, holding me firmly against the kitchen bench, how it felt, the power in him, the warmth of that memory is lighting me up. I look to Sam, walking towards him, standing close, without touching.

I ask Sam if I may please kiss him? He smiles and nods with permission. I place my hand on those shoulders and feel his lips with mine, tasting him playfully and gently. I step back from him saying, "Thank you, Sam."

He clears his throat, grabbing hold of my hand. "Evie," all gentlemen like, "Can I make love to you?" Tears well, in my eyes as he said, 'make love.' Sam feels my recognition.

Leaning forward, he whispers "yes, make love."

I nod. He takes my hand, guiding me into his bedroom. Sam takes his time undressing me, scattering kisses over my body, calling my love to him, claiming my body, my heart and my soul in this new layer of honest love.

He kneels before me, slightly moving my legs apart, kissing my inner thighs, smiling at me. I am literally all giggles from his light touch, until he holds my hips firmly and summons my wild self through pleasure. The sensation of Sam's tongue tasting me, his fingers. I instantly surrender myself to him. I am a ragdoll at the mercy of this man, and I feel worshipped, honoured, losing the ability to stand as he sucks on me hard. He holds me in this sacred space of bare emotion, expressed. I reach for him. His wanting written all over his face. I push him hard against my womanly centre, sliding myself down his body so I can take all of him into me. We find our flow quickly. I anchor to my man and we come together, surrendered, with raw groans from us both.

Sam stays inside me until my body finishes her aftershocks. He says the experience of my throbbing lady parts feels incredible in the aftermath of our love making. This is also the moment I feel ever so close to Sam. We both feel it, beginning to freely talk about it. Our conversation continues just as we are, in our raw selves, emotions expressed, playful stroking, lingering fingertips, tender kisses. I share with him my fears of being too damaged and he shares his feelings of being not enough. We genuinely listen to each other, not completely knowing the other story and still very able to understand the battles of inadequacy. Sam and I spend the afternoon in absolute vulnerability, honestly soothing each other's hurts.

"I am not BROKEN!" said aloud and embraced. Sam never argues with me about my feelings, my fears. He has never said my feelings are wrong or silly, he acknowledges them. He listens and holds my hand. This is most precious healing gift I have ever felt. Slightly snoozing after my mental exposure and deep in felt emotion, while Sam declares "Food! Feed the man."

I laugh and ask if we can shower together first, to wash a little of the emotion off. I want to bring him into how I manage my emotional self, how I fight back from my fears and how I embrace my emotional experiences by finding ways to acknowledge and spend them, like holding my heart with soothing water. Sam holds me while the water washes away the intensity of our day. Between, the strength of this man and the water, I have no words to describe, how cherished I feel. The silky feel of the water and his touch, my body covered in goosebumps and heat simultaneously, the ability to be held and not have to hold myself.

As we leave the house in search of food, I can feel some waves of angst, some over exposed, a new skin, our new level of honesty, I guess. I am walking in the new skin, like a new pair of shoes, and it's painful at first. I begin over thinking and vocally state "Stop!" reaching for Sam's hand.

He holds my hand tightly and says, "I know. I felt the uncomfortable space too, it's okay. Just ride the wave with me, beautiful." Finishing with a supportive kiss on the back of my hand, it's enough encouragement for me. We are sitting, waiting for the food to arrive when it dawns on me that I am releasing years of pain, of trauma, and learning to love instead of bear the pain. I'm opening parts of me that have never seen daylight and that it will feel completely foreign and painful to me, as until now I've never been loved correctly. 'Time, Evie, time!' I reassure myself and feel proud of what I am achieving in love. Not all of this is connected to Sam, and I am learning to love after being damaged. Wait, not damaged, injured, now mending and more than enough.

LOVING. LOUDLY.

It's late and I am awake, feeling my pain and monsters standing over me. Sam is next to me and I am still trying to protect him. Why am I still doing this? I've been so good lately and I'm being stalked by my monsters. Some days I feel like I am winning and others... It was a shit night. I was completely stupid; I wonder how much longer he will put up with me?

I know my fear thinking is here, I know those monsters are attempting to take control, to push him away. I can't stop them dragging me into the depths of despair. My body is pained, muscles completely engaged, while feeling the sensations of love next to me. I feel like my body has an entire story that I have never read before. I feel empowered and trapped by this past that is dragging me down, like I am struggling to swim in deep water; one-minute feeling free and the next being dragged to the bottom. I am surrounded by this beauty and yet this darkness is consistently haunting me. Am I even worthy of him? Can I truly love him? My demons came out strong tonight, but hope shines amidst my innermost thoughts. Those demons are making their loudest cry before I banish them. Encouraging thoughts and breathing through my torment.

"You are worthy." Battling my mind, battling my fears.

Left over shakiness from being triggered earlier reminding me that my pain won tonight. I froze in a full-blown memory, I didn't see Sam, I saw my monster, I shut down all of me. I did not have control, I tried to undo, it was like I became a witness to the moment, and no amount of pleading or strategies could get me out of that dark hole. My protection mode came on and turned everything off, and I just functioned in a zombie-like state. I engaged with Sam, although in a very mechanical way, without connection. I pulled the 'I have a headache' card and went to bed.

He knows. It's 3am and here I am waiting for emotional exhaustion to take me off to sleep. I'm trying to make myself small to hide from Sam. My shame, the unworthiness I feel. How could I do this to him? A storm swirls around outside the window, joining with the one inhabiting me. The droplets comfort my skin.

I sit up to close the window before it wakes Sam. He is awake and reaches over the top of me to close the window, frustratedly telling me to 'let me.' I knew he was awake! He was too quiet, usually he is a noisy breather in his sleep. Sam stretches out with a reassuring touch. "How is your head?"

I immediately tell him. "I don't have a headache, I was triggered earlier and couldn't escape it, and then I didn't know how to get back to you, it really all happened on its own and I really didn't know how to come back to you. My fears and monsters won today."

He simply says "I know. Can I hold you?"

I curl myself into him immediately and say, "I am trying." He pulls me closer and I kiss him, holding his lips in mine.

He acknowledges my efforts and that he is proud of me. It dawns on me that my monsters are not allowed here. They are not welcome in my world with Sam and I am going to fight back, take my world back. I am not going to make myself small for them, they no longer rule here.

"Sam, I'm going to love you so loudly my monsters run and hide."

I grab his hand and drag him out of bed. "Please indulge me."

I walk us outside to the patio in the rain. I pull over a chair and sit him down. I'm standing over him, the rain is heavy now, the storm building both inside and outside me. We are both totally naked and covered in goose bumps from the slight chill in the air, as the light from the kitchen guides my heart. Every part of me feels alive. The sensation of him, the exposure to the elements. His piercing eyes are alive. The rain stings my body with every droplet, as the heat builds between us, pausing in this instant of us. Steam rises from our skin, from the anticipation of us in desire. My womanly self is here to claim her man. I massage myself against his manhood, the way I know he likes, calling him to me. My body and heart are openly free from fear, free from my monsters, choosing how to love and choosing what my world with Sam is. I clumsily take as much of my man as I can. We are eye to eye, announcing to the world that this is our love. Sam seizes my hips and sets the flow, the rhythm of us. As he deepens his reach inside me, groaning loudly, he asserts his claim to me and to the world. "They can't have you anymore!" We express ourselves freely and show my monsters they can't exist here anymore. I out love them by claiming the love within me, accepting myself, while my beautiful man anchors me and we purposefully come together, owning our space, as we are love embodied. Sam and I hold each other tightly, my heart pressed over his, letting the rain wash over us as we recover from our orgasms, feeling his heart beating against mine.

I look to Sam and tell him it is this tenderness and acceptance of expression right now that holds my vulnerabilities that tells me it's okay. That five minutes where we are simply felt emotion together, that is my love received. A shiver runs through my body. Sam lifts me up, walking in silence to our bed, both ending up on the same side of the bed. Sam lays down, pulling me on alongside him and ushers me to rest part of my chest on him. "Evie, like your heart outside, I want to fall asleep feeling the sensation of your heart beating next to mine. It's like our naked cuddling but better."

Joy bounces around my heart and I can feel Sam's heart also bounce to our beat and like that, we sleep.

Since our night of heart connection as we have called it, we have been blissfully ordinary. I am more myself and less in my head about us. Sam and I have continued to talk about what we need and what is happening. We have practiced a lot of compassion towards each other, in that we both don't have to be on the same page, nor do we need to have the answers for one another. It is very freeing to remove the expectations from each other beyond friendship. I'm actively trusting Sam, actively loving him, not just expecting it to happen on its own. I trust Sam implicitly and I know he does me too.

A few days later, Sam is driving us up north to a famous beach spot. I have a picnic organised and I'm ready. I'm emotionally fierce. I'm unafraid of my history.

I'm prepared to free us both from my traumas. I'm not sure he knows what's coming, although he seems to know me better than I do sometimes. I'm nervous, which he notices. He holds my hand or has been stroking my thigh on the drive, always within touch, and the occasional kiss on the back of my hand. We have grown so close and shared so much. Our naked heart cuddling, holding our love in a space, were we actually spent time receiving each other's love, has become one of Sam's favourites and part of our daily routine. I think it's because we get our needs met in raw love and trust. He clearly understands my body, plus it keeps me 'out of my head,' as Sam puts it.

I feel loved every day. I give love every day to my man. All in the doing of 'loving', we can just stay in our bodies, avoiding crazy thinking. Although I have a little problem with fear thinking... We have a way of loving each other now. I learnt that I don't have to tell Sam what happened to me. It's something that happened to me, it is not who I am. Sam helped me to realise this and that I can be loved. I can love. We are not perfect and that's why I am comfortable and ready to tell Sam. The 'how' to tell Sam, is the difficulty. It is not something that can described in words. Horrors are horrors and words are not enough nor am I able to put a voice to indescribable things, while Sam's eyes are on me.

It is important for me to tell Sam and be free, not have anything controlling me. I don't believe I can look at this man while telling him. It's so hard to look at anyone and tell my story. Our kind of love and this story should never be in the same lifetime so I will tell him what happened to me and leave it at the beach. It no longer has a place in me. The final step to freeing myself, so I'm going to face the ocean, tell my Mother Nature, let her cleanse us both of my story with the ocean while Sam sits by my side, steadying me. Just as I did with him, that day on the beach.

A voice to it means there is no longer any secrets or anything between us, it's the final act of releasing myself from the past and completely stepping into our life together. We arrive at the beach, driving along the sand until I let Sam know that I want to stop. He trusts me and allows me to take the lead, knowing I need to. He must feel something different about today. I swim first while Sam sets up our spot for the day.

The ocean feels cool with a tiny swell. I kneel in the shallows and send a little prayer out to bring forth the strength of the ocean within me, to allow each word to unhook me from the pain, the monsters released from my heart, entirely. I picture the water unhooking me, removing the claws from under my skin, thanking them and gifting my pain to the ocean, to dissolve, picturing each hook coming out of my skin, out of my body, out of my heart. I no longer belong to you. I belong to me.

I stand and walk into her, submerging myself in the cleansing waves, feeling the ocean healing my skin, nurturing my heart, loving my body.

After the swim and with the courage of Mother Nature, beating throughout my body, I sit next to my love. "Sam, I'm ready for you to hear what happened to me…"

I've prepared him as best as I can. I let him know I want him to hear my story by way of me sharing it with Mother Nature, and if he could remember that I'm healed by love. I, of course, can't help but give him a few pointers, that he might feel angry, or hurt and all of that is okay. I am strong for a reason and I have fought hard battles, and this is a final battle to share my story with my love for the first and final time. I ask him to please, understand, I need him to steady me, hold my hand and after today for me, it is gone.

Sam is ever the man I dreamt of patient, loving, kind. I can see it's hard, the struggle in him, our pains in hearing the story aloud. The pain in telling it. As he listens, I am stripping away my armour, peeling off my scars, baring them to the shine of the sun, feeling my hurts while my pains are carried away by Mother Nature who tenderly absorbs them with each wave. Swallowing them, removing them to the depths, never to be found again. I run out of words, of sobs, steadied by a beautiful man. We sit in silence, Sam holding my hand to his heart. Emotionally bare.

ABOUT AUTHOR

Jess Kolbe was born and raised on the outskirts of Melbourne, Australia and has lived abroad in the UK and Ireland. She resides on the Sunshine Coast in Queensland and runs a successful Counselling practice. Jess has always loved writing and writes to make a difference in people's lives. She is passionate about helping others understand and relate to their emotional experiences and guides people to have accepted relationships with themselves.

This is her second book, The Naughty Therapist was published in 2015, reflections from a trauma therapist.

The Naughty Therapist 2015 ©

Made in the USA
Middletown, DE
26 October 2020

22776994R10144